Debra Shipley
and
Mary Peplow

THE OTHER
MUSEUM GUIDE

GRAFTON BOOKS

A Division of the Collins Publishing Group

LONDON GLASGOW
TORONTO SYDNEY AUCKLAND

Grafton Books
A Division of the Collins Publishing Group
8 Grafton Street, London W1X 3LA

A Grafton Paperback Original 1988

ISBN 0-586-07215-2

Printed and bound in Great Britain by
Mackays of Chatham Ltd

Set in Bembo

CONTENTS

Acknowledgements 7

How To Use This Guide 9

1. CUMBRIA 11

2. EAST ANGLIA 24
   Cambridgeshire
   Essex
   Norfolk
   Suffolk

3. EAST
   MIDLANDS 44
   Derbyshire
   Leicestershire
   Lincolnshire
   Northamptonshire
   Nottinghamshire

4. GUERNSEY 62

5. HEART OF
   ENGLAND 67
   Gloucestershire
   Hereford & Worcester

Shropshire
Staffordshire
West Midlands County

6. ISLE OF MAN 96

7. JERSEY 105

8. LONDON 112

9. NORTHERN
   IRELAND 134

10. NORTHUMBRIA 149
    Cleveland
    County Durham
    Northumberland
    Tyne and Wear

11. THE NORTH-
    WEST 167
    Cheshire
    Greater Manchester
    Lancashire
    Merseyside

12. SCOTLAND   180

13. THE SOUTH-
    EAST   207
    Kent
    East Sussex
    West Sussex

14. SOUTHERN
    ENGLAND   225
    Dorset
    Hampshire
    Isle of Wight

15. THE THAMES AND
    THE CHILTERNS   248
    Bedfordshire
    Berkshire
    Hertfordshire

Oxfordshire

16. WALES   263

17. THE WEST
    COUNTRY   283
    Avon
    Devon
    Somerset

18. YORKSHIRE AND
    HUMBERSIDE   297
    Humberside
    North Yorkshire
    South Yorkshire
    West Yorkshire

Regional Tourist
    Boards   313

Indexes   315

ACKNOWLEDGEMENTS

Many people have helped us compile this guide and we'd like to thank them all for their enthusiasm and support. Special thanks are due to Mr and Mrs John Oldacre, Paul Anderson, Mike and Margaret Atkinson, Sue Conner, Jenny Hanger, Joyce MacLennan, Rosemary and David Molesworth, Sarah Priday, Sarah Salway, Cath Shipley and Jane Saunders. And thank you, too, to the Regional Tourist Boards and their busy marketing and press officers, and to Hotel Nelson, Norwich, and Stakis Hotel, Glasgow, for their enjoyable hospitality and for providing excellent bases for visiting museums in the area.

HOW TO USE THIS GUIDE

The Other Museum Guide covers a wide cross-section of museums in England, Scotland, Wales, Northern Ireland, Channel Islands and the Isle of Man. It's divided into regional tourist board areas to provide you with a contact point where you can get more information about accommodation, travel facilities and other attractions (addresses on pages 313–14).

In each chapter the entries are arranged alphabetically by museum for quick reference. (Note that Museum of Childhood appears under 'C'.) Under the museum's title you'll find its telephone number and address. The text is our impression of the museum (naturally, it's only a taster), while under the heading 'Special!' we've highlighted in more detail a specific item of interest. At the end of each entry we've provided some practical details:

Open. The opening times were accurate at time of going to press, but if you're travelling any distance or planning to visit on a Bank Holiday, do check in advance.

Admission. Some museums are free, for others the admission charges can vary enormously. Where we've indicated a fee, you may like to contact the museum for a special reduction such as party or family rates.

Disabled access. Our assessment is meant only as a guide. All the museums we visited would be happy to advise you further.

Café/Picnic facilities, gifts, toilets. These are noted when available.

At the end of the book there's a coded index which is both a page reference and a subject guide.

Museums can be both fun and interesting, and we've travelled the country to prove it. We've included only those museums which we enjoyed visiting – hence the enthusiastic style! Some are huge and some are tiny; some are specialist and some general; but we feel they're all in their own way well worth a visit. This certainly isn't a comprehensive guide, so if you've a favourite museum do write and tell us about it.

Debra Shipley and Mary Peplow, 1988

CUMBRIA

THE MUSEUM OF THE BORDER REGIMENT AND KING'S OWN BORDER REGIMENT

Queen Mary's Tower, The Castle, Carlisle, Cumbria.
Tel: Carlisle 32774

Has anyone seen Lewis Brandon, '5ft 8ins high, a well fed man with fair hair, little squinting eyes and bow legs, about 30 years'! An advertisement in a *London Gazette* of 1703 offers a reward of between two and five guineas for information about Lewis Brandon or any other of the five deserters from Lord Lucas's Regiment of Foot, later to become the Border Regiment. This is just one of the many imaginatively presented exhibits, including models, dioramas, medals, uniforms, documents and battle trophies. Look out for the Russian Eagle taken at Sebastopol – a rather bulky mascot to carry around, to say the least! The displays trace the individual histories and campaigns of the Border Regiment and the King's Own Border Regiment, highlight their associations with Carlisle Castle, describe their amalgamation in 1959 and bring the story of active

11

service up to date. Queen Mary's Tower, home of the museum, was named after the last Royal to live here, Mary, Queen of Scots, and like the rest of the medieval castle is of great architectural and historical importance.

SPECIAL!
Queen Mary's Table, dating from the twelfth or thirteenth century, makes a good resting place for a set of regimental china plates and a silver candelabrum. The table is thought to have been used by Queen Mary when under guard at the castle in 1568.

Open: mid-March to mid-October, daily, 0930–1830. Mid-October to mid-March, Monday to Saturday, 0930–1630; Sunday, 1400–1630.
Admission fee: yes (includes entry to Castle)
Picnic facilities
Gifts: on sale
Toilets

BRANTWOOD
Coniston (east of lake), Cumbria. Tel: Coniston 41396

The views from Brantwood, home of critic, poet and artist John Ruskin (1819–1900), are breathtaking. Indeed, it was the view which first attracted him to this spot. It's difficult to imagine a more beautiful landscape than the view from the study window and even more difficult to describe it. But Ruskin himself captured the vision: 'I raise my eyes to these Coniston Fells, and see them, at this moment imaged in their lake in quietly reversed perfect similitude, the sky cloudless above them, cloudless beneath, and two level lines of blue vapour drawn across their sunlighted and russet moorlands, like an azure fesse across a golden shield' (12 February 1878).

Ruskin was perhaps one of the most eminent figures of the Victorian age. His admirers included Tolstoy, who described him as 'one of the most remarkable of men, not only of England and our time, but of all countries and all times'. Friends who visited Ruskin here included many famous people of the day: Harriet Martineau, Sir Edward and Lady Burne-Jones, William Holman Hunt, Charles Darwin.

For visitors today there's plenty to see and do. The house contains a lovely collection of Ruskin's own watercolour paintings as well as a number of personal items including his coach and boat, *Jumping Jenny*. Then there's a nature walk – three miles of Brantwood estate (best in spring when there are glorious displays of rhododendrons and azaleas and bright bursts of yellow daffodils, including many paths set out by Ruskin himself. Brantwood is most definitely an enchanting place to visit.

SPECIAL!
Views from the turret bedroom are particularly stunning. Ruskin's first addition to Brantwood was this picturesque turret built to provide him with an unrivalled panorama of the lake and mountains. Here he spent many hours contemplating the ever-changing aspect of light upon lakeland scenery.

Open: mid-March to mid-November, daily, 1100–1530. Mid-November to mid-March, Wednesday to Sunday, 1100–1430.
Admission fee: yes
Disabled access: slightly limited
Café
Picnic facilities

Gift shop: including a good book shop
Toilets

CUMBERLAND PENCIL MUSEUM
Southey Works, Keswick, Cumbria. Tel: Keswick 73626

How much do you know about pencils? If the answer's 'Not much', make for this unique museum – there's plenty to discover. The first pencils ever made were produced here in Keswick following the uncovering of Cumberland graphite during Elizabethan times. The museum's audio-visual display traces the development of the pencil from that early period, with the first hand-made pencils, to the modern mass-produced products we know today. On display are the three basic parts which constitute a pencil – the wood casing, the inner core and the outer finish – as well as some of the early machinery, like the shaping machine (*c.*1920), which made the first rounded pencils. All in all, it's a museum which will really make you think the next time you pick up a pencil or reach for a sharpener.

SPECIAL!
Because materials were limited during the Second World War, all pencils were made and sold unpainted – you can see examples on display. The one exception was a range of green pencils, each containing a map of Germany and a small magnetic compass, which were issued to the pilots of Bomber Command in case they were shot down during a mission. They were also sent in prisoner-of-war parcels to help people to escape from Germany.

Open: March to October, Monday to Friday, 0930–1430; Sunday, 1400–1700.

Admission fee: yes
Disabled access: good
Gift shop
Toilets

THE DOLL AND TOY MUSEUM
Bank's Court, Market Place, Cockermouth, Cumbria.
Tel: Lowton 259

While parents look around and remember their child-hoods, kids can push buttons and play! Part of the museum is a hoard of toys belonging to a self-confessed perpetual 'player', so children are made very welcome. The rest of the museum is a private collection of ethnic dolls; some of the figures are antique, but all are dressed in authentic costumes from across the world. The result is both unusual and very colourful. One thing you'll notice about the toys in general as you browse around is that over the years they seem to have shrunk! Finally, if you think you know a thing or two about toys, look carefully at each transport display case. The owner has put something into each which will make the expert stop and think.

SPECIAL!
The central railway circuit is spectacular in its own right. But take a closer look at the exquisite miniature (Hornby gauge 0 tinplate) milk tankers.

Open: Easter to mid–October, daily, 1000–1700.
Admission fee: yes
Gifts: on sale

KENDAL MUSEUM OF LAKELAND LIFE AND INDUSTRY

Kirkland, Kendal, Cumbria. Tel: Kendal 22464

The Kendal Museum of Lakeland Life and Industry is just the place to spend a wet afternoon (and there seem to be plenty of those in Cumbria!) when the weather doesn't permit you to explore the fabulous mountain scenery and serene lakeland beauty. Here you can discover an earlier Lake District, one little known to tourists. Converted from an old stable block, the museum manages to capture something of the atmosphere of days gone by. There are reconstucted workshops showing the local crafts and industry, dark farmhouse rooms crammed with oak furniture and a toy-filled nursery. It's an absorbing story of social and economic life told with hip-baths, sheep dips, bobbins, parasols and turbine engines. From the faded sepia images recorded over a half a century ago, to the large photographs showing man's more recent impact on the mountains and lakes, it's a tale well told and an excellent introduction to the lakeland area. Well worth a visit even if the sun *is* shining!

SPECIAL!
Lead was mined locally and the miners collected crystals to make glittering 'grottoes'. You can see one of these popular parlour decorations on display.

Open: Monday to Friday, 1030–1700; Saturday and Sunday, 1400–1700.
Admission fee: yes
Café
Picnic facilities
Gift shop
Toilets

KESWICK RAILWAY MUSEUM

28 Main Street (above National Westminster Bank),
Keswick, Cumbria. No telephone

Railway buffs and visitors to Keswick who want to kill an hour or so are both welcome! This is certainly a museum run by, and for, railway enthusiasts; but for stranded tourists in the Lake District, who've discovered the reason for the area's high rainfall figures, it's a haven. The museum endeavours to preserve Cumbrian railways by collecting all sorts of items which would otherwise have been lost. There are dozens of photographs and relics – cast-iron notices, enamel signs and signalling equipment, to mention a few. The museum may be small, but train enthusiasts appreciate its efforts. Judging from the visitors' book in which you are asked to comment, it has succeeded in reviving memories for lots of local people as well as saving wet tourists!

SPECIAL!
It's a measure of the museum's idiosyncrasy that the largest exhibit here – the working model railway layout – has nothing whatever to do with Cumbria. It represents an area of the Rocky Mountains in Canada and is the work of Bill Kellett, who spent twenty years constructing it in his bedroom.

Open: March to October, daily, 1400–1700. Cumbrian school holidays: Monday to Saturday, 1000–1700; Sunday, 1400–1700.
Admission fee: yes
Gifts: on sale

LAKELAND MOTOR MUSEUM

Holker Hall, Cark-in-Cartmel, Grange-over-Sands, Cumbria.
Tel: Flookburgh 328

One gleaming vehicle after another demands your attention here. There are cars, motorcycles and engines all set against a fascinating backdrop of automobilia such as lamps, badges, dashboard instruments. A collection of car number plates strung across the museum's walls makes an unusual garland, while petrol pumps and their 'romantic' glass signs are dotted around like pieces of sculpture. There are dozens of bonnet mascots including famous 'Old Bill' of Bruce Bairnsfather's cartoon fame. In the garage section you can see the dirtier side of motoring – grimy workbenches, oil-clogged cans, dusty tyres and all sorts of bric-a-brac associated with maintaining a smooth-running machine.

SPECIAL!
Your ticket includes entry into the grounds of Holker Hall, so you might as well make the most of it! There are extensive gardens, deer grazing in the park and an excellent local craft and countryside gallery. Children love the baby animal enclosure just next to the Motor Museum (no extra charge).

Open: Easter to end October, Monday to Saturday, 1030–1800. Last admission to Holker Hall grounds and therefore access to the museum, 1630.
Admission fee: yes
Disabled access: limited
Café
Picnic facilities

Gift shop
Toilets

MARYPORT MARITIME MUSEUM
Senhouse Street, Maryport, Cumbria. Tel: Maryport 3738

Though on the coast, there's very little to attract tourists
to Maryport today. It's a small, quiet town forgotten
by the visitor to Cumbria, who usually heads directly
for the picturesque Lake District. In its heyday, however, Maryport was a thriving harbour town famed for
its ship-building, sail-making, cordage and nail-
making. The quays were the hub of activity as anything
up to a hundred coal boats waited to enter the harbour
for reloading, and the launch of a new ship was an
exciting event watched by large crowds. It's this atmospheric past which Maryport Maritime Museum tries to
capture. There's the story of the 1448-ton iron ship
Netherby, which left Maryport on 21 June 1906 and was
lost with all hands less than a month later, and the tale
of Henry Ismay and the White Star Line. And if you're
interested in model ships, take a look at the fifty-six-
gun warship *Bulwark*, made in 1872 by a ship's carpen-
ter from Maryport.

SPECIAL!
The museum's most spectacular exhibits can be found
bobbing on the water in the harbour – three steamboats.
One of them, originally called *Flying Buzzard*, was sunk
by an American oil tanker just a few months after it
was launched, but it was eventually raised, rebuilt and
renamed Steam Tug *Harecraig II*.

Open: Monday, Tuesday, Thursday to Saturday,
1400–1600.

Admission fee: no
Gift shop
Toilets

STOTT PARK BOBBIN MILL

Finsthwaite (near Newby Bridge), Cumbria.
Tel: Newby Bridge 31087

Built in 1835 and remaining virtually unchanged since then, Stott Park Bobbin Mill is an atmospheric place to visit. It's been restored as a working industrial monument and much of the original machinery is still in position. By joining a guided tour (led by men who've worked here all their lives, as did their fathers before them) you can see the machines in action. There are roughing machines to take the bark from the wood, boring devices which made the holes through the bobbins, a turbine and a magnificent steam engine. But it's the social history, brought alive by the guide, which really makes this a unique museum to visit.

SPECIAL!
The small cottages nearby were once all inhabited by workers from the mill. In days gone by (*c.* 1835) there were some sixty people employed here. In 1938 the numbers were down to thirty. Now the museum is run by just a handful of people.

Open: end March to end September, Monday to Saturday, 0930–1830; Sunday, 1400–1830.
Admission fee: yes
Disabled access: limited
Gifts: on sale
Toilets

WINDERMERE STEAMBOAT MUSEUM

Rayrigg Road, Windermere, Cumbria.
Tel: Windermere 5565

Generation after generation has been attracted to Lake Windermere. The Romans made their camp, Galava, on its shore at Waterhead and in the Middle Ages monks fished its waters. Indeed, for communities through the centuries the lake has been the principal source of food. However, it was during the Industrial Revolution, with the advent of the steamboat, that Windermere came into its own. Tea parties on board a steamer became fashionable, and elegantly dressed ladies twirled their parasols. It is therefore fitting that a steamboat museum should be sited here on this former wharf. The craft on display have all been restored to full working order and can be regularly seen steaming on the lake. In the museum you can see them bobbing up and down in wet dock which has a high-level walkway for viewing from where you can fully appreciate their pristine condition!

SPECIAL!
Dolly is very special. She sank to the bottom of the lake during the great frost of 1895 and lay forgotten for almost seventy years. Now raised and fully restored, this fine steamboat can once again be seen chugging across the water. But why is she so special? *Dolly* is listed in the *Guinness Book of Records* as the oldest mechanically powered boat in the world.

Open: Easter to end October, daily, 1000–1700.
Admission fee: yes
Disabled access: good
Picnic facilities

21

Gift shop
Toilets

WORDSWORTH MUSEUM
Dove Cottage, Grasmere, Cumbria. Tel: Coniston 41396

Where once the Dove and Olive-Bough
Offered a greeting of good ale
To all who entered Grasmere Vale;
And called on him who must depart
To leave it with a jovial heart;
There, where the Dove and Olive-Bough
Once hung, a poet harbours now,
A simple water-drinking bard . . .
    (Wordsworth, 'The Waggoner', 1805)

Originally a small hostelry known as the Dove and Olive Branch, this beautiful small cottage was poet William Wordsworth's home during the happiest years of his life. The museum is split into two parts: Dove Cottage and a purpose-built exhibition building filled with all sorts of Wordsworth treasures. Dove Cottage may be visited only by joining a guided tour, but that's actually a real bonus as all the guides are very knowledgeable and keen to help you. The cottage, with its oak-panelled hall and floors of Westmorland slate, has been carefully restored; many of the objects on display once belonged to the poet and his family. The garden, too, which was especially loved by Wordsworth, has been carefully maintained. Next door, the well-presented permanent exhibition traces Wordsworth's life and works with original manuscripts, paintings and sketches.

SPECIAL!
Look out for the letter from Dorothy Wordsworth to
Coleridge, written from Goslar in Germany. As you'll
see, it's full of blots and crossing outs and is written at
all sorts of different angles. In fact, this letter is a key
document in the development of English Romanticism.
The manuscript is, in every way, priceless.

Open: Monday to Saturday, 0930–1730; Sunday,
1100–1730. Closed mid-January to mid-February.
Admission fee: yes
Disabled access: limited
Gift shop
Toilets

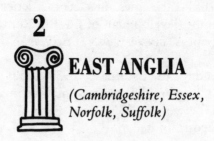

2

EAST ANGLIA

(Cambridgeshire, Essex, Norfolk, Suffolk)

THE A.T.J. MUSEUM

Old Regent Cinema, 43 High Street, Downham Market, Nortfolk. Tel: Downham Market 385307/387150

Why A.T.J.? Well, the newly-opened museum is a dream come true for Alfred Thomas Johnson ('A.T.J.' as he's known) – a self-confessed compulsive collector and cycle enthusiast. The 1930s cinema has been refurbished and converted as a showcase for his amazing array of bygones, around 2000 of them. It's a staggering sight – you just don't know where to begin. Every nook and cranny is filled with cycles, prams, radios, militaria, farm tools, organs, early musical instruments, office equipment, you name it, it's here – carefully restored to working order. The building is quite large but there's still not really enough space to display everything, so it's very much a case of discovering the delights for yourself. As a rough guide, the ground floor has a unique collection of vintage and veteran cycles dating from 1865 together with other wheeled items such as prams and invalid carriages; the gallery contains an old Victorian chemist shop; and the first floor is full of domestic and agricultural bygones. The rest, including such diversities as a reference library covering a hundred years of the history of the cycle and a series of photographs showing the changing face of archways in Downham Market, is crammed into every spare corner. You've got to see it with your own eyes to believe it!

SPECIAL!
A cycle-lover's dream – the library has a complete set of bound volumes of *Cycling* magazine from 1876 to 1975. It weighs two and a half tons!

Open: Wednesday, Saturday and Sunday, 1400–1700.
Admission fee: yes
Disabled access: very limited, telephone in advance
Café: opposite
Gifts: on sale
Toilets

CAMBRIDGE AND COUNTY FOLK MUSEUM
2–3 Castle Street, Cambridge, Cambridgeshire.
Tel: Cambridge 355159

Wonderfully situated for a leisurely stroll along the Backs, the beautiful riverside walk overlooking the backs of Cambridge's colleges, this museum shows the life and changing times of the people of the Cambridgeshire over the past three centuries. But it's more than a local history museum: there are eleven rooms full of exhibits such as strange-looking tools and implements of the brick-maker, boot-maker, chemist, tobacconist and chimney-sweep, among other trades; displays of rural and domestic crafts; toys and games; a bottle bar and Victorian kitchen. Particularly intriguing are the explanations of Fen legends and folklore. And, of course, there's a look at life in the university since Peterhouse, the first college, was founded by the Bishop of Ely in 1284. All in all, this museum, housed in a sixteenth-century building that was once the White Horse Inn, is an ideal introduction to the lovely city.

SPECIAL!
The collection of samplers on display here is one of the best in the country – just look at the dainty stitching, often worked by young children.

Open: Monday to Saturday, 1030–1700; Sunday, 1430–1630.
Admission fee: yes
Disabled access: limited
Café: nearby
Picnic facilities: nearby
Gifts: on sale
Toilets

CHRISTCHURCH MANSION
Christchurch Park, Ipswich, Suffolk. Tel: Ipswich 53246

The minute you walk in through the gates of Christchurch Park and catch a first glimpse of the sixteenth-centry mansion, you get that feeling that you're about to enjoy something very special – and you won't be disappointed. On paper, Christchurch Mansion might sound unremarkable – a country house collection of furniture, bygones, pictures and ceramics set in period rooms – but once inside you'll soon realize this is not only a real treasure-trove of fine craftsmanship and decorative arts but also an invitation into the past with everything so beautifully presented, it's a real pleasure to walk around. Allow plenty of time – it's hard to tear yourself away from the exhibits. There's everything from early examples of can-openers in the kitchen (they were often decorated with a bull's head because beef was one of the first foods to be canned) to the original hand-blocked, flocked wallpaper of the 1730s in the state bedroom. The lived-in atmosphere makes each room an adventure and inspires you to find out more about the past occupants and their way of life. Adjoining is the Wolsey Art Gallery with works by Gainsborough, Constable, Moore and other Suffolk artists.

SPECIAL!
Washday at Christchurch Mansion at the turn of this century was quite an event. Tune into the listening post in the laundry in the servants' wing to hear the Monday memories of Mrs Agnes Rogers, who worked here.

Open: Monday to Saturday, 1000–1700; Sunday, 1430–1630.
Admission fee: no
Disabled access: very limited
Picnic facilities: in the park
Gifts: on sale
Toilets

COLCHESTER CASTLE
Ryegate Road, Colchester, Essex. Tel: Colchester 712490

You're in for a real surprise – from the outside of the castle, you can have no idea of what's awaiting you inside! The massive Keep, begun by William the Conquerer *c.* 1076, is now home for the city's archaeological collections ranging from the Romans' early occupation of Britain (at nearby Clapton) to the dramatic siege of Colchester during the Civil War in 1648. The castle itself (well worth looking around) stands on the foundations of a Roman temple and the most extensive displays in the museum are from the Roman occupation of Colchester including mosaics, tombstones, burial jars, statues and many other items. The exhibits are all labelled to show their past use, and you're also told the story of how they were excavated and cleaned. It's a great favourite with children.

SPECIAL!
They might not have been adorned with sparkling gems, but the Romans still wore rings on their fingers and you can see some of their jewellery dating from the first to the third century on display in the museum.

Open: April to September, Monday to Saturday, 1000–1700; Sunday, 1430–1700. October to March, Monday to Friday, 1000–1700; Saturday, 1000–1600.
Admission fee: yes
Disabled access: limited
Picnic facilities
Gifts: on sale
Toilets

CROMWELL MUSEUM
Grammar School Walk, Huntingdon, Cambridgeshire.
Tel: Huntingdon 52861

Oliver Cromwell has special connections with Huntingdon. He was born here in 1599 and spent his early years in the town. The small stone building near the Market Square, which now houses a museum in his memory, was his school until 1616. Inside there are signed documents, coins, medals, personal artefacts and portraits of Cromwell, his family and leading personalities which help trace his life and times. If you plan your visit on a Sunday, you can combine it with a tour of nearby Hinchingbrooke House, the home of Oliver Cromwell's grandfather (telephone Huntingdon 51121 for details).

SPECIAL!
Looking distinctly like a large flying saucer under glass is the hat Oliver Cromwell wore at the Dissolution of the Long Parliament in 1653 – just look at the width of the brim!

Open: April to October, Tuesday to Friday, 1100–1300 and 1400–1700; Saturday and Sunday, 1100–1300 and 1400–1600. November to March, Tuesday to Friday, 1400–1700; Saturday, 1100–1300 and 1400–1600; Sunday, 1400–1600.
Admission fee: no
Disabled access: good
Café: nearby
Picnic facilities: by the river a short walk away

EASTON FARM PARK
Easton (off B1116), near Wickham Market, Suffolk.
Tel: Wickham Market 746475

It's a real country day out here at Easton Farm Park – a chance to see life down on the farm. It's still a working farm, producing some 1.5 million litres of milk and 1500 tonnes of wheat plus barley, sugar, oilseed rape and peas and beans for freezing, but 150 acres have been set aside to show visitors the contrast between the old and modern techniques of farming. There's lots to see so put on your sensible clothes and get stuck in! For children the main attraction is the farmyard animals – sheep, cattle, poultry, goats, pigs and horses – many of which are rare breeds. But there's much more to Easton Park than animals: there's a working blacksmith's shop, a Victorian dairy, a nature trail through meadows and woodland and along the river Deben, a pets' paddock and a fascinating display of early farm machinery and country bygones. And to bring you right up to date there's a highly automated dairy centre with a special viewing gallery where you can watch as 130 cows are milked by one man! Milking time is early afternoon, so plan your visit to be there then. And don't let the weather put you off, it's a 'rain *and* shine' museum. There are farming events throughout the season; ask for details.

SPECIAL!
The Victorian dairy with its wall tiles, marble shelves and stained-glass windows seems much too beautiful to use – but as the utensils on display show, this was where butter, cheese and cream were once made.

Open: Easter to end September, daily, 1030–1800 (telephone to check milking time).
Admission fee: yes
Disabled access: good
Café
Picnic facilities
Gift shop: bags of food for the animals also on sale
Toilets

GLANDFORD SHELL MUSEUM
Church House, Glandford (on B1156), Norfolk.
Tel: Cley 740081

This tiny museum, three miles north-west of Holt, is hard to find – but do persevere, it's well worth it. Shells, delicate and exquisite, of all shapes, sizes and colours from all corners of the world are housed in a curious Dutch-style building standing in the shadow of the beautiful St Martin's Church. The museum was built in 1915 by the late Sir Alfred Jodrell especially for the collection of shells he gathered over sixty years, and was considered of such importance it was kept open after his death. All the shells are carefully laid out and well labelled, explaining their origin and any special story – look out for the giant turtle shell brought over from the Ascension Islands in 1924! Obviously, shells are the main theme, but there are other exhibits too: jewels, pieces of pottery, agate ware, even a sugar bowl once used by Elizabeth I.

SPECIAL!
One wall is lined with a colourful tapestry showing scenes from the north Norfolk coast. This was worked by a retired local fisherman determined to keep busy through months of ill-health.

Open: March to November, Monday to Thursday, 0930–1230 and 1430–1630; Friday and Saturday, 1400–1630. December to February, Monday to Thursday, 0930–1230. Other times by arrangement.
Admission fee: yes
Disabled access: limited

GRANDAD'S PHOTOGRAPHY MUSEUM
91 East Hill, Colchester, Essex. Tel: Colchester 564474

Forget the happy snaps – this is serious photography! The museum has a wonderful collection of old still cameras, equipment and photographs all dating from before 1925. The fact that people actually carried around some of these weird-looking instruments is one thing, but to think they actually produced photographs is quite another! You'll find yourself amazed and amused at the four hundred or so cameras (the earliest dating back to around 1857), the stereoscopic viewers, magic lanterns, enlargers and other pieces of darkroom equipment. And to demonstrate that they really did work, photographs taken with these cameras are on display. To complete the visit (but at an extra fee) you can have your photograph, a sepia print of course, taken by an old wooden camera of *c*. 1895. Period clothes and Victorian props are provided.

SPECIAL!
The reconstruction of an Edwardian darkroom shows some of the antiquated equipment in its proper setting with a model of a photographer hard at work.

Open: Tuesday to Saturday, 1000–1800 (but check times if you're travelling any distance).
Admission fee: yes
Gifts: on sale, including collectables

GRIMES GRAVES

Weeting (3 miles north-east of Brandon on B1108), near Thetford, Norfolk. Tel: Thetford 810656

A long driveway along the edge of Thetford Forest brings you to a rather eerie and very isolated area of heathland known as Grimes Graves. Excavations at the end of the nineteenth century proved that this was the site of a Neolithic flint-mine. More recent excavations have discovered that there was actually a whole group of mines here, ranging from shallow pits to deep shafts with radiating galleries, and gradually the story of the site has evolved. The displays in the Visitor Centre show how the site was dug and mined, the qualities and different types of flint and how it was made into tools. There's often someone demonstrating flint-knapping – a skill that dates back some 4000 years. You can also go down one of the mines, Pit No.1, where a guide will explain the various features. And to finish off your visit, do have a walk around the site – the hollows, looking rather like bomb craters, mark the tops of the many deep shafts.

SPECIAL!
The main mining tool was a pick made from the antler of a red deer and there's one on display. Up to 150 such picks were used in digging each shaft.

Open: mid-March to mid-October, daily, 0930–1830. Mid-October to mid-March, Monday to Saturday, 0930–1600; Sunday, 1400–1600.
Admission fee: yes
Picnic facilities: nearby
Gifts: on sale

MUSEUM OF GROCERY SHOP BYGONES

70 High Street (just off Market Square), Wickham Market, Suffolk. Tel: Wickham Market 747207

This tiny museum in the beautiful Suffolk village of Wickham Market is little known but much loved by those who've discovered its olde-worlde charm. Set in a room within an antique shop and below an art gallery, it's chock-a-block with all sorts of curious grocery bygones, including an amazing collection of chocolate moulds, six sets of scales for weighing different items from sweets to chicken corn, and tins with half-sized labels, a wartime economy. The mahogany furnishings are original eighteenth century while the tins, packets, boxes and canisters show the stock that used to be sold in a pre-1930 grocery shop. It's small but most enjoyable, especially for those who can take a nostalgic step back to the days before supermarkets. Guided tours can be arranged.

SPECIAL!
Look out for the stuffed mouse – it's lurking somewhere!

Open: Wednesday to Saturday, 1000–1230 and 1430–1630. Other times by appointment.
Admission fee: no (donations welcome)
Disabled access: limited
Café: nearby

NATIONAL HORSERACING MUSEUM
99 High Street, Newmarket, Suffolk.
Tel: Newmarket 667333

If you've ever cheered from your armchair as the horses race to the finishing line, or had a flutter on a Saturday afternoon, then you'll love this museum devoted entirely to horseracing, the 'Sport of Kings'. There are galleries chock-a-block with saddles, trophies, paintings and portraits, all telling the story of horseracing and the great jockeys and horses through the ages. And to get the adrenaline flowing, there's an audio-visual display of some of the most thrilling races of the past. Appropriately set in the centre of Newmarket, the capital of horseracing, there are also displays on the history of the town and a humorous look at some of the scandals of bygone days! To make the most of your visit it's well worth joining a special Equine Tour (extra fee; telephone in advance for details). There are several to choose from, giving you the chance to watch the horses galloping on the heath, take a look at the stallions in the National Stud and visit a training yard to find out about the gruelling training programme involved in getting both horses and riders to peak fitness.

SPECIAL!
'Mill Reef' is a name well loved by racing enthusiasts and amateurs alike – a special display shows how this famous thoroughbred and many others are descended from 'Eclipse'.

Open: end March to end November, Tuesday, Saturday and Bank Holiday Mondays, 1000–1700; Sunday, 1400–1700. August, Monday to Saturday, 1000–1700. Sunday 1400–1700.
Admission fee: yes
Café

Picnic facilities
Gift shop
Toilets

JOHN JARROLD PRINTING MUSEUM
Jarrold Printing, Whitefriars, Norwich, Norfolk.

If you're lucky, you might catch someone working on the old hand-printing, composing and binding machinery on display here – the equipment might be rather out of date, but most of it can still be used, and this museum with its olde-worlde atmosphere is the perfect place for enthusiasts to practise the craft. To help you understand the intricacies of the various machines, tools and artefacts, a visit is always by guided tour, lasting around two hours. An expert will take you around, explaining the different techniques and traditions, and describing the history of printing and how it has been revolutionized in recent years. And to show you exactly how an old printing press works, you get the chance to print your own name on a poster and take it home as a souvenir.

SPECIAL!
As you'll soon discover, the whole process was all rather sticky and stinky, but the pen-pushing machine, built in 1924, must beat them all. Just smell the degreasant – it's disgusting!

Open: Weekends and evenings (except Tuesday) by appointment only. For full details of tours write enclosing an s.a.e.
Admission fee: yes
Toilets

THE MUSTARD SHOP MUSEUM
3 Bridewell Alley, Norwich, Norfolk.
Tel: Norwich 627889

Hot and spicy, mild and aromatic – no mustard connoisseur should miss this charming little museum tucked away down one of Norwich's eighteenth-century alleyways. The museum, part of Colman's specialist mustard shop, tells the story of mustard, its many uses and great importance through the ages from the days when Alexander the Great used a sack of mustard to symbolize the fiery energy of his soldiers! The displays are mainly pictorial with some memorabilia including packaging, advertising posters and mustard pots. There's even a gout bath – well, mustard oil was supposed to cure all ills!

SPECIAL!
The Mustard Club, launched in 1926, was one of the most successful advertising campaigns ever. The museum has posters explaining how to join the imaginary and amusing club, plus all the rules and regulations including the master rule: 'Every member shall once at least during every meal make the secret sign of the Mustard Club by placing the mustard pot six inches from his neighbour's plate.'

Open: Monday, Wednesday, Friday and Saturday, 0900–1730; Tuesday, 0930–1730.
Admission fee: no
Disabled access: limited
Café: nearby
Gift shop: a unique and extensive range of mustards and kitchenware

THE NORFOLK SHIRE HORSE CENTRE
West Runton Stables, West Runton (off A149), Cromer, Norfolk. Tel: West Runton 339

The children's delighted giggles say it all. There's nothing musty or dusty about this museum – it's lively, fun and an absolute must for all horse- and pony-lovers. All the animals are gentle-natured and every visitor, young and old, goes away with a favourite – whether it's Captain, Trooper, Jade or Judy! There are three main areas: the lower fields with a collection of all the breeds of mountain and moorland ponies – some with their foals in the season; the farm buildings which house examples of old horse-drawn machinery, waggons and carts plus a video on working horses and an intriguing display of photographs of draught-horses past and present; and the stables which are now the home of the museum's magnificent shire and Suffolk horses.

One of the highlights of a visit is the working demonstration held twice daily (at 1115 and 1515) and it's well worth planning your trip so you can watch it all. The demonstration lasts about one and a half hours and is included in the price of admission. First, you're shown how a shire horse is put into harness for ploughing or harrowing and you can watch as it goes about its work; then there's a parade of various breeds of horses in the stable yard. Finally, and a really nice touch, a horse is harnessed, hitched up to a cart or waggon and all the children are taken for a ride on West Runton Common. You're encouraged to ask questions and, by the end, you'll find you've learnt all sorts of facts about things you never knew existed! There are also special working days throughout the year – ask for details.

SPECIAL!
The tiny Shetland ponies are always a favourite, but did you know they used to work as a pack ponies for the

crofters on the Shetland Islands? An information plaque tells you all about them.

Open: beg. April to end October, Sunday to Friday, 1000–1700. (Open Bank Holiday Saturdays)
Admission fee: yes
Disabled access: good, but it can be rather muddy!
Café: with lovely views
Picnic facilities
Gifts: on sale
Toilets

THE OLD MERCHANT'S HOUSE AND ROW 111 HOUSES
Great Yarmouth, Norfolk. Tel: Great Yarmouth 857900

In the mid-sixteenth century great shoals of herring changed their pattern of migration and began appearing on the east coast of England – and it was on the herring trade that the prosperity of Great Yarmouth was founded. The town grew so quickly that more and more housing was needed and the result was the building of narrow alleyways lined with tall houses, known as 'rows'. The dwellings in these rows were unique to Yarmouth – with walls of brick or flint, tiled roofs and large wooden windows with leaded lights. The Merchant's House and the houses No. 7 and No. 8 in Row 111 have been preserved as examples. They're open by guided tour only, lasting around three-quarters of an hour. As you're shown around you'll hear the whole story of the rise and decline of the row area and the changing way of life from the days of ostentatious wealth to their deterioration into cramped, ill-lit and unhygienic properties. To give you a good picture of how they would have looked inside, the houses are fitted out with authentic furnishings dating between the sixteenth and nineteenth centuries, including doors, hinges, knockers, cupboards, fireplaces and overmantels.

SPECIAL!
Take a good look at the wall-anchors on display – these were a form of decorative wall-tie used extensively in Great Yarmouth.

Open: beg. April to end September, Monday to Friday, 0930–1800 (closed 1300–1400). Guided tours leave from the Custodian's office in Row 111 at regular intervals.
Admission fee: yes
Café: nearby
Picnic facilities: the beach is half a mile away

THE SCOTT POLAR RESEARCH INSTITUTE
University of Cambridge, Lensfield Road, Cambridge, Cambridgeshire. Tel: Cambridge 337733

In June 1910, the *Terra Nova* set sail for the Antarctic – the start of Captain Scott's famous expedition to the South Pole. The five leading explorers eventually reached the Pole on 18 January 1912, only to discover they weren't the first – the Norwegian flag was there to greet them. All five explorers, including Scott, died on the return journey, suffering from severe frostbite, malnutrition, sickness and accident. The full story of this, and other more recent expeditions to the Arctic and Antarctic regions, is told in this small museum with diaries, letters, photographs, drawings, manuscripts and relics including travelling equipment and clothing. The museum also has major displays on the native people and the arts and crafts of the region from the early nineteenth century to the present day plus an important section on scientific research being carried out today.

SPECIAL!
The preparation for the Scott expedition was quite staggeringly detailed and efficient – take a look at the records of the plan of action.

Open: Monday to Saturday, 1400–1600.
Admission fee: no
Toilets

THE SHIREHALL MUSEUM
Common Place, Little Walsingham, Norfolk.
Tel: Walsingham 510

Walsingham has been a place of pilgrimage since 1061 and this museum, housed in a fifteenth-century flint building just a short walk from the site of the first Shrine of Our Lady, tells the story of pilgrims through the ages. The other main feature is the Georgian courthouse complete with original fittings. You'll be given an information board as you enter which shows the layout with the cramped benches and prisoners' lock-up and then you're free just to wander around as you like. Don't miss the public gallery – it gives a good overall view of the courtroom. Incidentally, the town itself, historic and picturesque, is well worth a visit.

SPECIAL!
Details of court cases dated 1833 are on display in the courtroom. They make fascinating reading: Robert Blofield, for example, was accused of stealing two rat-

traps and Richard Wright was caught stealing twelve pecks of oats!

Open: Easter to end September, daily, 1100–1300 and 1400–1600. October, Saturday and Sunday, 1100–1300 and 1400–1600.
Admission fee: yes
Café: nearby
Gifts: on sale (the museum is part of the local Tourist Information Centre)
Toilets

THE THURSFORD COLLECTION
Thursford (off A148), Fakenham, Norfolk.
Tel: Thursford 477

There's a real fairground atmosphere in this museum as bright lights flash and wink at you from every direction. It claims to be the world's greatest collection of steam road locomotives, showman's traction, ploughing and barn engines, and certainly there's no denying the sheer size and number of exhibits, all beautifully restored to their former glory. In fact, it's one of those museums where you're never quite sure where to begin! But whatever you do, don't miss the spectacular sight and sounds of the Wurlitzer Organ – there are two half-hour shows (at 1500 and 1600) each day. The resident organist puts on a lively show of music and everyone's encouraged to sing along. There are also nine mechanical organs, all played during the afternoon – giving rousing background music. One of these organs is inside the Venetian gondola fairground ride, an exciting steam-operated switchback ride. It's in action every day so why not give it a go (extra fee)? Or if you'd prefer something rather less energetic, there's the narrow-gauge steam railway which runs every Sunday and on other days during the height of the season (extra fee). You'll need a whole afternoon here to enjoy it to the full.

SPECIAL!
The gondola fairground roundabout is thought to be the only one of its kind surviving from the nineteenth century. Built by Frederick Savage, pioneer of the steam-driven roundabout, it's wonderfully ornate and colourful.

Open: Easter to end October, 1400–1730. (July and August 1300–1700) Telephone to check railway timetable.
Admission fee: yes
Disabled access: good
Café
Picnic facilities
Gifts: on sale
Toilets

3 EAST MIDLANDS

(Derbyshire, Leicestershire, Lincolnshire, Northamptonshire, Nottinghamshire)

BATTLE OF BRITAIN MEMORIAL FLIGHT

RAF Coningsby (off A153), Lincolnshire.
Tel: Coningsby 44041

This is very much a 'take us as you find us' museum – you can never be quite sure what's going to be on show, but then that's what makes it so exciting! You might find a group of engineers in oily overalls checking over a Chipmunk, a pilot testing controls or, if you're lucky, you might see the mighty Lancaster, the only flying Lancaster bomber in existence, taxiing before take-off. The Battle of Britain Memorial Flight consists of nine working aircraft – four Spitfires, two Hurricanes, a Devon, a Chipmunk and, perhaps the most popular of all, the Lancaster. Based here at Coningsby, an operational RAF airfield, the Flight was formed in 1957 as a reminder of the defence role played by the Royal Air Force. The team of dedicated air- and ground-crew travel all over the country giving special air displays and even play starring roles on television and film! So just how many of the aircraft will be there

44

and exactly what you'll see all depends on circumstances. One thing's for sure, your guide (for obvious security reasons visits are by regular guided tours only; each lasts an hour and a half) will help you make the most of your visit, taking you first through a room devoted to memorabilia from the Second World War, and then around the huge hangar where the magnificent aircraft are housed.

SPECIAL!
If you've seen the film *Battle of Britain*, you might well recognize the Spitfire Mk II. Built in 1940, she's the oldest aircraft in the Flight. She was restored to flying condition especially for the film, then presented to the Flight in 1968.

Open: Monday to Friday, 1000–1600. Telephone first to book a tour.
Admission fee: yes
Disabled access: good
Café
Gift shop
Toilets

BELL FOUNDRY MUSEUM
Freehold Street, Loughborough, Leicestershire.
Tel: Loughborough 233414

You may well have heard the peals of 'Great Paul', the largest bell in Britain, as it rings out from St Paul's Cathedral in London. And here, at the Bell Foundry Museum, you can see the furnace where the bell was cast in November 1881. Lit at six in the morning, it burned until ten at night using eight and a half tons of coal to produce a heat intense enough for casting. Ask and you'll be treated to the story of how – with will and skill – the bell, which weighs a mighty 37,483 lb, was taken from Loughborough to London. The museum is housed in the former fettling shop of the John Taylor Bell Foundry, and is the only one of its kind in the country. Each exhibit is clearly labelled so you soon learn all about the various techniques of casting, tuning and fitting up of bells past and present – from cowbells to carillons. And, to bring you up to date, tours of the factory itself can be arranged if you book in advance (for safety reasons children under ten can't be included on the tour).

SPECIAL!
Don't miss the strange-looking instrument called a Trichordia. It was used to record the notes of bells so they could be tuned to perfection after recasting.

Open: Tuesday to Saturday, 0930–1630.
Admission fee: yes
Disabled access: limited
Gifts: on sale

WILLIAM BOOTH MEMORIAL COMPLEX
Notintone Place (east of city centre in Sneinton),
Nottingham, Nottinghamshire. Tel: Nottingham 503927

It was here, at 12 Notintone Place, that William Booth, founder of the Salvation Army, was born on 10 April 1829 and lived until 1831. The original house has been beautifully restored and behind the red front door with its polished brass knocker, the story of the man and his mission are told through artefacts, personal possessions, old photographs and drawings. There are six rooms, each devoted to a particular period, taking you from 1829 (Room 2 is Booth's actual birthplace and his christening gown is on display) to the early beginnings of the Salvation Army, right up to its present-day activities and international work. It's a stirring reminder of the great spirit and devotion of the founding members of the Sally Army. If you're a Salvationist yourself, or you find the exhibits have sparked off a new interest, you'll enjoy following the William Booth Walkabout through Nottingham. Leaflets are on sale (at a nominal price) at the museum shop.

SPECIAL!
A statue of William Booth stands outside, his first finger pointing heavenward in the traditional Salvation Army salute.

Open: daily, by appointment.
Admission fee: no
Gift shop

BREWHOUSE YARD MUSEUM
Castle Boulevard, Notttingham, Nottinghamshire.
Tel: Nottingham 411881

Beautifully situated at the foot of Nottingham Castle, five seventeenth-century cottages have been converted to give visitors a glimpse of daily life in Nottingham in the past. The exhibits, all either used or made in the area, are displayed in period room-sets so you get an insight into how people lived and worked. There's such attention to detail you really feel as though you're walking into a schoolroom of the 1930s – open the desk lids, there's something different in each! – or windowshopping back in the 1920s and '30s when ginger biscuits were 7d for a pound and chemists sold the most amazing pills and potions. Then there are the contrasting kitchen ranges of the seventeenth, eighteenth and nineteenth centuries, and the exhibits on popular pastimes – goose fairs, cockfighting, bingo and pub games. And don't miss the caves, or rock-cellars, hewn into the castle rock behind the houses. As you can see from the displays, they've been used for many purposes over the years – as workshops, wash houses, ale cellarage and, more recently, air-raid shelters. Whether you're from Nottinghamshire or further afield, there's something to capture everyone's imagination in this museum.

SPECIAL!
Can you recognize any of the toys in the 1930s toyshop? The old card and dice games might not be on sale now but they still look fun to play!

Open: daily, 1000–1200 and 1300–1645.
Admission fee: no
Disabled access: limited
Café: nearby
Picnic facilities
Toilets

CHURCH FARM MUSEUM
Church Road South (between A158 and A52), Skegness, Lincolnshire. Tel: Skegness 66658

Can you name two of the earliest breeds of chicken in Britain? And where do a share, coulter and mould board all belong? You'll find the answers, and a lot more, at this friendly, well-loved, well-looked-after museum centred round the old farmhouse and outbuildings of Church Farm. The only animals here now are bees and a duck, but the displays are so vivid you can almost smell the cows and hear the relentless 'oinking' of the pigs – for city-dwellers it's a real country treat, for locals a nostalgic step back in time. The museum really comes alive at its special events such as the craft displays and threshing demonstrations (telephone for details) but it's a pleasure to visit at any time. The farm buildings – the cow byre, barn and stables – house the Bernard Best Collection of local agricultural machinery, and there are some fascinating exhibitions on a farming theme including several relating to local livestock; look out for the Lincolnshire Curly Coat Pig! The farmhouse itself has been completely furnished as the home of a tenant farmer *c*.1900 and thanks to the memories and donations from local people, it's authentic right down to the scrub-topped table and peg rug in the scullery.

SPECIAL!
Withern Cottage, an original 'mud and stud' cottage, typical of the area, has been re-erected on the museum site and partly furnished in the style of 1800. Displays show exactly how it was constructed.

Open: April to October, daily, 1030–1730.
Admission fee: yes
Disabled access: limited
Café: in a traditional brick and pantile barn
Picnic facilities
Gifts: on sale
Toilets

NATIONAL CYCLE MUSEM
Brayford Wharf North, Lincoln, Lincolnshire.
Tel: Lincoln 45091

Take your camera with you – here's your chance to have your photograph taken sitting on a Penny Farthing! The museum tells the story of cycles and cycling through the ages right from the early Hobby Horse of *c.*1818 through the various incredible and clever inventions right up to the present day, with examples of the very latest racing bikes. But it's much more than just a collection of old bikes; each exhibit is carefully explained with special design features pointed out so you find out all about the MacMillan, the first mechanically propelled road vehicle, the difficult-to-master Otto Bicycle, the Ivel Tandem of 1886 and the Lincoln Elk, to name just a few. And as no cycle is complete without accessories, there are displays of bells, pipes, hooters, whistles and lamps through the ages. The staff are cycling experts, so they'll answer any queries.

SPECIAL!
One, two, three, four, five – the Ariel Squint really did seat five people. Built in 1896, it could reach speeds of up to 60 mph, but there were no brakes!

Open: all year, daily, 1000–1700.
Admission fee: yes
Disabled access: limited
Café: nearby
Gifts: on sale

EAST MIDLANDS AEROPARK
East Midlands Airport, Castle Donington, Derby,
Derbyshire. Tel: Derby 810621

If you don't know a thing about aeroplanes, don't worry – you will after an hour or so in the Visitor Centre here at East Midlands Airport. Covering a twelve-acre site, it's thought to be the only air museum in the middle of a busy, functioning airport. The best time to visit is at weekends or on weekday mornings when the air traffic is heavy and you can get an amazing, if rather noisy and windswept, view of the planes arriving and leaving. You're just 55 metres from the taxiway, so if you're a photographer here's your chance to get some action shots! The Visitor Centre is a short walk from the runway. Inside, you'll find videos, scale models and photographs describing the development of the airport, the story of civil aviation and the science of flight. Outside, there is a growing number of historic aircraft – including a Vickers Varsity and an Avro Vulcan bomber. It's designed as a place for the whole family, and it's just that. Flying displays and events are held during the year; ask for details.

SPECIAL!
Find out all about the intricate workings of a jet engine – there's a real one on display, an historic Whittle W2 of 1943.

Open: October to March, daily, 1000–1600. April, May, September, daily, 1000–1800. June to August, daily, 1000–2000.
Admission fee: yes
Disabled access: good
Picnic facilities: with an excellent view of the runway and taxiway
Gift shop
Toilets

GAINSBOROUGH OLD HALL

Parnell Street, Gainsborough, Lincolnshire.
Tel: Gainsborough 2669

The King is on his way . . . it's 1483 and the kitchen staff are busy preparing a feast for their royal visitor, Richard III. The chicken is on the spit, the loaves in the brick oven and the soup simmering in the cauldron – the Clerk of the Kitchen has everything well under control! The medieval kitchen of the Gainsborough Old Hall, with its displays of figures, food and equipment, is one of the highlights of a visit to this fifteenth-century manor house, considered to be one of the best preserved in the country. But don't imagine that's all you're going to see: every room is packed with interest. The building has been restored and furnished with many fine pieces to show its changing history, occupants and visitors – and it's not all royal grandeur; in its time the Old Hall has been used as a theatre, linen factory, tenements, corn exchange and town ballroom among other things! Today, it's a museum of living history open to everyone but designed with children very much in mind. There are quiz sheets and heraldry trails, and the Great Hall is lined with huge tables for projects and discussions. Sumptuous feasts, with everyone dressed in period costume, are held here from time to time!

SPECIAL!
Riches and rags – the differing clothes and lifestyles of the Lord and the Lady of the Manor and their tenant farmers are well illustrated with life-sized models upstairs in the solar room.

Open: Easter to October, Monday to Saturday, 1000–1700; Sunday, 1400–1700. November to Easter, Monday to Saturday, 1000–1700.

Admission fee: yes
Disabled access: limited
Gifts: on sale
Toilets

GREEN'S MILL AND SCIENCE CENTRE
Belvoir Hill, Nottingham (east of city centre, in Sneinton, off A612), Nottinghamshire. Tel: Nottingham 503635

George Green (1793–1841) was a miller by trade but his real interest lay in mathematics and science. And it's Green, who used the upper floor of this mill as a studio, whom we can thank for many of the discoveries that are the basis of modern technology. That his genius has changed our lives no one can dispute, but just how do you try to explain his theories? It's no easy task! The Science Centre, attached to the mill, has been turned into a museum and goes a long way towards simplifying the subject with lots of working models. Even if you don't fully understand everything, by the end of your visit at least you'll have had a good time experimenting with magnetism, optics and sound – pushing buttons and pulling levers! It's as fascinating for tiny tots as for learned professors of physics. The centre also has displays on Green's life and the history of milling. The mill itself, a post mill built in 1807, is now back in working order, even grinding flour, and open to visitors in the summer.

SPECIAL!
Among the milling exhibits is a grindstone – try making your own flour!

Open: *Centre*: Wednesday to Sunday, 1000–1200 and 1300–1700. *Mill*: summer only, telephone to check times.

Admission fee: no
Disabled access: Science Centre only
Picnic facilities
Gifts: on sale
Toilets

OAKHAM CASTLE

Off Market Place, Oakham, Leicestershire.
Tel: Oakham 3654

You won't believe your eyes when you walk into the
Great Hall of Oakham Castle – wherever you look the
walls are lined with horseshoes, large and small, decorative and plain, some weighing well over 50 lb. It's
long been a tradition that royalty and peers of the realm
who enter the Lordship of Oakham should pay forfeit
of a horseshoe of some description to the Lord of the
Manor of Oakham. The custom continues today so you
can spot many given by the present royal family,
including one from the Queen's racing horse. There are
around two hundred horseshoes – but try counting,
you always seem to lose one!

SPECIAL!
The Great Hall itself is of considerable architectural
importance. The only remaining part of the early
medieval fortified manor house, it's considered to be
one of the finest examples of Norman architecture in
the country. If you can take your eyes away from the
horseshoes, it's worth studying the fine and detailed
twelfth-century carvings, especially the musicians. Incidentally, a magistrates' court, dating back to the early
nineteenth century, is still held in a courtroom at one
corner of the Hall.

Open: *Castle*: Tuesday to Saturday and Bank Holiday Monday, 1000–1300 and 1400–1730. November to March, closed at 1600. *Grounds*: daily, 1000–1730.
Admission fee: no
Disabled access: limited
Picnic facilities: in the picturesque grounds

PEAK DISTRICT MINING MUSEUM

The Pavilion, Matlock Bath (just off A6), Derbyshire.
Tel: Matlock 3834

This museum, which traces the history of lead-mining in Derbyshire over 2000 years, is a gem for inquisitive children – visitors are positively encouraged to climb up and down shafts and crawl through a maze of narrow, twisted tunnels. It's fun at first but the exhibits are designed to show you just how cramped and uncomfortable conditions were for the miners – and before too long you feel as if you're on an assault course rather than enjoying a day out! The museum is so well presented there's something to capture your curiosity at every step: you can peer down into the stopes and shafts, work the noisy rag-and-chain pumps and handle pieces of galena (lead ore) and other mineral substances to find out what it actually feels like. There are displays of all the different tools and methods of working; the strange laws (unique to the area) that governed the miners' lives; the working conditions; and geology and mineralization. And to give you a picture of the different features in and around the lead-mines of the Peak District, there's an excellent audio-visual show.

By the end of your visit – and do set aside a good few hours – you'll probably be completely exhausted, your legs aching from climbing and crawling, your head spinning with facts about stemples and stowes, kibbles and wiskets, but if you've got any energy left, then just five minutes' walk away is Temple Mine, a real mine reconstructed with early-twentieth century workings. A guide takes you underground and explains all! (Additional fee.)

SPECIAL!
The centrepiece of the museum is the amazing giant water-pressure engine. Invented by Richard Trevithick, the famous Cornish engineer, and built in 1819, it was used to pump water from the lower workings of the mine.

Open: all year, daily, 1100–1600 (later in the summer).
Admission fee: yes
Disabled access: limited
Gifts: on sale
Toilets

RED HOUSE STABLES WORKING CARRIAGE MUSEUM
Old Road, Darley Dale (off A6), Matlock, Derbyshire.
Tel: Matlock 733583

This is very much a working museum; the aim is that the vehicles should be out on the road as much as possible, not kept behind closed doors. The carefully restored old carriages take visitors for rides through the Derbyshire countryside, they're hired out for weddings and television appearances, and are used to teach people all about driving. So whenever you visit you're sure to find it full of activity – with staff cleaning out the stables, grooming and tacking up the horses, harnessing the carriages and putting students through their paces. You might even find the blacksmith or wheelwright at work. It's always very busy but the atmosphere is informal and even if you're not tempted to have a go yourself (there's an extra charge for rides and lessons), you can enjoy browsing around the stables and collection of carriages. There are about thirty carriages including one of the old Hansom cabs that were so popular in the nineteenth century. There are also harnesses, collars, liveries, travelling chests, a collection of coach horns, and even a travelling tin bath!

SPECIAL!
The Gay Gordon Road Coach, which used to run between Edinburgh and London from 1832 to 1864, is a magnificent sight with its lovingly polished lamps.

Open: daily, 1000–dusk.
Admission fee: yes
Disabled access: for partially disabled riders and visitors
Picnic facilities: nearby
Toilets

ROYAL CROWN DERBY PORCELAIN CO. MUSEUM
194 Osmaston Road (A514, south of Derby), Derbyshire. Tel: Derby 47051

A room in the factory is set aside as a showcase for displays of world-famous Derby china and Royal Crown Derby china with exhibits dating back to the early 1750s when William Duesbury, an ambitious craftsman, first set up a factory in Nottingham Road, Derby, to create beautiful china. Among the artists he employed was William 'Quaker' Pegg, whose only surviving sketchbook is on show together with examples of his work. The majority of pieces in the museum are extremely rare and precious – and for the enthusiast and collector, a sight not to be missed. If you're less of an expert, it's a good idea to combine your visit with a guided tour of the factory (admission fee; telephone for details). Here you can see the sculptors, engravers and artists at work.

SPECIAL!
Among the most famous of the exhibits is the Kedleston Vase (*c.* 1790) with its distinctive snake handles and the two centrepiece paintings – one of the south front of Kedleston Hall and the other of 'Virgins Awakening Cupid'.

Open: Monday to Friday, 0900–1230 and 1330–1600.
Admission fee: no
Gifts: on sale, including pieces at reduced prices
Toilets

RUTLAND COTTAGE MUSIC MUSEUM
Millgate, Whaplode St Catherine (on B1165, 5 miles southeast of Spalding), Spalding, Lincolnshire.
Tel: Holbeach St Johns 379

This museum of mechanical musical instruments is an unexpected delight. The private collection of Ray and Iris Tunnicliff, it takes you right back to the early 1800s when music boxes entertained the family at home. The exhibits – including barrel organs, Edison phonograms, fairground organs, chamber organs and church organs – are housed in three barns, and although at first sight it's all rather overwhelming as there's so much to see, you'll find there's usually someone on hand to show you around and give a working demonstration of the various instruments. Do make sure you're shown the display featuring the history of gramophone records; it's a fascinating collection of records including the smallest playing record ever made: 'God save the King' – designed for Queen Mary's doll's house in 1924.

SPECIAL!
Unique to the collection are the Tillers Royal Marionettes, the original puppets which toured the country over 150 years ago.

Open: April to September, Saturday, Sunday and Bank Holiday Monday, 1000–1800.
Admission fee: yes
Disabled access: good
Café
Picnic facilities
Gifts: on sale
Toilets

NATIONAL TRAMWAY MUSEUM
Crich (just off B5035), near Matlock, Derbyshire.
Tel: Ambergate 2565

Make straight for the terminus at Town End and board a vintage tram heading for Glory Mine. There are usually two or three electric trams running each day and you can treat yourself to unlimited rides – all included in the price of your admission ticket. It's a mile-long route through scenic countryside with many points of local and tramway interest on the way. Once you've actually experienced the magic of travelling by tram, then the rest of the museum really comes to life. The terminus is part of the 'Tramway Period' street – a reconstruction of a street scene of the late nineteenth and early twentieth centuries with authentic buildings, hoardings and notices, iron railings and street furniture, even gas lighting. However, the main feature of the museum is its impressive collection of vintage trams, around fifty of them – horse-drawn, steam and electric, all built between 1873 and 1953, from Great Britain and overseas. Many have been fully restored and are put to work at special events.

SPECIAL!
There's an old cast concrete telephone callbox in the Town End square. The original 'Press Button A' mechanism is still there, but it's been adapted so you can use it today.

Open: Easter to end October, Saturday and Sunday, 1030–1830; Monday to Thursday (and Friday during August), 1000–1730. (If you're travelling any distance, telephone first to check opening times.)
Admission fee: yes
Disabled access: limited
Café
Picnic facilities
Gift shop
Toilets

THE WATERWAYS MUSEUM
Stoke Bruerne (just off A508 between Junction 15 of M1 and A5), near Towcester, Northamptonshire.
Tel: Roade 862229

The setting is perfect – a restored grainhouse on the banks of the Grand Union Canal in a spot that was once a popular meeting place for boat people. The smithy and rope works are no longer here, but it's still a centre for canal life as brightly coloured barges cruise up and down and holidaymakers tackle the intricacies of the lock. Indeed, the museum is almost as much fun outside as inside, with the old canal signs, ideal for brass-rubbing, and the boat-weighing machine once used to check toll charges. There's a café on the canalside, pretty walks along the towpath and even the chance to take a boat trip. The museum itself – all three floors of it – gives a lively picture of how the working boatmen and their families lived and describes over two hundred years of history of the canals and waterways of Britain. There are plans, prints and photographs, tools and teapots, models and mementoes, and, in pride of place, the full-sized replica of a 'butty' boat showing the layout inside. It's almost impossible to imagine how a family could have fitted in – until you see how the table folds up to form the cupboard door and the double bed folds away. The detailing is superb; look out for the lace-edged plates, collected as souvenirs of the boatman's annual holiday at the seaside.

SPECIAL!
Children love the model of the horse showing its traditionally painted feeding bowl and crocheted cap to keep the flies away in the summer!

Open: Easter to October, daily, 1000–1800. October to Easter, Tuesday to Sunday, 1000–1600 (telephone to check opening times during winter months).
Admission fee: yes
Disabled access: limited, notify in advance
Café: nearby
Gifts: on sale
Toilets

4

GUERNSEY

CASTLE CORNET

Castle Emplacement, St Peter Port, Guernsey.
Tel: Guernsey 26518

The confusion of walls and buildings of all dates and sizes will tantalize your imagination the moment you set eyes on Castle Cornet; indeed, its very name conjures up a delicious image. Pass through its six gateways and you'll eventually find yourself at the citadel, which dates back to medieval times. It isn't known when the first castle was built here, but it's mentioned in King John's accounts for 1206 – just two years after he lost Normandy. You'll find out more about its turbulent history in the museum – look out for a seventeenth-century oil painting showing Castle Cornet in all its splendour. And there's plenty more to see: medals and honours won by Guernsey people, trophies and, in the German Occupation Room, a thought-provoking exhibition of articles recalling the sad years of German rule. Then there's the armoury, the section devoted to militaria, filled with silverware and mementoes, a collection of buttons, badges and insignia. Finally, look out for the collection of uniforms displayed in the Hospital Building; they date from the time of the Redcoats. When you've seen all you want, wander outside and enjoy the castle's gardens. Its gardening tradition dates back to the sixteenth century when flowers were grown by its most famous prisoner, General Sir John Lambert. Lambert introduced the lily *Amaryllis sarnenisis* to Guernsey – it's now the island's floral symbol.

SPECIAL!
A noonday cannon is fired by two soldiers dressed in Victorian military uniform.

Open: 1 April to 31 October, daily, 1030–1730.
Admission fee: yes
Café
Gift shop
Toilets

FOLK MUSEUM
Saumarez Park, Castel, Guernsey. Tel: Guernsey 55384

The kitchen, the largest room in the house, was once the centre of domestic life on Guernsey. The fire in the hearth burned continuously, a kettle steamed gently on the 'terpid' and maybe some bread would be baking in the oven. There would have been sand on the floor, a bacon hanging from an overhead rack and probably a dresser full of china. Just such a scene forms the nucleus of this fascinating Folk Museum. There's also a wash-house dairy where butter and curd were made by the farmer's wife and a tool-room filled with the special implements needed to make barrels and to thatch roofs. In the cart room you can see, among other vehicles, a horse bus, while in the plough room you can see the all-important bird-scarer!

SPECIAL!
Out in the courtyard you'll find the Cider Barn, which contains a magnificent press dated 1734. At one time just about every farm of any size on Guernsey made its own cider and the intriguing display of photographs will give you some idea of the processes involved.

Open: mid-March to mid-October, daily, 1000–1730.
Admission fee: yes
Picnic facilities
Gift shop
Toilets

FORT GREY MARITIME MUSEUM
Rocquaine Bay, St Peter Port, Guernsey.
Tel: Guernsey 65036

Amazing scenes of drunkenness, free fights and encounters with the law were witnessed . . . Men pounced on the barrels as they came in, broached them and licked up the liquid as it streamed out. Some of the elite even brought wine glasses to sample the liquid. (Local newspaper report).

Have you guessed? This is a museum devoted to shipwrecks! And there have certainly been plenty of them; Guernsey's west coast forms the easternmost border of one of the world's oldest shipping lanes. Many ships have been lost on this dangerous stretch of coastline, which remained unsigned until the building of Hanois lighthouse in the mid-nineteenth century;

you can see a solid granite contemporary model of the lighthouse on display in the museum. Other exhibits include part of a silver teapot, a candlestick and some spoons and forks from SS *Yorouba*, which was wrecked in 1888, and the ship's bell from the *Channel Queen*, wrecked off Portinfer in 1898.

SPECIAL!
Fort Grey (which is, in fact, white) is itself a mariners' seamark. One of a string of coastal forts built in 1804 to defend Guernsey from French invasion, Fort Grey holds a commanding position and was manned during both world wars, serving as a German anti-aircraft battery during their occupation of the island.

Open: daily, mid-April to mid-October, 1030–1230 and 1330–1730.
Admission fee: yes
Picnic facilities: on nearby beach
Gifts: on sale
Toilets: in nearby car park

GUERNSEY MUSEUM AND ART GALLERY
Candie Gardens, St Peter Port, Guernsey.
Tel: Guernsey 0481

The museum and art gallery tells the story of the island and its people, so if you're a first-time visitor to Guernsey this is the place to learn about its past. There's a small theatre which shows audio-visual programmes relating to the island's heritage while the main display gallery is devoted to Guernsey's history from its separation from the mainland after the Ice Age to its occupation by the Germans during the Second World War. You can see pottery excavated from prehistoric chambered tombs, bronze-age swords and seventeenth-century official measures. There's a section on natural history – Guernsey's shores are rich in marine life – and some interesting paintings and photographs. You'll undoubtedly leave this attractive museum knowing considerably more about Guernsey's unique heritage.

SPECIAL!
Time for tea! And it's in a very special place – a once-dilapidated Victorian bandstand has been restored and converted for use as a tea-room. So sip a cuppa and enjoy the view across the harbour to Castle Cornet (see page 62).

Open: daily, winter, 1030–1630. Summer, 1030–1730.
Admission fee: yes
Disabled access
Café
Picnic facilities
Gift shop
Toilets

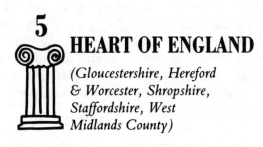

5 HEART OF ENGLAND

(Gloucestershire, Hereford & Worcester, Shropshire, Staffordshire, West Midlands County)

ACTON SCOTT WORKING FARM

Wenlock Lodge, Acton Scott, near Church Stretton (off A49), Shropshire. Tel: Marshbrook 306/307

What makes this farm museum so special, and it is indeed very special, is that it's a real working farm. Walking into the farm courtyard you'll be met by a row of waddling geese, a worker out to scythe grass, a Dorking hen or a majestic shire horse being driven out to the fields. Acton Scott Working Farm Museum was established in 1975 to preserve the traditions of south Shropshire farming in the pre-tractor age and in this unique museum items aren't simply on display, they're in use! Workers and volunteers farm the twenty-three-acre site as it would have been farmed in the period from 1875 to the 1920s. During that time horses were the main source of power and the work was hard:

> You had to get up about six or quarter to in the morning to feed them and get them ready see. And you went out to work at half-past seven when it

was light. I've seen them out with hurricane lamps, hung on the hames of the horse harness waiting for the light to come to start. And you went out till 12 o'clock when you came in and had two hours for dinner so as you had an hour getting your food ready for the horses for night . . . And then you went out to work again till it got dark in the winter, 6 o'clock in the summer, the six days a week like. There was no August Bank Holidays and them sort of things! (Oscar Morgan, formerly a farmer at Acton Scott)

Every day there's something to see at this primarily outdoor museum: hay being harvested on to a picturesque Shropshire waggon, the blacksmith shoeing a team, a Tamworth sow feeding her piglets. There are also regular craft demonstrations (telephone in advance for specific dates and times) which include making dyes from plants, hay pressing, smocking, wood-turning and traditional sheep shearing. This is an excellent museum which provides a great family outing and one which should not be missed. It's often wet and muddy so wear strong shoes or boots.

SPECIAL!
You can watch butter being laboriously churned in the dairy. In the words of George Eliot: 'the dairy was certainly worth looking at – such coolness, such purity, such fresh fragrance of new pressed cheese, of firm butter, of wooden vessels perpetually bathed in pure water' (*Adam Bede*, 1858).

Open: April to end October, Monday to Saturday, 1000–1700; Sunday, 1000–1800.
Admission fee: yes
Disabled access: yes, and guidebooks available in braille

Café
Picnic facilities
Gift shop
Toilets

AVONCROFT MUSEUM OF BUILDINGS
Stoke Heath, Bromsgrove, Hereford & Worcester.
Tel: Bromsgrove 31886/31363

A unique collection of buildings spanning seven centuries of English history and set in fifteen acres of Worcestershire countryside, Avoncroft is a museum with a difference. Each building has been carefully removed from its original site (thus often saving it from destruction) and then painstakingly restored and reconstructed. There's a counting house from Bromsgrove cattle market, an ice-house from Tong in Shropshire, an eighteenth-century Worcestershire granary and a thatched barn from Cholstrey in Herefordshire. Inside the Merchant's House you'll be transported back to the fifteenth century, while on wandering into the 1946 prefab you'll find it hard not to chat to the attendant as though she really lives in this austere and nostalgic setting!

SPECIAL!
Avoncroft is also a working museum where you can experience the real thrill of being inside an operational windmill. When conditions are favourable, stone-ground flour is milled here – it's absolutely delicious (on sale in the gift shop).

Open: June to August, Tuesday to Sunday, 1100–1730. March and November, Tuesday to Thursday, Saturday and Sunday, 1100–1630.

Admission fee: yes
Disabled access: limited
Café
Picnic facilities
Gift shop
Toilets

THE BASS MUSEUM OF BREWING

Horninglow Street, Burton upon Trent, Staffordshire.
Tel: Burton 42031/45301

Real-ale enthusiasts might be rather shocked at the museum's description of their favourite tipple: 'Strictly speaking, it's made without hops or sugar and is the sort of drink the Anglo-Saxons enjoyed. If it was served in pubs today, customers would refuse to drink it!' The museum is the country's most important open brewery museum, tracing the history of over two hundred years of brewing in Burton upon Trent. There are so many exhibits both inside and outside, it's impossible to give a detailed account. Suffice it to say you'll need a good half-day to take it all in: the working models, audio-visual displays, photographs and drawings, reconstructions of rooms, three-dimensional glass paintings and actual objects, and look out for the extensive collection of drinking glasses and the amusing 1920s Daimler Bottle Car. And you must meet the magnificent Bass shire horses stabled at the museum and used for special events around the country; gentle and kind, they're always a favourite with children. A visit to the museum doesn't include a guided tour of the brewery. Tours are by arrangement only (telephone for details).

SPECIAL!
Monday 10 October 1921 at 1030 – that's the moment captured by the Burton model. This large and

extremely detailed working model re-creates life in the brewery town just as it was – right down to the washing on the line!

Open: Monday to Friday, 1030–1630; Saturday and Sunday, 1100–1700.
Admission fee: yes
Disabled access: limited
Café: and the licensed Burton Bar
Picnic facilities
Gift shop
Toilets

BLISTS HILL OPEN AIR MUSEUM
Madeley Road, Coalport, Telford, Shropshire.
Tel: Telford 58639

A really fabulous museum where you can easily spend a whole day, Blists Hill takes you back in time. You can ride in an open horse-drawn carriage, watch candles being hand-dipped, see a locksmith at work, visit a nineteenth-century chemist, a bank, where you can change your money into the currency of the period, sweetshop, builder's yard and foundry. The museum, which shows how people lived and worked towards the end of the last century, was set up in 1967 to preserve the buildings and machines which would otherwise have been lost for ever. When you've walked for a few hours (and there's plenty of walking to be done on this 50-acre site) treat yourself to a well-deserved pint in the 'spit-and-sawdust' setting of a Victorian pub. You can sample traditional food served by bar staff in period costume, and soak up the atmosphere.

SPECIAL!
One exhibit will make you think more than any other – Squatter Cottage. This single-storey building, just 20

71

feet by 12 feet, was in 1861 home for a family of nine: Michael Corbett, a forty-four-year-old cobbler; his wife Sarah; sons Thomas (aged twenty-four), William (twenty-two) and John (seventeen) – all coalminers; his daughters Sarah (twenty) and Susana (fourteen) – both worked picking iron ore on pit banks; his schoolboy son Matthew (five) and another youngster, William (ten). You can judge for yourself what life was like for them.

Open: March to October, daily, 1000–1800.
Admission fee: yes
Disabled access: limited (lots of pushing)
Café
Picnic facilities
Gifts: on sale
Toilets
See also: Ironbridge Gorge Visitor Centre, page 86.

CHATTERLEY WHITFIELD MINING MUSEUM
Tunstall (off A527), Stoke-on-Trent, Staffordshire.
Tel: Stoke-on-Trent 813337

Kitted out in miner's safety helmet and lamp, it's off for a real taste of the coalface. Inside counterbalanced cages you're dropped into a 1930s-style pit bottom. But you're soon transported back in time even further, to around 1850. Time changes continue throughout the guided section of this thought-provoking museum: 1900, Longwall face; 1920s, pony stable; 1937, semi-mechanical cutterface; 1970s, loco railway. Until the late nineteenth century mining was a small-scale activity and colliers came from the local rural community. However, the growing demand for coal during the Industrial Revolution encouraged the growth of colliery villages where almost everyone depended on the pit for a living. Chatterley Whitfield was just such a community, and at the mining museum you can experience for yourself what life and working conditions must have been like. Coal was last drawn from the colliery in 1976 and the museum was opened in 1978. New areas of the site are gradually being opened to the public. It's an exciting museum to visit every couple of years or so, if only to keep an eye on its progress.

SPECIAL!
There's more to a colliery than its underground seams. Most impressive of the above-ground machinery on show is the steam winding machine which at one time regularly raised four mine cars (1½ tons each) in a double-deck cage some fifty times an hour.

Open: March to October, daily, 1000–1700. November to February, Monday to Saturday, 1000–1700.
Admission fee: yes
Disabled access: limited
Café: in the old colliery canteen
Picnic facilities
Gift shop
Toilets

CHELTENHAM ART GALLERY AND MUSEUM
Clarence Street, Cheltenham, Gloucestershire.
Tel: Cheltenham 237431

What makes this museum of more than just local interest are galleries 7 and 8 which house an excellent collection of objects and artefacts made by members of the Arts and Crafts Movement. There's a good range of furniture designed by Ernest Gimson (described by

Nikolaus Pevsner in 1939 as 'the greatest English craftsman'), including a sideboard in walnut and ebony, a cabinet of drawers in mahogany, whitebeam, ebony, walnut and holly, and an oak coffer with an unfinished foliage design in gesso on its front made by craftsmen at his Daneway workshops. The contrasts within the Arts and Crafts Movement are well illustrated: take a look at the simple oval pine table designed by Philip Webb for Kelmscott Village Hall, then compare it with the decorative writing table by C.R. Ashbee. Other galleries to see include seventeenth-, eighteenth- and nineteenth-century Dutch watercolours; local archaeology and history; collections of ceramics, pewter and glass; and an oriental gallery.

SPECIAL!
High on the wall in gallery 7 you can see part of a set of leather panels designed by Ashbee for James Rankin's country house. They're the earliest known examples of leatherwork made by the Guild of Handicraft and are decorated with popular guild motifs.

Open: Monday to Saturday, 1000–1730.
Admission fee: no
Disabled access: good
Gift shop
Toilets: disabled only

MUSEUM OF CIDER
Whitecross Road (off A438), Hereford, Hereford &
Worcester. Tel: Hereford 54207

It's the smell that hits you first – the powerful odour of fermenting apples. Cider has been made here in Hereford for centuries and the story of cider-making –

harvesting, milling and pressing – is told from the traditional days on the farm to the present-day mechanical production and modern factory methods. Among the highlights are the huge seventeenth-century French Beam cider press and the reconstruction of a farm cider house complete with working equipment. There's also a cooper's shop where you can see barrels being made and plenty of working models, photographs, tools and genuine pieces of equipment used on local farms for over three hundred years. And, perhaps the most intriguing of all, displays tell you about the old traditions, customs and recipes: one eighteenth-century recipe for English port begins: 'Take 42 gallons of cider'! Downstairs are the original Champagne cider cellars of the early 1900s; wherever you look there are bottles all neatly stacked in tiers. It's enough to give anyone a thirst but, sorry, there's no sampling!

SPECIAL!
The museum's King Offa Distillery has been granted a licence for distilling cider brandy, the first to be issued for over a hundred and fifty years. Visitors can watch production in progress – notice the beautiful copper stills.

Open: April to October, daily, 1000–1730 (April, May, October closed Tuesday).
Admission fee: yes
Disabled access: limited
Gift shop
Toilets

CLIVE HOUSE MUSEUM
College Hill, Shrewbury, Shropshire.
Tel: Shrewsbury 61196

A pretty building in the Georgian part of Shrewsbury, occupied by Clive of India when he was Mayor of the town in 1762, Clive House Museum holds one of the country's finest collections of Caughley and Coalport porcelain. Small-scale and domestic, it's a pleasant place to browse and you don't need to be an expert – there are helpful notices throughout the house.

SPECIAL!
It's impossible to select one item from the collection, they're all ravishing; so instead, make for the gardens – they're quite special too!

Open: Monday, 1400–1700; Tuesday to Saturday, 1000–1300 and 1400–1700.
Admission fee: yes
Picnic facilities
Gift shop
Toilets

COALPORT CHINA WORKS MUSEUM
Coalport, Telford, Shropshire. Tel: Telford 580650

Jiggering, jolleying, sheards and slip, gilding, glazing, fliny, flux and frit, they're all processes in making china. There's more: luting, kneading, fettling, and how about the terms Kaolin, Petuntse and India Tree? You'll learn just what they all are inside the original nineteenth-century factory building which has now been converted into the Coalport China Works Museum. Carefully laid out, it provides an excellent introduction to the reconstructed workshops which show the techniques of making creamware and earthenware. When you think you've seen everything you go round a corner and there's more – a display of 'The Coalport Years from 1750–1975'. Then, quite suddenly, you'll find you're inside a bottle kiln!

SPECIAL!
In the old kiln where glazes were once fired there's now an attractive display of Coalport china. Look out for the richly decorated plates made specially for the opening of the Royal Exchange by Queen Victoria in 1844.

Open: March to October, daily, 1000–1800. November to February, 1000–1700.
Admission fee: yes
Disabled access: limited
Café
Picnic facilities
Gifts: on sale
Toilets
See also: Ironbridge Gorge Visitor Centre, page 86.

THE COMMANDERY

Sidbury, Worcester, Hereford & Worcester.
Tel: Worcester 355071

The Commandery is an imposing title for a museum, and in this instance a fitting one. It's a Civil War centre which records the battles and events which changed the face of English history. Founded in the late eleventh century as the Hospital of St Wulston, the Commandery became in 1545 the country house of the Wylde family. The present building dates from 1500 when it was used by monks to tend the sick and poor – medieval wall-paintings of the saints can be seen in the room where the dying were laid. The hammer-beam roof of the Great Hall is impressive despite the fact that in the nineteenth century a carriageway was driven through it! In the hall you'll be treated to an excellent and entertaining audio-visual display. Real effort has been made to bring home the experience of the Civil War, making it a particularly good place to bring children for an unusual history lesson.

SPECIAL!
Wear a metal helmet of the type worn during the Civil War, and while you're about it, try handling the nearby cannon ball – that's if you're strong enough!

Open: Monday to Saturday, 1030–1730; Sunday, 1400–1700.
Admission fee: yes
Disabled access: limited
Café
Picnic facilities
Gift shop
Toilets

CORINIUM MUSEUM
Park Street, Cirencester, Gloucestershire.
Tel: Cirencester 5611

How many towns can boast that Roman pavements are being discovered frequently? That somewhat blasé claim, however, has not led to complacency: Cirencester is proud of its heritage, as the large gallery in its musem showing the development of Roman Corinium as a centre of production during the third and fourth centuries reveals. There are six large mosaics on display and in the reconstructed mosaic workshop you can get some idea of the craftsmanship involved. Most appealing, perhaps, is the hare mosaic, but it's in the reconstructed Roman dining-room that you can see how the decorative flooring might have looked in a Roman home. It's worth focusing on the smaller items in the Roman collection too: coins and vases, lock mechanisms, carved stone heads of gods. Excellent though the Roman exhibits are, there's much more to see in this museum, which was conceived as a regional centre for the Cotswolds. There are displays of iron-age and Saxon settlements, the Norman invasion, and a major display of the medieval period – particularly Cirencester Abbey and its extensive influence upon life in the town for four centuries.

SPECIAL!
The Cirencester Word Square is very special indeed. It's an acrostic scratched on a piece of painted wall plaster found in a garden during excavations in 1868. Experts from far and wide have all tried to break its code. The most popular explanation to date is that it was a secret Christian talisman composed sometime before 79 A.D.

Open: Easter to end September, Monday to Saturday, 1000–1730; Sunday, 1400–1730. October to Easter, Tuesday to Saturday, 1000–1700; Sunday, 1400–1700.
Admission fee: yes
Disabled access: excellent (award-winning)
Gift shop
Toilets

COTSWOLD WOOLLEN WEAVERS

Filkins (¾ mile off A361), near Lechlade, Gloucestershire.
Tel: Filkins 491

With the whirring of machinery at work in the lower-floor rooms you can't forget that you're visiting an active weaving-mill. As a notice points out: 'No one in the world now makes replacements for these looms. When this machinery finally grinds to a halt, small-scale cloth production will disappear.' It's a perfect setting for the display, which shows how wool becomes cloth and the history of wool production in the Cotswolds. There are examples of handlooms, stitching-machines, early knitting-machines and an evocative selection of old photographs. Twelfth-century weavers sang: 'In Europe the best wool is English, in England the best wool is Cotswold'; after a visit here you'll understand why.

SPECIAL!
It was difficult to measure the thickness of a piece of woollen material so a traditional method was developed; look out for the yarn counter and you'll discover just what that method was.

Open: Monday to Saturday, 1000–1800; Sunday, 1400–1800.
Admission fee: no
Café
Picnic facilities
Gifts: on sale
Toilets

DYSON PERRINS MUSEUM

The Royal Worcester Porcelain Works, Severn Street,
Worcester, Hereford & Worcester. Tel: Worcester 23221

The Worcester Royal Porcelain Company was founded in 1751, which makes it the oldest china manufacturer in Britain. Much of the extensive collection in the Dyson Perrins Museum dates from this early period, but it also has pieces from all periods right up to the present day. The museum is divided into two galleries – Warmstry and Diglis. In the Warmstry Gallery you can see examples of famous Worcester underglaze blue grounds decorated with patterns of flowers and exotic birds, all inspired by the Orient. Look out, too, for the rare lilac decorative enamels and the fine selection of onglaze prints over black. A large percentage of pieces exhibited in the Diglis Gallery formed the original company museum, which was founded in 1878. You can combine a visit to the museum with a factory tour where you can see the craftsmen of today at work (telephone in advance for details).

SPECIAL!
The Chicago Exhibition Vase is the largest piece of porcelain Worcester has ever made. It took the modeller and painter one year to produce this huge object for the exhibition of 1893.

Open: Monday to Friday, 0930–1700; Saturday, 1000–1700.
Admission fee: no
Disabled access: good
Café
Gift shop
Toilets

FORGE MILL NEEDLE MUSEUM

Needle Mill Lane (off A441), Redditch, Hereford &
Worcester. Tel: Redditch 62509

Picturesquely restored, Forge Mill is the only remaining
water-driven needle mill in the world. It provides a
good insight into the production of needles – that's if
you can manage to find it off Redditch's ring-road
system! The mill dates from 1725, but its attractive
pond is much older and was probably constructed by
monks from Bordesley Abbey (the site of the abbey is
now being excavated nearby) to grind their corn. Once
inside the museum you can take a close look at the
machinery used during the eighteenth and nineteenth
centuries to manufacture needles – it's a dirtier process
than you might imagine – including the water wheel,
some 14 feet in diameter.

SPECIAL!
The Queen opened the Needle Museum at Forge Mill
on 5 July 1983 – you can see a replica of the paperweight
presented to her. It's made from a block of Perspex
inset with two needles: one, threaded with twine from
the yucca plant, surrounds the other, a surgical needle
used by NASA to attach the thermal barrier to the
Space Shuttle.

Open: April to October, Monday to Friday, 1100–
1630; Saturday, 1300–1700; Sunday, 1130–1700. March
to November, Monday to Friday, 1100–1630.
Admission fee: yes
Disabled access: limited
Café
Picnic facilities
Gift shop
Toilets

GLADSTONE POTTERY MUSEUM

Uttoxeter Road, Longton, Stoke-on-Trent, Staffordshire.
Tel: Stoke-on-Trent 319232/311378

Television cameras have often filmed the picturesque cobbled courtyard of Gladstone, and it's easy to see why. Beautifully preserved and dominated by four spectacular and distinctively shaped bottle ovens, the potbank yard is the hub of this once thriving china factory. Your imagination will need little further encouragement to conjure up the bustling atmosphere of the nineteenth century when the air was filled with smoke and some sixty men, women and children went about their work. For almost two hundred years china was manufactured here and you can see some of its old and traditional skills demonstrated in the workshops which surround the yard; maybe casting and making of bone china floral jewellery or perhaps painting and decoration. The noise of the machinery beckons you into the engine house; more noise, this time an oozing gurgling sound, leads you on into the slip room. There's also the opportunity to see how a potter would have lived at the end of the nineteenth century, and it was a poor and unhealthy existence:

> 'life's pure stream is poisoned by the dust that floats around, and in, and like the sea, makes the employ of potters a toiling tempest curse' (Medical officer's report, 1840). Ninety per cent of potters died before the age of forty-five.

SPECIAL!
Make sure you don't miss the large collection of 'bathroom furniture' – basins, bowls and 'pos'!

Open: Monday to Saturday, 1030–1730; Sunday, 1400–1800.

Admission fee: yes
Café
Gift shop
Toilets

MUSEUM OF IRON
Coalbrookdale, Ironbridge, Telford, Shropshire.
Tel: Ironbridge 3418

Nowhere in the world could there be a more appropriate setting for the Museum of Iron; in the eighteenth century, Coalbrookdale was at the very centre of a whole series of innovations in the manufacture of iron without which the Industrial Revolution could not have taken place. Iron has been worked in the region for well over four hundred years – there's evidence of a furnace at the Wenlock Priory at the time of the 1530s dissolution of the monasteries – and in the museum you can see some of the wide range of uses it has been put to from bicycles to balustrades, firegates to firearms, seats, statuettes and street furniture. There's also an introduction to the Darbys and the Reynolds, the strong Quaker families who masterminded and managed the production and development of this precious ore.

SPECIAL!
The haystack boiler on display is one of only a handful left in the country – and no, it's not for boiling haystacks! The distinctive haystack shape developed at the beginning of the nineteenth century was, in fact, a very poor design as it could withstand a pressure of only about 10 lb per square inch.

Open: March to October, daily, 1000–1800.
Admission fee: yes

Disabled access: good
Café
Gifts: on sale
Toilets
See also: Ironbridge Gorge Visitor Centre, page 86.

THE IRON BRIDGE AND TOLLHOUSE
Telford, Shropshire. Tel: Telford 882735

Now a small museum illustrating the history of the Iron Bridge, the tollhouse was once the place where travellers would stop to pay a toll to cross the river Severn. For a person on foot the toll was ½d, and the charge was the same for a calf, sheep, pig or lamb, but a carriage drawn by six horses would have to pay a full two shillings (10 pence).

SPECIAL!
A particularly special exhibit is the Iron Bridge itself. Made from cast iron and majestically spanning the river, it was the first bridge of its kind – a spectacular advertisement for the materials and skills to be found in the gorge area. Even during the eighteenth century it was a tourist attraction, with one stage-coach proprietor listing among the advantages of his service the fact that the route crossed 'that striking specimen of Art and so much admired object of travellers'.

Open: March to October, daily, 1000–1800. November to February, daily, 1000–1700.
Admission fee: no
Picnic facilities
Gifts: on sale
Toilets: across the bridge
See also: Ironbridge Gorge Visitor Centre, page 86.

IRONBRIDGE GORGE VISITOR CENTRE

Ironbridge Gorge Museum Trust, Ironbridge, Telford, Shropshire. Tel: Ironbridge 3522

When you arrive in Ironbridge make directly for the Ironbridge Gorge Visitor Centre and you'll receive a fascinating introduction to the gorge area and its extraordinary history. Housed in a converted warehouse which was built on the banks of the river Severn during the 1840s for the Coalbrookdale Company, the centre sets the atmosphere for a trip back to the Industrial Revolution. Don't miss the excellent audiovisual programme which covers the five main museums to be seen:

Museum of Iron (see page 84)
The Iron Bridge (see page 85)
Jackfield Tile Museum (see page 87)
Blists Hill Open Air Museum (see page 71)
Coalport China Works Museum (see page 76)

SPECIAL!
The wealth and development of Ironbridge depended to a large extent on the extraction of iron ore, coal, clay and lime from underground, but there's now only one place in the area where you can go under the surface – the Tar Tunnel. Follow the disused trolley rails down a hundred yards of this 1000-yard tunnel; it's an eerie experience, particularly if you venture in alone. But don't worry, you're perfectly safe fitted with a safety helmet. There's only one exhibit in this most unusual museum – and it isn't tar! Natural bitumen oozes down the sides of the tunnel, gathering in dark pools – you can find out more in the Visitor Centre.

Open: daily, 1000–1800.
Admission fee: yes

Disabled access: good
Gifts: on sale

JACKFIELD TILE MUSEUM
Jackfield, Telford, Shropshire. Tel: Telford 882030

Decorative Victorian tiles can still be found covering the walls and floors of old houses, railway stations, public houses, churches and schools. Many of them originated from the tile factory belonging to Maw and Company at Jackfield which, by the 1880s, was the leading decorative tile factory in the world. At Jackfield you can see some of the many tiles and architectural ceramics which form the collection of this light, airy, well-laid-out museum. They make for an exceptionally colourful exhibition with swirling Art Nouveau flowers, pictorial panels for butchers' shops, silk-screen decorations, Art Deco work for 1930s fireplaces, mosaics and a whole host of lively patterns. If you aren't a Victorian tile enthusiast before your visit, Jackfield will certainly make you think again.

SPECIAL!
In the 'Punch and Judy' tile panel (*c.*1920), a small cluster of children stare at Mr Punch and his dog in their striped box beside the blue, blue sea.

Open: March to October, daily, 1000–1800.
Admission fee: yes
Disabled access: difficult
Picnic facilities
Gifts: on sale
Toilets
See also: Ironbridge Gorge Visitor Centre, page 86.

MIDLAND MOTOR MUSEUM

Stourbridge Road (A458), Bridgnorth, Shropshire.
Tel: Bridgnorth 61761

A car enthusiast's dream world filled with Lamborghini, Ferrari, Lotus, Jaguar and Porsche motorcars, that's the Midland Motor Museum. And motorcyclists haven't been forgotten either, with Nortons, Rovers, Sunbeams and Triumphs all in pristine condition. Housed in the stable block of the 8-acre gardens of Stanmore Hall, the collection is shown off to advantage. Some ninety vehicles are on display in this museum, which claims to be the only one of its kind in Europe specializing in sports racing cars and racing motorcycles. Many of the motors are still used by their owners in parades and competitions so there are frequent changes in the exhibits, but whatever's on show, you can be sure it will be worth seeing.

SPECIAL!
Most popular of all exhibits is John Cobb's Napier Railton, which holds the Brooklands Outer Circuit record for all time at 143.44 miles per hour. It was first raced in 1933.

Open: Monday to Saturday, 0930–1700; Sunday, 0900–1800.
Admission fee: yes
Disabled access: good
Café
Picnic facilities
Gifts: on sale
Toilets

THE ROBERT OPIE COLLECTION

Albert Warehouse, Gloucester Docks, Gloucester, Gloucestershire. Tel: Gloucester 32309

A century of shopping has been vividly captured in this, Britain's first museum of advertising and packaging. For some it's a nostalgic journey back to childhood memories – Omo 'the safe whitener and cleanser', Mansion Polish, Rowntree's Motoring Chocolate, Kolynos Dental Cream, Pearce Duff's Creamy Custard – for others it's a witty record of the evolution of graphic design and packaging technology. For everyone it's both colourful and captivating. Everything for the home, and in particular the larder, seems to be here: tins, bottles, posters, display cards, popular cigarette brands, patent medicines. You feel as though you're looking into a series of well-stocked shop windows: grocers, tobacconists, confectioners, chemists, super-markets. It's an uncanny experience to trace social taste and even tempo through the adverts of its age, but it's all here to see – fashion, the family car, the Jazz Age. Biggest of all advertising media is, of course, television; a continuous tape (guaranteed to keep children quiet) plays early TV commercials from the 1950s and 1960s.

SPECIAL!
Make sure you don't miss the biscuit tin collection. The decoration of Victorian tins (promoted as objects in their own right to be kept long after the contents had been eaten) became ever more elaborate as biscuit manufacturers tried to outdo each other. When the printed designs became unimaginably intricate, the manufacturers started to experiment with the shapes of tins. Increasingly inventive, tins began to appear in the form of baskets, books, vases, furniture and toys.

Open: Tuesday to Sunday, 1000–1800.
Admission fee: yes
Disabled access: good
Café
Gift shop
Toilets

BEATRIX POTTER MUSEUM

House of the Tailor of Gloucester, 9 College Court,
Gloucester, Gloucestershire. Tel: Gloucester 422856

'No more twist' – the note pinned to the embroidered waistcoat made by the grateful mice in Beatrix Potter's *The Tailor of Gloucester* is known to countless children across the world and inside this minute museum you can see some modern mechanical mice at work. Nine College Court, the very building Beatrix Potter used to illustrate her tale, is now a museum devoted to her life and work. There are photographs, sketches and paintings, together with examples of her children-sized books. Do pay it a visit when you're in Gloucester.

SPECIAL!
Beatrix Potter carefully researched before drawing the now famous Mayor's waistcoat, copying an elaborate one from the Victoria and Albert Museum (London). Gloucester Women's Institute have painstakingly produced a copy of the V&A garment and it's on show beside the reconstructed study.

Open: Monday to Saturday, 0930–1730.
Admission fee: no
Gift shop

REDHOUSE CONE MUSEUM

Stuart and Sonsa Limited, Redhouse Glassworks, Wordsley, near Stourbridge, West Midlands. Tel: Brierley Hill 71161

You'll easily spot the red-brick cone from the road and know that you've arrived at the Redhouse Cone Museum. Built between 1788 and 1794, the cones have long been distinctive landmarks – the Redhouse is the last surviving – in this glass-blowing region. Inside you can see the blowing process (telephone for demonstration times) and there's a small local collection relating to the industry. It's an atmospheric place which certainly makes you think about the craft; do remember to look up to see the fantastic structure of the cone.

SPECIAL!
Take a look at the lehr – two men fitted into this narrow tunnel area working the chain of the winding pulley to operate the annealing lehr (you'll discover what that is during your visit!).

Open: daily, 1000–1700.
Admission fee: no
Disabled access: limited
Gift shop

STOKE-ON-TRENT CITY MUSEUM AND ART GALLERY

Bethesda Street, Hanley, Stoke-on-Trent, Staffordshire. Tel: Stoke-on-Trent 273173

Although undoubtedly serving the local community, the City Museum has earned itself an international reputation for its ceramic collection, for Stoke-on-Trent has been the centre of English ceramic production since

91

the seventeenth century. Exhibits are imaginatively presented; ceramics, natural history, fine art, social history, archaeology and decorative arts all have their own galleries of permanent displays. In addition there are two galleries devoted to temporary exhibitions covering a variety of subjects in the arts and sciences.

SPECIAL!
The City Spitfire has its own room in the museum. As every local will tell you, it used to be housed in a 'greenhouse' outside: they're rightly proud of the new setting for 'their' Spitfire.

Open: Monday to Saturday, 1030–1700; Sunday, 1400–1700.
Admission fee: no
Disabled access: good
Café
Picnic facilities
Gift shop
Toilets

TUDOR HOUSE MUSEUM
Friar Street, Worcester, Hereford & Worcester.
Tel: Worcester 25371

Wandering through Worcester's atmospheric streets, there's an overwhelming urge to peep into the windows of old buildings whose overhanging galleries shade the pavement and whose black beams are so evocative of a time gone by. Then, quite unexpectedly, there's an invitation to step inside Tudor House. It's a delightful place for children as it isn't plastered with 'Do Not Touch' notices and very little is cordoned off. In the Tudor and Stuart room you can see the method of wall construction – a framework of oak beams fastened together with oak pegs infilled with wattle and daub. There's a distinct lack of furniture here, reflecting the sparse way in which houses of the sixteenth and seventeenth centuries were furnished. Much more cluttered, as you might expect, is the Victorian bedroom where everything, including the brass bedstead, seems to have been designed to attract dust! Down in the kitchens you can see a nineteenth-century attempt at making a dust-removing machine; as it relied on blowing rather than sucking, you can imagine the results.

SPECIAL!

From around 1614 to the end of the nineteenth century, Tudor House was a tavern called Cross Keys. Beer pumps were first installed about a century ago and you can have a go at 'pulling a pint' – sorry, they're not connected!

Open: Monday to Wednesday, Friday, Saturday, 1030–1700.
Admission fee: no
Disabled access: limited
Gift shop

THOMAS WEBB MUSEUM

Dennis Hall, King William Street, Amblecote, Stourbridge, West Midlands. Tel: Stourbridge 392521

In a Georgian mansion, in the heart of the West Midlands, this museum of glassware is a joy to visit. Its collection includes superb examples by well-known artists and craftsmen such as Jules Barbe and William Fritsche, as well as all sorts of items of historical interest: twinkling crystal, beautifully hand-drawn record books of coloured vases and bowls. A helpful video will introduce you to the mysteries of glass-blowing (discover what a 'glory hole' is), but better still you can join a factory tour and see pieces being made – no doubt some of them are destined to become the treasures of the museums of tomorrow!

SPECIAL!
The 42-inch-high trumpet vase on display may be a lurid shade of red and green; nevertheless it's a superb example of the great skill of the glass-blower.

Open: June to September, Monday to Friday, 1000–1500; Sunday, 1000–1500.
Admission fee: no
Disabled access: limited
Café
Picnic facilities
Gift shop
Toilets

WEDGWOOD MUSEUM
Barlaston, Stoke-on-Trent, Staffordshire.
Tel: Barlaston 3218/4141

If you've ever admired Wedgwood ware you'll certainly enjoy a visit to this museum, which houses some 15,000 ceramic exhibits together with numerous objects and manuscripts. The museum illustrates the founding of the Wedgwood company from the early days during the mid-eighteenth century, when the firm produced cream-coloured earthenware known as Queen's Ware, right up to the present day. Until *c.* 1764 the company's founder, Josiah Wedgwood, produced 'useful wares' while experimenting with 'Egyptian Black' ceramics.

The result of his numerous tests was the development of a new black basalt. Josiah used this fine-grained and very smooth product for his distinctive relief plaques, busts, medallions and cameos. However, his most famous invention was 'Jasper' – an unglazed, vitreous, fine stoneware. Once stained, 'Jasper' was used as a colourful background for white classical reliefs and portraits. The museum is grouped in period settings which include the Etruria workshops, Victorian and Georgian rooms. Finally, at the end of the museum, there's an art gallery where you can put a face to the famous names behind the ceramics you've just seen.

SPECIAL!
You can watch modern Wedgwood ware being made by experts – throwing, decorating, casting and figure-making.

Open: Monday to Friday, 0900–1700 (all year); Saturday, 1000–1600 (April to December only).
Admission fee: yes
Disabled access: good
Café
Gift shop
Toilets

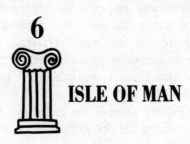

6

ISLE OF MAN

CREGNEASH VILLAGE FOLK MUSEUM
Cregneash (Near Port Erin and Port St Mary), Isle of Man.
Tel: Douglas 75522

The more you explore the Isle of Man, the more curious you'll become about its traditional way of life. Here at Cregneash, one of the last strongholds of the skills and customs which characterized the crofters' way of life, it's been preserved for you to see. The museum comprises the whole village of Cregneash, an isolated self-sufficient community who lived by farming and 'the fishing'. You can walk through its narrow lanes, exposed to the harsh sea winds, and enter Harry Kelly's low thatched cottage where a turf fire burns to welcome the visitor. Dating back to the early eighteenth century, it is furnished with items belonging to Kelly himself – a Cregneash crofter and fluent Manx speaker who died in 1934. Across the road is the wood-turner's shed and not far away there's the weaver's house where, during the summer months, you may see spinning demonstrations. Demonstrations are also given at the forge, where

96

the air is filled with the distinctive clanking and wheez-
ing of the hand-operated bellows. The smith was an
essential craftsman in this rural community, repairing
agricultural equipment as well as shoeing horses. You
can easily enjoy a whole day in this evocatively preserved and picturesque spot.

SPECIAL!
Sheep are very special here; you can usually see a flock
of Loghtans in the field behind the wood-turner's shed.
A native breed of the Isle of Man, Loghtans are clearly
recognizable as the rams have two or even three pairs
of horns.

Open: May to September, Monday to Saturday,
1000–1300 and 1400–1700; Sunday, 1400–1700.
Admission fee: yes
Disabled access: slightly limited
Café
Picnic facilities
Gift shop
Toilets

THE GROVE RURAL LIFE MUSEUM
Andreas Road, near Ramsey, Isle of Man.
Tel: Douglas 75522

Passing through the front door is like walking into a
friend's house, but inside 'The Grove', time has stood
still. This Manx Victorian house, once the home of the
Gibb family, will give you a clear idea of Victorian life
on the Isle of Man. The dining-room stands ready for
the maid to bring in the dinner – which is to be served
'à la Russe', as was fashionable during the 1850s – with

a cold dessert decorating the table throughout the meal. The kitchen, which looks like something out of Mrs Beeton's cookery book, is dominated by a cast-iron coal-burning range, while on the table preparations for cake-making seem to be in progress. Has the cook popped out to fetch some forgotten ingredient? Upstairs in the main bedroom a half-unpacked trunk reveals souvenirs of a trip to France, while in the child's bedroom there are a young person's treasures – a mussel-shell penguin, a moorhen's egg and a frog with a guitar. In each room of 'The Grove' you can't help feeling that you've just missed its occupant, and when you leave the house you feel you have learned something special and very personal about its owners.

SPECIAL!

One of the most popular exhibits in this museum is very much alive – the resident Manx cat. Tales of the Isle of Man's tailless moggies abound, but the best relates to Noah and his Ark. Legend has it that Noah sent for the animals to come to the Ark two by two but the Manx cats said, 'Oh, traa dy liooar' (which means in Manx 'time enough') and carried on playing. Finally, they scampered into the Ark just as Noah was slamming the door, and it chopped off their tails!

Open: May to September, Monday to Friday, 1000–1700; Sunday, 14000–1700.
Admission fee: yes
Disabled access: limited
Gifts: on sale
Toilets

ISLE OF MAN RAILWAY MUSEUM
Station Road, Port Erin, Isle of Man. Tel: Douglas 74549

A working steam railway with its own associated museum is a railway enthusiast's dream, and here in Port Erin there's just that! You can take a trip from Douglas along the original track to Port Erin on board an original carriage pulled by an original locomotive. Where the train terminates you walk along the platform and into this fascinating museum. Old photographs and tickets, pamphlets and posters conjure up a world which is far from forgotten – it can be authentically enjoyed today.

SPECIAL!
Caledonia, or 'Cale' as she is known, is unique to the Isle of Man. When she was built in 1885, the foreman painter was offered a new hat in return for a fine finish – he won his hat!

Open: Easter to September, Sunday to Friday, 1000–1600.
Admission fee: yes
Disabled access: limited
Gifts: on sale
Toilets

THE LAXEY WHEEL (The Lady Isabella)
Laxey, Isle of Man.

Built in 1854, the wheel is known as the Lady Isabella is the largest working water wheel of its kind in the world – a truly spectacular example of Victorian engineering. A few facts about its proportions will give you an idea of both its size and awe-inspiring appearance: circumference 228 feet; diameter 72½ feet; breadth 6 feet; it developed 200 horsepower and pumped 250 gallons per minute from a depth of 1200 feet below the surface. You can walk up a dramatic spiralling staircase to the high-level viewing platform, some 72 feet above the ground, and see this magnificent piece of machinery in action. The wheel's job was to keep the lead mines at Laxey free from water, and when you've watched the water splash off its buckets you can descend to the valley and walk the mine trail. It's quite a steep walk in parts and takes about an hour to do the full circuit. From the wheel, walk up the valley taking in the old quarry – here you can have a picnic overlooking a waterfall and the original 200-year-old mine entrance. Then a zigzag path takes you up the hill and through the woods, turning to descend again by skirting the quarry. You then follow the viaduct and take the stepped path beside the wooden trough which carries water to the Lady Isabella. At the upper path, turn south and you'll see the water-gathering cistern and the massive spare iron crank. From here it's just a short walk past the water wheel, over the footbridge near the wheel's counterbalanced weight, and you're in the car park near the point where your walk started. All in all this is a remarkable outdoor industrial museum and the spinning Lady Isabella provides a stunning centrepiece.

SPECIAL!
You can reach the Laxey Wheel by taking the Manx electric railway (extra charge). A museum exhibit in its own right and the last word in Victorian and Edwardian engineering, the railway is in full working order – so climb aboard and enjoy the experience!

Open: for details contact the Isle of Man Tourist Board (see page 313)
Admission fee: yes

Picnic facilities
Gift shop

THE MANX MUSEUM
Crellin's Hill, Douglas, Isle of Man. Tel: Douglas 75522

The Manx Museum covers just one subject – the Isle of Man – which gives it a very distinct character. However, this topic is extremely wide-ranging, encompassing the island in all its aspects from prehistoric flints to Celtic crosses, from natural history to crafts and trades. You can see jewellery found in a Viking boat grave, Neolithic pottery, Manx coinage and much, much more. In fact, the museum, which also houses the National Art Gallery and archives and is headquarters to the Manx National Trust, is an ideal first stop if you want to learn about the Isle of Man.

SPECIAL!
Take a close look at the exquisite Calf of Man Crucifixion altar panel. It's a unique and beautiful carving dating from the eighth century and is an outstanding example of Christian art.

Open: Monday to Saturday, 1000–1700.
Admission fee: no
Disabled accesss: limited (alterations in progress, telephone for details)
Picnic facilities
Gifts: on sale
Toilets

MURRAY MOTORCYCLE MUSEUM
The Bungalow, TT Course, Isle of Man. Tel: Laxey 719

The Murray Motorcycle Museum, like so many motor museums, is owned and run by a real enthusiast. There are over a hundred bikes on show, but it does take a little motorcycling knowledge to appreciate the collection fully as very few exhibits are labelled. However, there are enough quirky items to keep the non-expert occupied: nostalgic old photographs, collections of accessories, carburettors, speedometers, petrol tanks, a sidecar made from cane and motorcycling leathers. But the real bonus to this museum is its position on a bleak windswept hillside; Murray's is sited on one of the highest parts of the Isle of Man TT race course.

SPECIAL!
Take a close look at the display case of goggles. Several pairs (*c.* 1914) are made from aluminium with just small slits to see through. They're special rain goggles which were said to give the motorbike racer an unmisted view of the track.

Open: mid-May to mid-September, Monday to Sunday, 1000–1730.
Admission fee: yes
Disabled access: telephone in advance to arrange lift up entrance stairs
Café
Picnic facilities
Gifts: on sale
Toilets

NAUTICAL MUSEUM
Castletown, Isle of Man. Tel: Douglas 75522

You won't be disappointed with an excursion to Castletown, a lovely historic town, once the island's capital, dominated by an impressive fortress. A visit to the Nautical Museum will give you an interesting insight into the maritime life of the Isle of Man in the days of sail. The building which houses the museum, a small three-storeyed late-eighteenth-century boathouse, is very appropriate, but all is not as it seems . . . The boathouse belonged originally to George Quayle, a merchant financier with an inventive flair, and in the 'Cabin Room' you can see the work of his unusual imagination. There's also a small map room containing early maps and charts of the Isle of Man, a sailmaker's loft and displays of fishing boat models and equipment.

SPECIAL!
The museum centres round schooner-rigged yacht called *Peggy*. You can find her down in the boat cellar where she lay walled up and forgotten for over a century. *Peggy* dates from 1791 and is a typical small coastal vessel of her day. However, her preservation is remarkable and she is in fact the oldest known boat of her type surviving.

Open: May to September, Monday to Saturday, 1000–1300 and 1400–1700; Sunday, 1400–1700.
Admission fee: yes
Gifts: on sale

PORT ERIN SEASHELL MUSEUM
Strand Road, Port Erin, Isle of Man. Tel: Port Erin 4075

This is a tiny museum, but the variety of shells on show is wide. You can see the Giant Clam which it takes two people to lift, but most are much smaller, like the Nautilus – the sea creature which has the submarine-like ability to move up and down in water. Experts appreciate the examples of venomous shellfish – members of the cone family – like the Textile Cone which is mentioned (as something to be avoided) in the navy handbook for survival at sea. Then there's the Geographic Cone, whose venom kills people every year. Other shells are intriguing: the Contraria, which has a left-handed spiral rather than the usual right; and Marmoratus Turbo, known as the 'large green snail', which was used by the Victorians to make mother-of-pearl prayer-book covers.

SPECIAL!
Shell collectors visit this museum specially to see one particular shell – 'The Glory of the Sea'. It's very rare because until recent years its habitat was unknown.

Open: May to September, Monday to Saturday, 1000–1700.
Admission fee: yes
Disabled access: limited
Gifts: on sale

JERSEY

BATTLE OF FLOWERS MUSEUM
La Robeline, Mont des Corvées, St Ouen, Jersey.
Tel: Jersey 82408

Just the name, Battle of Flowers Museum, is enough to arouse curiosity. Islanders know all about the Battle of Flowers, it's long been part of their heritage, but for visitors to Jersey it's a mystifying title conjuring up images of thorny roses in combat with battalions of brightly coloured bedding plants. And Jersey would be an ideal setting for such a tournament, with its profusion of wild flowers, to say nothing of its acres of cultivated blooms sold for export and the Jersey Orchid Foundation, which boasts one of the finest orchid collections in the world. However, the Battle of Flowers isn't a battle at all, it's an annual parade of beautiful floral floats. Almost every year since she started making floats for the parade, Miss Bechelet, owner of this unique museum, has won an award. When you look at the exhibits in the museum, which are all her own work, you'll easily see why. There are horses, lambs, elephants and, most popular of all, 101 Dalmatians. They're all made from two types of grass – marram and harestail – both found on the island, which have been carefully dyed then painstakingly attached to frames of wood and wire. Looking at these carefully crafted (though now rather dusty and slightly faded) works, you won't be at all surprised to learn that each takes some 1400 hours to make.

SPECIAL!
Miss Bechelet's favourite float is the Flamingo Lake made for the Queen's visit in 1978. It's a stunning ensemble based on the flamingos at Buckingham Palace.

Open: March to end November, daily, 1000–1700.
Admission fee: yes
Disabled access: good
Café
Picnic facilities
Gifts: on sale
Toilets

ELIZABETH CASTLE
St Helier, Jersey. Tel: Jersey 23971

You can reach the castle by a causeway at low tide (about half a mile long); it's a beautiful walk with the damp sand glistening from the retreating sea. The castle itself is fascinating – it's one of the finest fortified sites in Western Europe – and its history, which is long and chequered, is told in the museum. There's a short audio-visual presentation which covers Jersey's fortifications including Elizabeth Castle, then you're free to wander around the museum displays which are housed in various buildings in the castle compound including the Governor's House, the barracks and the German bunker. You'll no doubt take the opportunity to scan the horizon, but nearer the castle, as you look out to sea, you can see the Hermitage Rock. During the sixth century a hermit, Helier, the son of a Belgian nobleman, lived here for fifteen years and the capital town of Jersey was named after him.

SPECIAL!
The museum is proud of its Victoria Cross, awarded to George Henry Ingouville. This gentleman, who was born in St Helier on 7 October 1826, also won the Conspicuous Gallantry Medal, Crimea Medal, Baltic Medal and Turkish Crimea Medal.

Open: mid-March to end October, daily, 0930–1730.
Admission fee: yes
Disabled access: limited
Café
Picnic facilities
Gift shop
Toilets

GERMAN UNDERGROUND HOSPITAL
St Peter's Valley, St Lawrence, Jersey. Tel: Jersey 63442

The seemingly endless corridors of the German Underground Hospital were hewn from rock by slave labour. That is a fact you'll never forget after visiting this particularly disturbing museum. The hospital was never used but various rooms have been created to show what it was meant to be like in operation. One area displays the tunnelling conditions which the prisoners of war and the slave labourers were forced to endure; it includes a realistic impression of a rockfall underground. There's also a German officers' mess, the

Kommandant's office, and an operating theatre. Together they help the visitor to step back in time and imagine what it must have been like down here and to consider the mentality that designed such a place.

SPECIAL!
Most memorable of all the exhibits is the collection of artefacts and panels which record lives lost and the horrors inflicted upon human beings.

Open: summer, daily, 0930–1730. Winter, Thursday, 1200–1700; Sunday, 1400–1700 (last admission, 1615).
Admission fee: yes
Disabled access: good
Gift shop

LA HOUGUE BIE MUSEUM
Grouville, Jersey. Tel: Jersey 53823

'Hogue' or 'Haugr' means barrow or burial mound in old Norse and 'Bie' is thought to signify a Norman settlement. That should give you some idea of what you can see here: a 40-foot-high mound over a grave which dates back to *c.*7000 B.C.. You have to be good at bending to make your way through the long megalithic passage leading to the burial chamber which contained the remains of four, or maybe five, men; it's worth the effort. Incidentally, the niche at the far end of the cave is known as the 'robing chamber' and it was built on such an axis to the entrance that at a particular time of the year the sun shines directly into it. But there's more to the museum than its namesake: an agricultural section is crowded with carts, including one for liquid manure; and there are all sorts of artefacts dating back to the early 1800s – jam-making pans, mole-traps, distinctive Jersey butter stamps. The archaeology gallery has a fine collection of rocks, all related to the islands; look out for the boulder of flint which was pulled up in a fisherman's net from a depth of 35 fathoms – if tapped it rings like a bell. And for train enthusiasts there's the last remaining carriage of the Jersey Western Railway. For a small charge you can activate a recording which re-creates a journey along the six-mile line.

SPECIAL!
Make sure you see the small boat (1.5 metres long) in which Denis Vibert escaped occupied Jersey. He was the only Jersey man to make it to England (a number escaped to France) by rowing this tiny boat across the open sea.

Open: mid-March to end October, Tuesday to Sunday, 1000–1700. November to mid-March, Monday to Friday, 1000–1500 and Sunday 1000–1500.
Admission fee: yes
Disabled access: limited
Picnic facilities
Gifts: on sale
Toilets

THE ISLAND FORTRESS OCCUPATION MUSEUM
9 Esplanade, St Helier, Jersey. Tel: Jersey 34306

Jersey was occupied during the Second World War by the Germans and this small museum sets out to record that occupation, not the war. Everything is authentic, down to the last ration book, and it all originated here in Jersey. If you're a visitor to the island, it's a good introduction to this unhappy period in its recent history.

SPECIAL!

Without doubt, the audio-visual presentation is worth watching (40 minutes long). The commentary is spoken by people who lived here during the occupation, like the French priest who secretly made crystal radio sets, and there are many original film clips.

Open: mid-March to mid-May, daily, 1000–1700. Mid-May to mid-October, daily, 1000–1200. Mid-October to end November, daily, 1000–1700.
Admission fee: yes
Disabled access: good
Gifts: on sale

JERSEY MUSEUM
9 Pier Road, St Helier, Jersey. Tel: Jersey 75940

This is the best place for any visitor to Jersey to go to find out more about the island's unique constitution, its history and some unusual facts. Jersey operates one of the oldest democratic systems in the world with a three-division constitution: Crown Appointments, States and Courts. You can discover just what this means to the island from the museum displays, but there's much more to see, like the atmospheric Victorian pharmacy filled with fascinating pots and potions. Then there's the fine collection of seventeenth-to-nineteenth-century silver including distinctive 'Jersey' bowls and some local pewter – standard measures, plates and flagons from the seventeenth century. Most intriguing of all is the wonderful collection of snuff boxes – some cheap and commercial, others exquisite and expensive!

SPECIAL!

For most visitors, the Lillie Langtry Room is the most absorbing in the museum. An actress and a particular friend of the Prince of Wales (later King Edward VII), Lillie was born on Jersey in 1853. Among the many personal items on display you can see her travelling case with all its bottles, brushes, manicure tools and mirrors. If you're a special fan you might like to visit her grave, which is marked with a marble bust, in St Saviour's churchyard.

Open: Monday to Saturday, 1000–1700 (closed first two weeks in January).
Admission fee: yes
Disabled access: limited (telephone in advance)
Gifts: on sale
Toilets

8

LONDON

APSLEY HOUSE
149 Piccadilly, London W1. Tel: 01-449 5676
(Underground: Hyde Park Corner)

Apsley House was once called Number 1, London –
that was when it was the address of the 1st Duke of
Wellington. Now it's a museum to the Duke and a
haven off busy Hyde Park Corner. If you're interested
in battles you'll enjoy the plate and china room, which
not only has exquisite Sèvres china but also houses the
magnificent Wellington Shield, the French sabre carried
by the Duke at Waterloo, and an unusual collection of
medals and decorations. If you prefer art, make for the
90-foot-long Waterloo Gallery with its extensive collection of paintings; filled with golden frames and with
huge candelabra, it's an impressive room. More
restrained are the Piccadilly drawing-room and the
Yellow drawing-room, both originally designed by
Adam but since substantially altered. Finally, mention
must be made of the nude statue by Canova of Napoleon Bonaparte. Try as you might you won't be able to

miss this colossal marble, which dominates the otherwise quite pretty cantilevered staircase. It was commissioned by Napoleon – who hated it – but was later,
surprisingly, bought by the British government and
presented by George IV to the Duke of Wellington;
Wellington also hated it! You're likely to share Napoleon's and Wellington's point of view!

SPECIAL!
Look carefully at the painting of 'The Agony in the
Garden' (in the Waterloo Gallery). Not only is this
beautiful little painting by a major artist, Correggio
(c. 1495–1534), it was also the Duke's favourite picture.
Note the lock on its frame; the Duke always carried its
key and when he wanted to contemplate the painting
he would unlock the picture glass.

Open: Tuesday to Thursday and Saturday, 1000–1800;
Sunday, 1400–1800.
Admission fee: yes
Disabled access: limited
Gifts: on sale
Picnic facilities: nearby Hyde Park
Toilets

CHARTERED INSURANCE INSTITUTE'S MUSEUM
*20 Aldermanbury, London EC2. Tel: 01-606 3835
(Underground: St Paul's, Bank, Mansion House or
Moorgate)*

This museum is all about fire insurance and fire-fighting
through the ages. It's tiny – one room within the
Chartered Insurance Institute – but packed with items
of interest: helmets, old fire buckets, documents and a
mind-boggling array of fire-fighting equipment dating

right back to the seventeenth century when it took three strong men to operate the hand-squirt. There are even three old fire-engines, including one which is over 860 years old and still in working order! However, it's the collection of British and foreign fire-marks and fire-plates that really takes pride of place within the museum and on the walls of the Institute's stairway. The earliest, which is in the form of a sheaf of arrows, is made of lead and dated 1682. If you'd like to know more about the collection, telephone in advance so you can arrange to be taken round by an expert.

SPECIAL!
The walls of the museum are decorated with an eye-catching mural painted by C. Walter Hodges in 1934. It represents the three kinds of insurance – marine, life, and accident and fire.

Open: Monday to Friday, 1000–1600.
Admission fee: no
Toilets

DENTAL MUSEUM
British Dental Association, 64 Wimpole Street, London W1. Tel: 01-935 0875 (Underground: Bond Street, Oxford Circus or Regent's Park)

If the thought of going to the dentist makes you go weak at the knees, take heart – things aren't nearly as bad as they used to be, as a visit to this small but impressive museum soon reveals. In days gone by, tooth-pullers had no qualifications or training and even less skill. A tooth operation was not only sheer agony, but sometimes fatal too. Charlatans worked from market stalls advertising miracle cures and barbers often doubled as dentists. And to prove it, there's a collection of dentist's tools from the past including a well-worn wooden chair belonging to a family of barber-surgeons in the sixteenth century and some ferocious-looking instruments whose names alone are enough to send shivers down your spine – forceps, pelcians, elevators, screws and keys! There are also paintings and drawings to help you picture the painful scene. Thankfully, the museum also brings you up to date with the modern – and far less frightening – advances in dentistry.

SPECIAL!
Look out for the reconstructions of dentists' surgeries dated 1860 and 1899. All the furniture is original.

Open: Monday to Friday, 0900–1730 by appointment.
Admission fee: no
Toilets

FREUD MUSEUM
20 Maresfield Gardens, Hampstead, London NW3.
Tel: 01-435 2002 (Underground: Hampstead or Finchley Road)

From outside, the house looks much the same as the others in the street – a 1920s neo-Georgian red-brick. But step inside and you enter the fascinating world of Sigmund Freud, 'Founder of Psychoanalysis'; this was where he lived and worked during the last months of his life. Freud moved from his home in Vienna to London with his wife and daughter, Anna, in June 1938. A refugee from the Nazis, he was eighty-two and weak from constant operations for cancer of the jaw. Fortunately he managed to bring with him most of his furniture, carpets, correspondence, extensive library and collection of Greek, Roman, Oriental and Egyptian

115

antiquities so he could be surrounded by familiar objects. He died the following year, but Anna, an eminent child psychoanalyst, kept the study and library just as they were as a memorial to her father. Her wish was that the house be turned into a museum when she died and in 1986 it was opened to the public. There are exhibitions of family memorabilia and explanations of the work of both Sigmund and Anna Freud, but the real beauty of the place is the wonderfully lived-in atmosphere – you can just picture Freud at his desk in his book-lined study surrounded by antiquities (there are over 1500 on display in the library alone!).

SPECIAL!
Freud's famous consulting couch is in the study – a comfortable chaise-longue, covered with a colourful Persian rug, carpet cushion and embroidered cloth.

Open: Wednesday to Sunday, 1200–1700.
Admission fee: yes
Gifts: on sale
Toilets

MUSEUM OF GARDEN HISTORY
St Mary-at-Lambeth, Lambeth Road, London SE1.
Tel: 01-261 1891 (Underground: Lambeth North)

This pretty church, standing at the gates of Lambeth Palace, London home of the Archbishop of Canterbury, was saved from demolition in the 1970s and, thanks to the determined efforts of the Tradescant Trust, turned into the world's first museum of garden history. Why was this church on the banks of the Thames chosen for such an honour? Well, you'll find the answer in the graveyard. Here lie the bodies of the two John Tradescants, father and son, famous royal gardeners in the seventeenth century who travelled the world hunting for 'all things strange and rare' – not only spices, shells, stones and trinkets but also unusual and unknown plants and seeds which they brought back to England and planted in the gardens of country houses. Their collections thrived; it's the Tradescants we can thank for many of our favourite and familiar garden flowers, shrubs and trees today, and it's their life and work that is the theme of this museum. However, as well as a special exhibition on the adventures of the Tradescants, you'll find out about the history of the church itself and the figures associated with it including William Bligh (1754–1817), also buried in the churchyard, who is best known as Captain of the *Bounty*.

SPECIAL!
Don't miss the Tradescant Garden in the graveyard. This has been specially created with a whole variety of seventeenth-century plants brought to England by the Tradescants – stocks, larch, Michaelmas daisies and, of course, Tradescantia.

Open: Monday to Friday, 1100–1500; Sunday, 1030–1700.
Admission fee: no
Disabled access: limited
Café: home-baked refreshments served by volunteers
Picnic facilities: in the garden or, if it's wet, in the museum
Gifts: on sale
Toilets

JEWISH MUSEUM
Woburn House, Upper Woburn Place, London WC1.
Tel: 01-387 3081 (Underground: Euston)

The Jewish Museum is tiny, quite difficult to find in an upstairs room of the Jewish Communal Centre, and a little intimidating to visit if you're not Jewish. However, do persevere because it's a fascinating collection which well illustrates Jewish life, religion and history. There are Scrolls of Law, Torah mantles, Sabbath lamps, candlesticks, pictures and all the things needed for the rite of circumcision. If you're not Jewish you probably won't know what all the items are used for, but the curator is very helpful so don't be afraid to ask! In addition, to help you understand more about the Jewish religion and rituals, there are audio-visual programmes – it's best to telephone in advance to find out when these are being shown. All in all it's an unusual but exquisite collection well worth visiting if you're in this part of London.

SPECIAL!
Make sure you take a look at the gold votive plaque with a Greek inscription, thought to date from the seventh or eighth century – it's unique. You'll find it in one of the central glass cases.

Open: Monday to Thursday, 1230–1500; Sunday, 1030–1245.
Admission fee: no

DR JOHNSON'S HOUSE

17 Gough Square, London EC4. Tel: 01-353 3745
(Underground: Chancery Lane)

Even with the help of an *A–Z of London*, Dr Johnson's House is difficult to find, tucked away in Gough Square just off busy Fleet Street. And it's little use asking passers-by for directions; most people have no idea it's here at all. However, you can console yourself that Carlyle had just the same problem and recorded the fact in his diary. Dr Johnson lived in this tall narrow house from 1748 to 1759. Today, in every room you'll find detailed hand boards telling you about him, his works and what there is to see in the museum: like the portraits of Johnson, Boswell, Sheridan and Reynolds, a stone from the Great Wall of China and all sorts of letters, books and playbills. Most interesting and atmospheric of all the rooms is right at the top of the house – the garret. Here Johnson, with the help of six scribes, compiled his famous dictionary.

SPECIAL!
Don't miss the opportunity to study a first edition of Johnson's *Dictionary* which is on display in the dining-room. Two thousand copies were printed in 1755 and they were all sold during that year.

Open: October to March, Monday to Saturday, 1100–1700. April to September, Monday to Saturday, 1100–1730.
Admission fee: yes
Gifts: on sale

KEATS' HOUSE

Wentworth Place, Keats Grove, London NW3.
Tel: 01-435 2062 (Underground: Hampstead or Belsize
Park)

The sensitive presentation of the items in this beautiful
museum devoted to the life and works of poet John
Keats makes it a joy to visit. They are, in fact, displayed
in the house which was home for Keats from 1818 to
1821 – the most prolific period of his writing career. It's
here that he wrote, among many other works, 'To a
Nightingale'; here too he met the great love of his life,
Fanny Brawne. Keats' life was short (1795–1821), but
he left such a wealth of memorabilia – books, letters,
manuscripts, pictures – that as you move from room to
room it becomes easy to imagine the young man living
and working here; after a visit you'll almost certainly
want to read his poetry again.

SPECIAL!
There are many drawings and paintings of Keats – most
of them very much idealized works by friends who
admired him. However, you can get a good idea of
what he looked like from a life-mask in the Chester
Room. It was made by Benjamin Robert Haydon
(1786–1846) as a study for a painting called 'Christ's
Entry into Jerusalem'. Keats appears in the crowd scene
to the right of the picture.

Open: Monday to Saturday, 1000–1300 and 1400–1800;
Sunday, 1400–1700.
Admission fee: no
Gifts: on sale
Picnic facilities
Toilets

KEW BRIDGE ENGINES TRUST

Green Dragon Lane, Brentford, Middlesex.
Tel: 01-568 4757 (Underground: Gunnersbury [and 20-minute walk]. British Rail: Kew Bridge)

This is a must for every steam enthusiast – a living steam museum. Here, housed in the Kew Bridge Pumping Station, you can see some of the world's largest and oldest steam engines in action. And it's an experience you'll never forget! Whether you understand the technicalities or not, you can't help but marvel at the power of these massive engines. There are many smaller examples on display showing how water was pumped in smaller waterworks, but most people come to see the biggies – the Maudsley, which began work at Kew in 1838, the first on the site; the Boulton and Watt beam engine built built in 1820, and, in the 90-inch and 100-inch engine house, two magificent Cornish Beam Engines. The latter is sadly not working at present but claims the title as the largest in the world; the former is most definitely the largest under steam – a marvellous monster that can pump 717 gallons of water at a single stroke. As you leave the pumping station – look up, the 192-foot-high Victorian standpipe is almost an exhibit in itself!

SPECIAL!
The museum is run by a team of enthusiastic volunteers and experts and if you look in the forge and machine shop next to the tea-room, you can see them at work restoring the old engines – they still use Victorian belt-driven machines!

Open: Saturday, Sunday and Bank Holiday Monday, 1100–1700 (telephone first to check the times when engines are under steam and for special events).

121

Admission fee: yes
Café
Gifts: on sale
Toilets

LINLEY SAMBOURNE HOUSE
18 Stafford Terrace, London W8. Tel: 01-994 1019
(Underground: Kensington High Street)

As you walk through the door of Linley Sambourne House you seem to step back in time. Home for an uninterrupted sequence of no fewer than four generations, and originally belonging to *Punch* cartoonist Edward Linley Sambourne, this ordinary terraced house in Kensington has a quite extraordinary interior. It remains today as it was in the 1870s and 1880s – the perfectly preserved home of a Victorian artist. An intriguing place to visit with its dark wallpaper and crowded furniture, it somehow retains the atmosphere of a home – an atmosphere rarely captured by a museum. Indeed, the staff in the house are at pains to create a welcoming environment and they've succeeded – if Edward Linley Sambourne came home today he'd recognize much and would certainly appreciate the fresh flowers beside his bed and the photographs on his desk. Such small touches keep the house a home and keep it 'alive'.

SPECIAL!
It's easy to miss the ground-floor lavatory, tucked beneath the stairs, but it's undeniably special! Tile-lined and marble-floored with an early tip-up type basin and an equally early water-closet; a visit is an experience!

Open: Wednesday, 1000–1600; Sunday (March to October only), 1400–1700.
Admission fee: yes
Disabled access: very limited
Gifts: on sale
Toilets

LONDON TAXI MUSEUM
1–3 Brixton Road, London SW9. Tel: 01-735 7777
(Underground: Oval)

Score ten points if you manage to find the London Taxi Museum easily – it's very well hidden off Brixton Road behind a large petrol station and beside a television studio. If you get lost, do the obvious, ask a taxi driver! – there are an estimated 30,000 cruising in the London area. In the museum you'll discover just how the ubiquitous black cab developed its highly distinctive shape. After a visit you'll never again take your comfortable taxi ride for granted! Just think, it wasn't until the diesel-powered Austin FX3 came into use (first manufactured in 1948) that heaters were fitted. But more hair-raising than that, the earliest taxi on show in the museum, the Unic (1907), had no front brakes – the regulations of the day forbade them! This particular model, which worked London's streets until 1931, is still used for special functions, films and television. It's also very popular with local couples getting married.

SPECIAL!
One taxi in the museum is unusual – the Lucas Electric (1975–6). Commissioned by Lucas Industries Limited and designed by David Ogle Associates, it's powered by a 50 BHP 216-volt CAV motor. Though it has all the correct specifications for a London taxi, this battery-

driven cab is unique – you certainly won't spot one on the streets waiting to pick up fares!

Open: Monday to Friday, 1100–1500; Sunday, 1030–1700 (closed second Sunday in December and second Sunday in March).
Admission fee: no
Disabled access: good

WILLIAM MORRIS GALLERY
Water House, Lloyds Park, Forest Road, Walthamstow, London E17. Tel: 01-527 5544 ex 4390 (Underground: Walthamstow Central)

Walthamstow is certainly a far-flung and often-forgotten corner of London, but it's well worth making the effort to visit the William Morris Gallery. Morris – designer, publisher and socialist – was born in Walthamstow in 1834 when it was still a pleasant country village. And this building, Water House, was his home during his childhood and student years. As you wander around the gallery, Morris's view that 'apart from the desire to produce beautiful things, the leading passion in my life has been . . . hatred of modern civilization' is manifest. The beautiful arts on display – stained glass, ceramics, furniture, wallpapers, textiles – all show a nostalgia for what he considered idyllic pre–industrial times, for example the 'Sussex' rush-seated armchair made by Morris and Co. *c.* 1868. The medieval age appealed to him particularly, which made the Gothic Revival architects and artists of the time sympathetic to his practices; most notably John Ruskin, champion of the Pre-Raphaelites, with whom Morris was involved (a drawing, 'West Porch of Rouen Cathedral', by Ruskin, *c.* 1864, is on display). Unfortunately, Morris's craft techniques were costly, putting his products beyond the reach of the very people whom he had aimed to provide with good design. But over the years, modern methods have been employed to reproduce his work and you're almost certain to recognize some of the original ideas you see exhibited here.

SPECIAL!
Many of the lovely Morris fabrics were printed with wood blocks and you can see a selection used to print 'Wandle Chintz' on display.

Open: Tuesday to Saturday, 1000–1300 and 1400–1700. Also on the first Sunday of each month.
Admission fee: no
Picnic facilities: in Lloyds Park
Gifts: on sale

THE MUSICAL MUSEUM
368 High Street, Brentford, Middlesex. Tel: 01-560 8108 (Underground: Gunnersbury, then bus 237 or 267. British Rail: Kew Bridge, then bus 65)

It's easy to miss this amazing museum of mechanical instruments housed in a disused church near Kew Bridge. But once found, never forgotten – re-enacting pianos and pianolos, re-producing pipe organs, orchestrions, orchestrelles, music boxes, barrel organs and gramophones, they're all here crammed into this tiny church. And, of course, there's the mighty Wurlitzer theatre organ which, with lights flashing dramatically, sends a whole host of instruments dotted around the room into musical harmony. It's a quite extraordinary collection; a feast of colourful sights and sounds – just try to stop your toes tapping! A visit always takes the form of a guided tour, taking about one and a half hours, You're lovingly shown each instrument in turn, given a potted history and explanation about how it works and then told just to stand back and listen as it plays a tune from a special music roll. To enjoy the music you need absolute quiet, so make sure children are well behaved. Concerts are held throughout the summer.

SPECIAL!
The Steinway Duo-Art Re-enacting Grand Piano is a great favourite, and historically very important. Once the 'constant companion' and cherished possession of Princess Beatrice, the youngest of Queen Victoria's nine children, this beautiful instrument is still, as you'll hear for yourself, in working order and is often used for concerts and television appearances.

Open: April to October, Saturday and Sunday, 1400–1700 (tours at 1400 and 1530).
Admission fee: no
Gifts: on sale

OLD ROYAL OBSERVATORY
Greenwich Park, London SW10. Tel: 01-858 1167
(British Rail: Maze Hill)

Put on your walking boots – it's a steep climb up through Greenwich Park to the Old Royal Observatory! But you'll be well rewarded. The museum, which is now part of the National Maritime Museum, has an extensive collection of weird, wonderful and positively ingenious historic timekeepers and astronomical instruments, originals and replicas. All have easy-to-follow descriptions which explain in simple terms the complex field of astronomy and the important work that has been carried out here. It's educative but great fun too and children love the museum. A favourite feature is the Greenwich Meridian marked on the ground in the courtyard of the Meridian building – stand with one foot either side of the line and you're in both the Eastern and Western hemispheres at once. You can also check your watch against the red time ball on the roof of Flamsteed House. Dating back to 1833, it was built as a time signal to ships on the river Thames and still drops at exactly 1300 local time every day. The Royal Observatory has now moved to Herstmonceux Castle in Sussex, but the old buildings, designed by Sir Christopher Wren and used as home and workplace for Astronomers-Royal from 1675 to 1948, make the ideal setting for the museum and the many exhibitions, lectures and special events throughout the year.

SPECIAL!
The museum is now the home of the largest refracting telescope in Britain. The 28-inch refracting telescope, built in 1893, is still in good working order – indeed, it was used in 1985 for observations of Halley's Comet.

Open: Monday to Saturday, 1000–1800 (1700 in winter); Sunday, 1400–1730 (1700 in winter).
Admission fee: yes
Café: in National Maritime Museum and Greenwich Park
Picnic facilities: in Greenwich Park
Gift shop
Toilets

ST BRIDE'S CRYPT MUSEUM

St Bride's Church, Fleet Street, London EC4.
Tel: 01-353 1301 (Underground: Blackfriars)

At night, the spire of St Bride's, a masterpiece by Wren and the inspiration for many a wedding cake, is floodlit to show off its full splendour. By day, it acts as an invitation to visitors to come inside the historic church dating back to the sixth century, and browse around its intriguing museum. Peaceful and atmospheric, the crypt has been converted into a showcase of relics, excavated during bombing in 1940, which reveal the turbulent story not only of the church, the seventh on the site, but a wealth of London's history from Roman times to the present day – a tale of fire, flood, plague and the power of the press. The church, tucked away behind Fleet Street, is known as 'The Printers' Church' and has always, as you will see from the exhibitions about the personalities who lived and worked nearby, had close associations with journalism and print. The museum manages to pack in a great deal – everything from a Roman pavement to the font where Samuel Pepys was baptized in 1615! You'll need plenty of time to take it all in, especially if you want to enjoy the beauty of the rest of the church too.

SPECIAL!
Why were so many wedding cakes modelled on the spire of St Bride's? A display centred round the party dress of his wife explains how William Rich (1755–1811), a pastry cook at Ludgate Hill, could see the steeple from his window and used it as the plan for his cakes. You'll also find out about the secret ingredient that made Rich's wedding cakes so popular!

Open: Monday to Sunday, 0900–1700.
Admission fee: no (donations appreciated)

SIR JOHN SOANE'S MUSEUM

13 Lincoln's Inn Fields, London WC2. Tel: 01-405 2107
(Underground: Holborn)

You'll never forget a visit to this very unusual museum. In the heart of London's legal quarter, Sir John Soane's Museum is an eccentric gem. From 1813 to 1837, this Georgian terraced house was Soane's home and, by Act of Parliament in 1838, his private museum. Into what is a relatively small space are crammed the fruits of his very individual taste in art and antiques, the result of his magpie instinct for collecting. However, Soane was a leading architect of his day – responsible for the design of the Bank of England and the Dulwich Picture Gallery – and for his museum/home he created a special environment. Walls revolve to provide extra picture-hanging space; mirrors trick the eye; whole walls open unexpectedly. A cloister and a tomb have been built from fragments of the Old Palace of Westminster and squeezed into a seemingly impossibly small courtyard; while the tiniest of studies has also been pressed into use to display an interesting collection of classical stones and friezes. All in all, the house is a triumph of architectural design and the museum a compelling place to visit.

SPECIAL!

Searching for a central object for his museum, Soane lighted on the sarcophagus of Seti I (1303–1290 B.C.). Without doubt this tomb, discovered in the Valley of the Kings, is the single most important item on display. Hieroglyphics, carved into the alabaster, are texts from *The Book of the Gates* – the religious book of the worshippers of Ra and Osiris. By standing in the gallery above the sarcophagus, you'll be able to look down on to the figure of the Goddess Nut – to whose keeping

129

the body of the dead King was given. Soane must have been very keen to own this beautiful tomb because he had to take down a wall of his home to get it inside!

Open: Tuesday to Saturday, 1000–1700.
Admission fee: no
Disabled access: limited
Picnic facilities: in Lincoln's Inn Fields
Gifts: on sale
Toilets

THEATRE MUSEUM
1e Tavistock Street, London WC2. Tel: 01-836 7624

The Old Flower Market in Covent Garden, with its undulating floor levels, low ceilings and numerous load-bearing columns, has been transformed into a museum devoted to the performing arts – opera, ballet, music-hall, puppetry and, of course, drama. The ground floor of the museum is really one big stage set which gives you the first hint of the rich theatrical treasures to be found on display here. You'll feel excitement mount as you walk down the long ramp which leads you to the exhibits – costumes, models, designs, jewellery, props, paintings, engravings and playbills. But hidden behind this make-believe world there's a whole host of facilities including study space for students of the performing arts. The second part of the museum has been designed specifically to display temporary exhibitions on particular themes; supplemented by a small auditorium where you can watch a workshop performance or attend a lecture. For theatre enthusiasts this is a museum not to be missed, and fittingly it's situated in the heart of London's glittering theatre-land and among the bright lights of the West End.

SPECIAL!
Ask to see the costume designs for the Court Ballet of Louis XIII. In the history of French ballet the drawings are unparalleled. Daring, grotesque, witty and extremely elaborate, they vividly illustrate the dazzling spectacle of the early-seventeenth-century French Court.

Open: Tuesday to Saturday, 1100–1900 (foyer open until 2000 for pre-theatre drinks); Sunday, 1100–1900.
Admission fee: yes
Disabled access: good
Café
Gift shop
Toilets

WALLACE COLLECTION

Hertford House, Manchester Square, London WI.
Tel: 01-935 0687 (Underground: Bond Street)

The Wallace Collection is perhaps one of the most overlooked museums in London, yet its magnificent contents should make it a 'must' for anyone interested in fine art and furniture. Amassed by the 3rd and 4th Marquesses of Hertford and by Sir Richard Wallace, the collection was bequeathed to the nation in 1897 by Lady Wallace. Under the terms of the bequest no additions or loans may be made; the resulting coherence produces a stunning effect. Well-known paintings include: Rembrandt's 'Titus', Poussin's 'Dance to the Music of Time', Fragonard's 'The Swing' and, most famous of all, Hals' 'The Laughing Cavalier'. But don't overlook the exquisite furniture, each piece is a work of art: such as the delightful oak and walnut console table, *c*. 1724, with its brass marquetry on tortoiseshell or the pedestal cabinet of oak veneered with ebony and decorated with Boulle marquetry of pewter and brass on tortoiseshell over red foil. They're all displayed in the elegant and luxurious surroundings of Hertford House, with its twinkling chandeliers and heavy draped curtains.

SPECIAL!
Take a look at Boucher's painting 'An Autumn Pastoral' – it is reproduced on a piece of Sèvres porcelain which can also be seen in the Wallace Collection. Indeed, highly decorative Sèvres porcelain is well represented here with, among other things, Madame de Pompadour's toilette service.

Open: Monday to Saturday, 1000–1700; Sunday, 1400–1700.
Admission fee: no
Disabled access: good
Gift shop
Toilets

WIMBLEDON LAWN TENNIS MUSEUM
All England Club, Church Road, Wimbledon, London SW19. Tel: 01-946 6131 (Underground: Southfields)

This is the story of Lawn Tennis from its early beginnings in Real Tennis through its 'ins and outs' to the present day. The museum, with views over the famous Centre Court, has displays of everything a tennis enthusiast could possibly want to know – and more! For some, it's the exhibits about past champions and tennis personalities that are the main attraction; others revel in the showcase of tennis memorabilia and trophies and the re-creation of an Edwardian summer party with tennis on the lawn. Then there's all the old equipment and the illustrated explanations showing how tennis balls are made and tennis rackets strung, including a reconstruction of a racket-maker's workshop. The question on everyone's lips is: did people really dress like that to play tennis? The old costumes are quite amazing! Don't miss the display about how 'gorgeous' Gussie Moran caused a stir at Wimbledon when she wore lace-trimmed knickers!

SPECIAL!
So you think you know about the tennis championships at Wimbledon? Try testing your knowledge with the special computerized quiz!

Open: Tuesday to Saturday, 1100–1700; Sunday, 1400–1700 (open to ticket-holders only during the Championships).
Admission fee: yes
Disabled access: good
Gift shop
Toilets

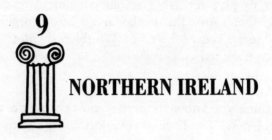

NORTHERN IRELAND

9

ANNALONG CORNMILL
Marine Park, Annalong, County Down.
Tel: Annalong 68746

This picturesque early-nineteenth-century cornmill beside Annalong harbour was the last working mill in Mourne – it was commercially operational until the 1960s. Now restored and preserved as a museum, it illustrates the power of the water wheel, a form of technology which is more than 2000 years old. To visit the mill you must join a guided tour which gathers in the mill entrance – an area which also houses an exhibition about mills and milling. Before the tour starts there's an opportunity for you to try stone-milling by hand – you'll soon realize why water-power was so important! The tour includes a look at a grain-drying kiln, three sets of millstones, hoppers and sack-hoist (note the roof beams, which are made from a ship's mast). You'll also have the chance to see the water wheel in action – always a beautiful sight.

SPECIAL!
The mill is operated by water from the river Annalong.
You can take a walk along its course to see the weir
which forms an integral part of the water-power
system.

Open: June to September 1100–1300 and 1400–1800
(groups by prior appointment)
Admission fee: yes
Café
Picnic facilities
Gifts: on sale
Toilets

ARMAGH COUNTY MUSEUM
The Mall East, Armagh, County Armagh.
Tel: Armagh 523070

This museum seeks to present the rich and varied
history of Armagh. Military items – uniforms, medals,
weapons – are here to be studied, and alongside you can
see displays of folk craft, coins, prehistoric tools, jewellery and some beautiful needlework: Irish lace, cro-
chet, broderie anglaise and embroidery. There's even
an exquisite pair of kid gloves which are so soft that
they can be packed into the empty halves of a walnut
shell.

SPECIAL!
In their own display case you can see a couple of ancient
and enigmatic 'crotals'. The word 'crotal' is thought to
have originated from the Irish word for husk or pod
which was later used, metaphorically to mean a cymbal.
Pearshaped and containing a metal or stone bead,

'crotals' ring like a bell when shaken. Their precise use is unknown but it's thought that they may have been ceremonial bells used by Irish druids to pronounce oracles.

Open: Monday to Saturday, 1000–1300 and 1400–1700.
Admission fee: no
Gifts: on sale

BALLYCOPELAND WINDMILL
One mile west of Millisle (B172), County Down.

There are many ruined mills dotted around East Down, a good grain-growing area. However, Ballycopeland Windmill is the only one restored to working order. A photograph inside shows just how derelict it was in 1935, and its condition today is a tribute to the patience and skill of craftsmen determined not to let it fall to rack and ruin. The mill, a tower mill, was built of local stone in the 1780s or 1790s and used until the First World War. A detailed plan shows you what you'll see on each floor and explains the different terms and milling techniques. Several tools found nearby are also on display, such as the old stone-chipper, used for roughing up the the grinding stones when they became too smooth.

SPECIAL!
The main beam is still the original one – made from the mast of a ship found in Millisle.

Open: April to September, Tuesday to Saturday, 1000–1900, Sunday 1400–1900. Closed for lunch 1300–1330. October to March, Saturday, 1000–1900; Sunday, 1400–1800.

Admission fee: yes
Picnic facilities
Gifts: on sale

FERMANAGH COUNTY MUSEUM

Castle Keep, Enniskillen Castle, Enniskillen, County Fermanagh. Tel: Enniskillen 25050

This is a good, small museum which tells the colourful history of Fermanagh. Oldest exhibits include flint tools found in the tombs of the earliest Fermanagh farmers, while temporary exhibitions show more recent history. Perhaps most interesting of all is the audio-visual presentation, which takes an imaginative approach to the information it conveys – you certainly won't fall asleep!

SPECIAL!
Interesting carved stones from the first centry A.D. have been found in Fermanagh and you can see a particularly good example on display, the Oghan Stone, which was used to mark a land boundary.

Open: all year, Monday to Friday, 1000–1300 and 1400–1700. May to September, Saturday, 1400–1700. July and August, Sunday, 1400–1700.
Admission fee: no
Disabled access: limited
Gifts: on sale

GIANT'S CAUSEWAY CENTRE
Causeway Road, Bushmills, County Antrim.
Tel: Bushmills 31855

The Giant's Causeway Centre is an informative introduction to one of Ireland's most spectacular attractions. It provides a valuable insight into the sociological history of this major tourist spot as well as a useful geological survey of its unusual and dramatic rock formation. A tramway, opened in 1887, running from the causeway to the nearest town of Bushmills proved very popular with holiday-makers and on display you can see some of the souvenirs they could buy. Great rivalry soon developed between local men who were quick to recognize the lucrative possibilities of being a tourist guide. Many touted for business along the public road and one Richard Lovett recorded his experience of their efforts in *Ireland Illustrated*: 'The next turn down the path will bring you either to a beggar, or a seller of spring water, or to a vendor of minerals of the neighbourhood, goes to banish all higher enjoyments of the place.' But you're safe from the 'remnant of Chaos', as Thackeray summed up his experience of the causeway area, when you visit today.

SPECIAL!
The Giant's Causeway itself can be reached by a steep path from the Visitor Centre (there's also a minibus which will take the effort out of the trip if you prefer). Legend has it that the causeways's bundles of hexagonal rock towers were the work of giant Finn McCool. What actually carved these astounding shapes was volcanic activity some 50 million years ago. Deep pools of molten lava cooled slowly and evenly, resulting in columns of basalt.

Open: daily, all year, 1000, closing November to April 1600, May and October, 1700, June and September, 1800, July and August 1900.
Admission fee: no
Disabled access: good
Café
Picnic facilities
Gifts: on sale
Toilets

LISBURN MUSEUM

The Assembly Rooms, Market Square, Lisburn, County Antrim. Tel: Lisburn 672624

A massive fire swept through Lisburn in 1707, leaving few buildings standing apart from this seventeenth-century market-house. A museum piece in itself, it's now the home of a permanent display of the history and development of the linen industry in the Lagan valley. Among the most interesting exhibits are the old spinning-wheels and hand-looms – do ask to be shown how they work, it's intriguing! And just to prove they're authentic, there are photographs of them in use. The story of this important local industry is told through prints, maps which locate the mills and factories, examples of the different materials and processes, and samples of work. It's all very well presented in a welcoming atmosphere. Upstairs, the eighteenth-century Assembly Rooms are used for temporary exhibitions.

SPECIAL!
Beautiful pieces of damask made by a local firm, Coulson's, hang on the walls. Of particular note is the sample hand-woven on a loom in 1849 to commemorate the visit of Queen Victoria to Belfast.

Open: Tuesday to Friday, 1100–1645 (April to end September, open Saturday).
Admission fee: no
Disabled access: limited (telephone in advance)
Café: nearby
Gifts: on sale
Toilets: nearby

NEWRY AND MOURNE MUSEUM
The Arts Centre, 1A Bank Parade, Newry, County Down. Tel: Newry 66232

It's said that *c.*460 St Patrick planted a yew tree around which a monastic settlement grew and which over the centuries developed into the town of Newry. However, it took a long time for the town to get around to organizing a museum; this, its first, opened in 1986. Apart from ancient objects, like a rare 3000-year-old bronze socketless axe-head, there are items of more recent domestic interest – a wickerwork pram, servant indicator bells and all sorts of photographs dating from a time when Newry was the most important town in Ulster.

SPECIAL!
The museum's pride is a preserved eighteenth-century room complete with Venetian window and carved archway. It used to be part of 19–21 Upper North Street, Newry, and was saved from demolition only at the very last minute. Today it provides an interesting, panelled backdrop for other exhibits in the museum.

Open: Monday to Friday, 1100–1600; Saturday, 1100–1300.
Admission fee: no

Café
Toilets

REGIMENTAL MUSEUM OF THE ROYAL INNISKILLING FUSILIERS
Castle Keep, Enniskillen Castle, Enniskillen, County Fermanagh. Tel: Enniskillen 23142

The memorabilia displayed alongside the more formal military exhibits help to provide an intimacy rare in this category of museum. One startling inclusion is the orange Japanese flag – the Japanese characters written on it are messages to the soldier who owned it from his family and friends. Prized possessions include the bugle which sounded at the charge of the Battle of the Somme in 1916. But it is the uniforms, standards, medals, badges and engravings which really tell the story of the regiment from its origins in the seventeenth century.

SPECIAL!
In pride of place is the display of no fewer than eight Victoria Crosses awarded during the First World War.

Open: Monday to Friday, 0930–1230 and 1400–1630.
Admission fee: yes
Disabled access: limited
Gifts: on sale
Toilets

REGIMENTAL MUSEUM OF THE ROYAL IRISH FUSILIERS

The Sovereign's House, The Mall, Armagh, County Armagh. Tel: Armagh 522911

If you're interested in army history you shouldn't miss this fascinating museum. It covers the history of five regiments – all raised in 1793 in response to French expansion after the Revolution. In 1881 they were merged into one regiment of five battalions. In the hall you can see a family tree which shows the development of the regiment from 1793 to 1968. Other exhibits include a soldier's uniform from the Peninsular War period – a rare item as uniforms of the time were worn until they fell apart – and a Christmas card from Adolf Hitler.

SPECIAL!
Don't miss the staff of the French Eagle Standard. It had been presented to the 8th French Infantry Regiment personally by Napoleon but was captured by the Fusiliers during the Battle of Barrosa on 5 March 1811.

Open: Monday to Friday, 1000–1300 and 1400–1600 (telephone for an appointment).
Admission fee: no
Disabled access: limited (flight of steps at entrance)
Gifts: on sale
Toilets

SAINT PATRICK HERITAGE CENTRE AND DOWN MUSEUM

The Mall, Downpatrick, County Down.
Tel: Downpatrick 5218

This as yet small museum attempts to tell the truth about St Patrick, rather than repeat the numerous myths which surround Ireland's patron saint. Such an aim has an immediate and obvious problem – lack of verifiable information to exhibit. However, there are two documents attributable to St Patrick and these have been used to tell his story. Large-scale illustrations show the strong link between south-east Ulster and early Christianity while small models of early Irish village life help you imagine what this part of the Ireland was like when St Patrick lived here.

SPECIAL!
The building which houses the Heritage Centre was once Down County Gaol. It dates from 1789–96 and is the most complete surviving Irish gaol of its type. The whole gaol complex, including the three-storey cell block has undergone restoration and is now the headquarters of Down Museum. Note the red brickwork over the front doorway – it indicates the entrance to what used to be the gaol gallows.

Open: Tuesday to Friday, 1100–1700; Saturday, 1400–1700 (July and August, extended opening: telephone for details).
Admission fee: no
Disabled access: very limited (telephone for details)
Gifts: on sale
Toilets

143

TRANSPORT MUSEUM
Witham Street, Belfast, County Down.
Tel: Belfast 451519

You can see the biggest locomotive ever built in Ireland and the smallest car here in the Transport Museum, a sadly often forgotten offshoot of the Ulster Folk and Transport Museum (see page 146). Old Maeve, a 3-cylinder express locomotive, was built in 1939 and weighs a massive 135 tons. An amusing contrast is the tiny car made for Davy Jones, the smallest man in the world. It's powered by a lawnmower engine! With steam locomotives, street trams, road vehicles, even wheelbarrows, the museum traces the history of Irish transport over 200 years. The vehicles are restored to good order and you can step inside the driver's cab in some of the locomotives. It's one of those museums that seems to have a surprise at every turn – and as there's no guidebook, you get an exciting feeling that you're discovering everything for the first time.

SPECIAL!
The No.118 double-decker horse-tramcar was a familiar sight on the streets of Belfast from about 1885 to 1905. The one on show has been rebuilt by the museum and is in working order.

Open: Monday to Saturday, 1000–1700.
Admission fee: yes
Disabled access: good
Gifts: on sale

ULSTER-AMERICAN FOLK PARK
Camphill, Omagh, County Tyrone.
Tel: Omagh 3292/3293

Have you ever wondered where the saying 'burning your candle at both ends' originated? Well, surprisingly, this is the place to find out. Make for the Pennsylvania Log Cabin and all will be revealed in a setting which seems to have jumped across continents and time. The Ulster-American Folk Park shows, through original and reconstructed buildings, the many links between Ulster and the New World. It is a tale of migration which shows both what the people left behind and what they established across the water. Weaver's Cottage is a typical dual-purpose dwelling which could be found throughout Ulster during the eighteenth and nineteenth centuries; here tweed or linen was made by a weaver family. The nearby Log Cabin, with its sparse facilities, is the sort of house early emigrants first occupied in America; it's an adaptation of European log construction to the possibilities offered by the New World forests. But before they could build, emigrants had to search for land, travelling in Conestoga Waggons: 'We slept by night in the waggon and in the evening and the morning prepared our food at a camp fire by the side of the road, as was then the custom of emigrants.' You can see one such wagon on show in the park along with a host of other details which graphically illustrate this tremendous story.

SPECIAL!
A chance for an American-style feast! Well, at least a taster or two as there's often a pot of corn chowder simmering on the fire in a cottage or a batch of corn-meal muffins baking in the oven.

Open: Easter to early September, Monday to Saturday, 1100–1830; Sunday, 1130–1900. Mid-September to Easter, Monday to Friday, 1030–1700.
Admission fee: yes
Disabled access: good
Café
Picnic facilities
Gift shop
Toilets

ULSTER FOLK AND TRANSPORT MUSEUM

Cultra, near Holywood (on A2), County Down.
Tel: Belfast 428428

This museum is huge – covering around 136 acres – and so fascinating you'll want to see it all. So set aside a whole day, put on a good pair of walking shoes and enjoy yourself! The aim is to show the traditional way of life of people living in Ulster over the past couple of centuries. Extensive research ensures that everything is authentic and new additions and projects are under way all the time, so you can never be quite sure what you'll find.

Your first port of call is Cultra Manor, a Visitor Centre with exhibition galleries showing domestic life and farming practices. Here you can pick up a much-needed plan to help you make your way around the open-air folk park. All the buildings in the park have been removed stone by stone from different parts of the Ulster countryside and rebuilt here in settings as close as possible to the originals. There are farmhouses, cottages, water-mills, a school and a small village with a thatched house, church, shops and a terrace of industrial workers' houses, the interiors of which are refurbished right down to the tiniest of details, so that each

146

building is a mini-museum. In some there's an attendant to answer your questions, in others you get the strange feeling that the owner has just popped out and will be back in a minute to put on the kettle! The scenery as you walk between exhibits is beautiful; notice the fields around you – the crops are still harvested in the traditional way and you're welcome to lend a hand.

The Transport Galleries can boast just about every kind of ancient vehicle including donkey creels and Scotch carts, with exhibits continuing the story of transport up to the present day with a modern proto-type of a military vertical-take-off-and-landing aircraft. It's a really comprehensive collection including trans-port on the roads, air, sea and inland water – look out for the three-masted schooner *Result*, built at Carrick-fergus in 1893.

A miniature steam railway, the only one in Northern Ireland, runs from here at weekends.

SPECIAL!
The thatched, whitewashed cottier's house from Dun-crun, County Derry, was the first outdoor exhibit at the museum. As you look around, it's worth remem-bering that it was lived in until about 1952. The owner, Mrs Margaret Clyde, who died in her late nineties, was quite a character and the house was well known as a centre for 'ceilidhing' and playing cards!

Open: April to September, Monday to Saturday, 1100–1800; Sunday, 1400–1800 (May and June, Wednesday, open until 2100). October to April, Monday to Saturday, 1100–1700; Sunday, 1400–1700.
Admission fee: yes
Disabled access: limited
Café
Picnic facilities

147

Gift shop
Toilets

ULSTER MUSEUM
Botanic Gardens, Belfast. Tel: Belfast 668251

Situated in the Botanic Gardens, one of Belfast's oldest green spaces, the Ulster Museum is an impressive place to visit. It's noted particularly for its Irish antiquities, but you'll discover in its labyrinth of galleries sections devoted to natural history, geology, archaeology, engineering, fine art, technology and much, much more. The earliest museum collection in the city belonged to the Belfast Reading Society (founded 1788) which was described, when it was handed over to the Belfast Natural History Society, as a 'cabinet' – you'll quickly realize on visiting this vast museum today that there have been a lot of changes over the last century and half since this, 'the first ever museum erected in Ireland by public subscription', was opened to the public.

SPECIAL!
The most recent addition to the museum has been the 'World of the Dinosaur'. The story is told with bubble captions and ends with a real dinosaur skeleton.

Open: Monday to Friday, 1000–1700; Saturday, 1300–1700; Sunday, 1400–1700.
Admission fee: no
Disabled access: good
Café
Picnic facilities
Gift shop
Toilets

10
NORTHUMBRIA

(Cleveland, County Durham, Northumberland, Tyne and Wear)

BEAMISH NORTH OF ENGLAND OPEN AIR MUSEUM
Stanley (off A693), near Chester-le-Street, Co. Durham.
Tel: Stanley 231811

Acres and acres of different museums all rolled into one – that's Beamish, and it all adds up to a day out you'll find hard to beat. The idea behind the 200-acre site is to preserve the North of England's recent past and show the everyday life of ordinary folk going about their business, whether it's growing leeks in the back garden or working down the mine, or even sitting in the dentist's chair.

There are five main areas including Rowley Station, a country railway station complete with signal-box, goods shed, coal cells, weighbridge and, often, locomotives under steam; Home Farm, a traditional working farmstead with farm animals, farmhouse and an intriguing collection of old agricultural implements and exhibitions on farm life at the turn of the century. Then there's the Transport Collection – a huge variety of steam and horse-drawn vehicles, electric tram cars, commercial vehicles and fire-engines. The Colliery closed in the 1950s but has been reopened with guided tours taking you down a 'drift mine' to show working conditions in around 1910. Nearby you can meet some of the retired pit ponies grazing peacefully in the fields, and have a good look around a row of original pit cottages fully furnished right down to the smell of freshly-baked bread in the coal-fired oven. And as though that's not enough, you've got another treat in store, Beamish's latest addition – the 1920s High Street where electric trams come and go, giving visitors rides to other parts of the museum. The row of Georgian-style terraced houses contains a fully equipped solicitor's office, dentist's home and surgery. Next door is The Sun Inn, a 1920s-style public house, and the stables of the Newcastle Breweries dray horses with the real thing on show! There's also the Co-op, fully stocked with 1920s goods at 1920s prices, and hand-printing demonstrations in the print works. Exhausted already? Well, just wait until you've actually been to Beamish!

SPECIAL!
Listen to the rousing sound of the brass bands playing in the bandstand in the Victorian park – music while you enjoy your well-deserved picnic lunch!

Open: Easter to mid-September, daily, 1000–1800. Mid-September to Easter, Tuesday to Sunday, 1000–1700 (last ticket, 1600).
Admission fee: yes (includes tour of mine and tram and horse-drawn carriage rides)
Disabled access: limited (telephone in advance)
Café: or enjoy a pint in The Sun Inn!
Picnic facilities
Gifts: on sale
Toilets

BEDE MONASTERY MUSEUM
Jarrow Hall, Church Bank, Jarrow, Tyne and Wear.
Tel: Tyneside 4892106

Before you go inside the museum, take a look across Drewett's Park to St Paul's Church. It was here in 68 A.D. that Benedict Biscop founded St Paul's Monastery where the Venerable Bede, one of the great Northern saints and scholars, spent his life and where he wrote *History of the English Church and People*. The museum itself, housed in the eighteenth-century Jarrow Hall, will tell you more about both Bede and the history of the monastery. There's an audio-visual presentation which takes you behind the scenes of monastic life, and a scale model of St Paul's in the seventh century showing the various rooms and buildings. And as solid evidence, archaeological finds are on show, discovered on the site of the Saxon and Norman monasteries. An important feature of the museum is the glass displays. Stained glass has been found on the site dating back to around 685 A.D., the earliest of its kind yet uncovered, and exhibits show how it was manufactured – an intricate and skilled process. And now you know more, it's worth actually looking around St Paul's Church, just a short walk away, and the picturesque ruins of the monastery.

SPECIAL!
The garden is planted with many of the herbs that would have been used by the monks for culinary and medicinal purposes.

Open: April to October, Tuesday to Saturday, 1000–1730; Sunday, 1430–1730. November to March, Tuesday to Saturday, 1100–1630; Sunday, 1430–1730.
Admission fee: yes

Café
Picnic facilities
Gift shop
Toilets

BERWICK BARRACKS

The Barracks, off Church Street, Berwick-upon-Tweed,
Northumberland.

Berwick, with its medieval castle and walls and the
Elizabethan ramparts that encircle the town, is one of
the best-fortified towns in Europe. As you might
expect, the Barracks, first occupied in 1721, are impressive buildings. Designed to accommodate thirty-
six officers and 600 men, they're built round a square
and entered by a splendid gatehouse. The Barracks have
been recently restored and are now home for three
museums – all worth a visit in their own right.

BOROUGH MUSEUM AND ART GALLERY
Tel: Berwick-upon-Tweed 308473
Housed in the Clock Block, this museum is a little-
known treasure-house of priceless fine art. While the
Burrell Collection in Glasgow has become internation-
ally famous, few people realize that here in Berwick are
over 800 paintings and artefacts donated to the town by
the eccentric Sir William Burrell himself, a regular
visitor to the Borough Museum before it moved to the
Barracks. Displayed in an imaginative setting, surrounded by packaging cases and straw, this Burrell
collection, a tenth of the total, is a hidden gem. Other
exhibits in the museum show the history of the
Borough.

'BY BEAT OF DRUM'
Tel: Berwick-upon-Tweed 304493

An original eighteenth-century barrack block is the perfect home for this exhibition tracing the history of the British infantryman from 1660 to the end of the nineteenth century. With life-sized models, room-sets, maps, mementoes and medals you can find out exactly how the soldiers lived and worked. If you weren't interested in military history before, you certainly will be after a visit here! Everything is beautifully detailed – right down to a typical meal – and so well explained with information boards and illustrations you just can't help but be enthralled. Of special interest is the reconstruction of a barrack room of 1757.

KING'S OWN SCOTTISH BORDERERS REGIMENTAL MUSEUM
Tel: Berwick-upon-Tweed 307426/7

The KOSB have long associations with the Barracks – their Regimental Headquarters are still in 'O' Block, where you'll also find their museum. Displays trace the history of the regiment from the year it was raised, 1689, right to the present day, and each exhibit has a story to tell: there's a shoulder-pad covered with mud from Gallipoli, chocolate bought from the fund for 'Scottish Comforts', and a traycloth embroidered by the owner of a coffee-shop with the names of over fifty soldiers. There are medals, weapons, pictures, models and a reconstruction of an officers' mess through the ages.

SPECIAL!

A good way to complete your visit is by a guided tour (extra fee) of Berwick and its fortifications. You'll be shown around by an expert and taken into places not usually open to the public. Tours leave regularly during the summer.

Open: Hours subject to change, telephone for details.
Admission fee: yes
Café
Gifts: on sale
Toilets

THE BOWES MUSEUM
Barnard Castle, Co. Durham. Tel: Teesdale 37139

At first sight this huge French Renaissance-style building is really quite overpowering – it's tempting just to admire it from the outside and walk away. But don't: an absolute wealth of fine and varied collections is waiting for you inside. Head straight for Room 10 – here you can enjoy the romantic story of John and Josephine Bowes, a couple with a passion for collecting who set their hearts on opening a purpose-built public museum, a novel and original enterprise for the mid-nineteenth century. After long delays, The Bowes Museum finally opened in 1892, too late for the couple to see the fruits of their labours. But as you walk around, you'll thank the Bowes for their efforts. There's something of exquisite beauty or special interest wherever you look: porcelain, tapestries, embroideries, English and French furniture and clocks from the sixteenth to the nineteenth centuries, period room-sets and an important collection of European art including works by El Greco, Goya and Tiepolo. There are also displays of folk life, children's toys and games, musical instruments and regional archaeology dating back to the Mesolithic period.

SPECIAL!
A silver swan floating gracefully on water in the entrance hall has a wonderfully calming effect on visitors. Dating back to before 1774, this life-sized automated swan is played regularly once or twice a day.

Open: May to end September, Monday to Saturday, 1000–1730; Sunday, 1400–1700. March, April, October, Monday to Saturday, 1000–1700; Sunday, 1400–1700. November to February, Monday to Saturday, 1000–1600; Sunday, 1400–1600.
Admission fee: yes
Disabled access: good
Café
Picnic facilities: in grounds
Gifts: on sale
Toilets

THE CAPTAIN COOK BIRTHPLACE MUSEUM
Stewart Park, Marton (off A172), Middlesbrough, Cleveland. Tel: Middlesbrough 311211

A tall totem pole and Wa'alele canoe greet visitors to this museum, a colourful and imaginative tribute to a great navigator. Set in the lovely Stewart Park, the Captain Cook Birthplace Museum is just a few yards away from the site of the cottage where James Cook was born in 1728 and traces his early days, epic worldwide expeditions and major 'discoveries' – among which were the first crossing of the Antarctic Circle and the 'discovery' of many Pacific islands. Cook was killed on his third voyage, clubbed to death in Hawaii in 1779 – the actual clubs reputed to have been used are among the many exhibits on display.

There are also galleries showing the ethnography and natural history of the countries Cook visited during his naval career – look out for the impressive collection of Aborigine artefacts which has traditional music in the background. The museum is the start of the Captain Cook Heritage Trail around the area; ask at the desk for details.

SPECIAL!

A granite vase marks the site of the cottage where Cook, the son of a farm labourer, was born. It was described in 1810 as 'a low cottage, of two rooms, one within the other, the walls of mud and covered with thatch'. There's a reconstruction of one of the rooms in the museum.

Open: May to September, daily, 1000–1800. October to April, 0900–dusk (last ticket, 45 minutes before closing).
Admission fee: yes
Disabled access: good
Café
Picnic facilities
Gift shop
Toilets

CATHERINE COOKSON EXHIBITION

Central Museum and Art Gallery, Ocean Road, South Shields, Tyne and Wear. Tel: Tyneside 456 8740

South Shields is deep in the heart of Cookson Country – Catherine Cookson Country, that is, and if you're not already acquainted with her novels, they include *The Mallen Trilogy*, the *Mary Ann* series and her moving autobiography *Our Kate*. She was born, the illegitimate daughter of a service maid, in 1906 at 5 Leam Lane, at the foot of Simonside Bank, Tyne Dock, then moved at the age of five to 10 William Black Street, East Jarrow, and it's her memories of that house which feature so vividly in her writing. This permanent exhibition, housed in the Central Museum, traces her life through its sad and happy times with photographs, memorabilia and a display showing the frontage of

William Black Street complete with the corner shop. The museum is part of the Catherine Cookson Trail around the area; ask at the desk for free leaflets highlighting the different places to visit in Cookson Country.

SPECIAL!
You can almost feel the warmth and smell the baking in the re-creation of the kitchen at William Black Street. It's modelled on the description in *Our Kate*.

Open: Monday to Friday, 1000–1730; Saturday, 1000–1630; Sunday, 1400–1700.
Admission fee: no
Disabled access: good
Gift shop
Toilets: disabled only

THE HANCOCK MUSEUM
Barras Bridge, Newcastle-upon-Tyne, Tyne and Wear.
Tel: Tyneside 232 2359

Hancocks, as this friendly museum has become known, is laid out with children in mind – an exciting way of introducing them to the wonders of the natural world. There are even special Professor Hancock Trails around the exhibits to help children learn in a fun way. It's a huge museum: the last count totalled some 171,000 specimens of animals, plants, fossils, minerals and rocks – and that doesn't include the insects, over 160,000 of them! Despite its size, there's a very personal atmosphere and, as you'll soon discover, a touch of humour too. It would be impossible to single out items of interest, but to give you some idea of the scope of the museum the main sections are on Geology, Zoology,

'Magic of Birds', and Ethnography with different displays on these and other related topics. One of the main aims of the museum is to encourage children and adults to become more aware of the world around them – and it certainly succeeds.

SPECIAL!
The animals came in two by two . . . Abel's Ark has been built as a home for a motley crew of stuffed animals that had no real home in the museum. It's a fun show for yougsters, rather like a zoo with the sounds but not the smells!

Open: Monday to Saturday, 1000–1700; Sunday, 1400–1700.
Admission fee: yes
Disabled access: limited
Gifts: on sale
Toilets

HUNDAY NATIONAL TRACTOR AND FARM MUSEUM
Newton (off A68 and A69), Stocksfield, Northumberland.
Tel: Stocksfield 842553

Llamas, goats, donkeys, pigs and ponies – they're all here at the Hunday Museum. You'll probably see a proud peacock strutting around the grounds and some Highland cattle grazing in the fields too. The atmosphere is friendly and the variety of farmyard exhibits absolutely absorbing – it's not surprising Queen Elizabeth The Queen Mother spent three hours looking around at the official opening in 1979! The collection of vintage tractors is one of the most comprehensive in Europe and the engines, driven by steam, oil and gas, are in full working order and often put to work to prove it! There's also a restored eighteenth-century water-powered corn-mill, a large display of country crafts and utensils, and all sorts of weird and wonderful domestic and agricultural bygones. And to take you on a scenic route around the parkland, lake and wildfowl, the 2 foot 6 inch gauge railway runs at regular intervals. Quiz sheets are available for children and special events are held throughout the year (ask for details).

SPECIAL!
Don't miss the Gin Gan – no, not some sort of gin palace, but a Northumbrian round house built as a wheel-house for providing motive power. Horses would trudge round and, through a special gear mechanism, drive the farm machinery.

Open: April to end September, daily, 1000–1800 (last ticket, 1700).
Admission fee: yes
Disabled access: good
Café: serving home-baked food
Picnic facilities
Gift shop
Toilets

JOHN GEORGE JOICEY MUSEUM
City Road, Newcastle-upon-Tyne, Tyne and Wear.
Tel: Newcastle 324562

The intimacy of the seventeenth-century building that houses the museum is what really makes a visit so memorable. Built in 1681 as an almshouse, its winding stairs, creaking floorboards, narrow corridors and tiny rooms add character and charm to the exhibits. The first floor is the official regimental museum of the 15th/

159

19th King's Royal Hussars and the Northumberland Hussars and there are also displays on weights and measures through the ages and a four-minute diorama, complete with crashing sounds and flashing lights, of two great disasters in Newcastle – the flood of 1771 and the fire of 1854. The second floor is devoted to period room-sets starting in early Stuart times and continuing to the Victorian era and Art Nouveau. The sixteenth-century Austin Tower is now a showcase for guns and gun-makers' tools, with a reconstruction of the nineteenth-century Alnwich Armoury and audio-visual display.

SPECIAL!
Shotley Bridge in nearby County Durham became a leading area for sword-making in the late seventeenth century. Look out for displays of the mean and magnificent swords together with old prints and drawings showing the sword-makers' craft.

Open: Monday to Friday, 1000–1730; Saturday, 1000–1630.
Admission fee: no
Toilets

MONKWEARMOUTH STATION MUSEUM
North Bridge Street, Sunderland, Tyne and Wear.
Tel: Sunderland 5677075

There's just one thing missing, and that's the actual trains steaming in and out. But use your imagination to conjure up the majestic sights and sounds and this museum is just like taking a step back to the age of steam. The station, built in 1848, has been restored to show life in its heyday – a model of a top-hatted passenger stands by the ticket window of the booking-office which is fully furnished in Edwardian style, and the porter is ready with a barrow to carry his bags. Also on show is the duty rota (with misdemeanours well noted!) of the railwaymen. You're free to wander outside on to the platform, walk over the original footbridge, sit in the waiting room and admire the old rolling stock! Back inside, there's a large exhibition area with models, plans and photographs highlighting the development of the British steam locomotive from 1804 to 1954 and sections tracing the decline of the tramways and changing modes of road transport – including some strange-looking Edwardian cycles!

SPECIAL!
If you think the station is rather grander than you would have expected, you're right! The reason it was built in such an impressive style is that George Hudson the 'Railway King' had just been elected MP for Sunderland and this was his celebration. Displays show his life and times.

Open: Monday to Friday, 1000–1730; Saturday, 1000–1630; Sunday, 1400–1700.
Admission fee: no
Disabled access: good
Gifts: on sale
Toilets

MORPETH CHANTRY BAGPIPE MUSEUM
The Chantry, Bridge Street, Morpeth, Northumberland.
Tel: Morpeth 519466

This intriguing and extensive collection of bagpipes is one of the largest in the world. Set in a restored thirteenth-century building, the collection contains Northumbrian Small Pipes, Scottish Kirkish Pipes, Border Half Longs and many, many more from three continents. So if you thought bagpipes were peculiar to Scotland, think again! As well as seeing the magnificent pipes, you can hear them too. The idea is to introduce everyone to the many different sounds of the bagpipe – from the solid mellow tones of the Northumbrian Small Pipes to the plaintive swirl of the Great Highland Pipe. By using a special infra-red system, the music of each pipe comes alive through headphones and you have your own personal performance!

SPECIAL!
The museum is rapidly becoming a folk centre for the area with recitals in the building and ceilidhs in the courtyard. Ask at reception for details.

Open: Monday to Saturday 0930–1730 (last admission 1700)
Admission fee: yes
Disabled access: good
Gift shop: (crafts on sale)
Toilets

PRESTON HALL MUSEUM
Preston Park, Yarm Road, Stockton-on-Tees, Cleveland.
Tel: Stockton-on-Tees 602474 (weekends: 781184)

It's worth visiting this museum just to see The Street – an open-air replica of a typical late-nineteenth-century high street in a north-eastern town such as nearby Stockton. There's the grocer and tobacconist, the chemist and draper, a bank and a pawnshop; there's even a Victorian pillar box and decorative cast-iron public

urinal. You'll probably find craftspeople at work too –
a blacksmith shaping horseshoes over a hot furnace, a
farrier shoeing a horse, a weaver using a traditional
loom and woodworkers practising their skills on Victorian machinery. But there's more to Preston Hall than
just the period street. Inside there are fully furnished
room-sets showing domestic life in the nineteenth century; and galleries full of collections of pewter, costumes, sewing-machines, arms and armour, snuff
boxes, toys and much, much more. What makes the
museum so entertaining is that the exhibits are thought-
fully labelled so you can discover all about their past
history and uses.

SPECIAL!
Carefully placed in a room with dimmed lighting is
Georges de la Tour's masterpiece 'The Diceplayers',
bequeathed to the museum by art collecter Edwin
Clepham but unrecognized as a major work of art until
the early 1970s.

Open: Monday to Saturday, 1000–1800; Sunday,
1400–1800 (last ticket, 1730).
Admission fee: no
Disabled access: limited to ground floor and period
street
Café: in Preston Park
Picnic facilities: in Preston Park
Gifts: on sale
Toilets

THE ROMAN ARMY MUSEUM
Carvoran, Greenhead (on B6318), Northumberland.
Tel: Gilsland 485

If you're on Hadrian's Wall near the Walltown Crags, you'll be just a few yards from the unexcavated fort of Magna (the modern name for Carvoran) and the Roman Army Museum which will answer all your questions about both the 80-mile-long wall that Hadrian built to separate the Romans from the Barbarians and the Roman soldiers who stood guard by it. Exhibits of Roman objects discovered at this and other sites along the wall help to create a picture of Roman times, while life-sized models, push-button displays and film shows really bring it to life. By the end of your visit you'll know exactly what a Roman soldier wore (the mail tunic alone weighed 35 lb!), how he trained, even how much he was paid a day. It makes an ideal introduction to a walk or drive along Hadrian's Wall.

SPECIAL!
To find out more about the Carvoran fort, take a look at the huge scale model. Just press the button and you'll be given a commentary!

Open: March to October, daily, 1000–1700 (April and September, 1730; May and June, 1800; July and August, 1830). November and February, Saturday and Sunday, 1000–1700.
Admission fee: yes
Disabled access: good
Café
Picnic facilities
Gift shop
Toilets

LADY WATERFORD HALL

Ford, near Berwick-upon-Tweed, Northumberland.
Tel: Crookham 224

Open the doors of the former village school at Ford and you'll be treated to a unexpectedly pleasant surprise – the walls of the schoolroom are completely covered with magnificent paintings of Bible scenes, all the work of Louisa, Marchioness of Waterford. Using the children of the school and their parents as models (they sat for a reward of 'sixpence and a jelly-piece'!), she painted the scenes in watercolour on paper stretched on wooden frames then washed over with distemper. It took her twenty-one years from 1862 to finish and, although damaged to some degree by condensation and smoke, the paintings are still a breathtaking sight. But don't think the achievement of the Marchioness has gone unnoticed – the visitors' book shows royalty and statesmen have been among her admirers. The building is now a showcase for the paintings and their history with displays showing the life and times of the Waterford family, especially Louisa.

SPECIAL!
The west wall is covered by a scene of Christ Blessing the Children. It contains twenty-two life-sized figures, all portraits of people from the village.

Open: daily, 0930–1830.
Admission fee: yes
Disabled access: good
Picnic facilities: nearby

WINE AND SPIRIT MUSEUM AND POTTERY
Palace Green, Berwick-upon–Tweed, Northumberland.
Tel: Berwick-upon–Tweed 305153

You've probably heard of the famous Lindisfarne Mead – now here's your chance to see how it's been made over the years and have a free tasting too! Mead isn't actually manufactured on the premises, but the museum does have a wide and unusual selection of artefacts from the wine and spirit trade, past and present: everything from a collection of cooper's tools to a set of scales and a display showing how corks are cut from the bark of a tree in Portugal. There's also a selection of old and new stone and earthenware pottery – and to bring you right up to date, you can watch Lindisfarne pottery being made in a nearby workshop.

SPECIAL!
Look out for the drinking glass 'thumpers'. These date back to the days before there was any legislation on weights and measures. The landlord would have his own measure, which was marked by a ring around the neck of the glass. When the customer wanted a refill he would simply thump the heavy base of the glass on the table – hence the name!

Open: Easter to October, Monday to Saturday, 1000–1700.
Admission fee: no
Disabled access: good
Café
Gifts: on sale
Toilets

11
THE NORTH-WEST
(Cheshire, Greater Manchester, Lancashire, Merseyside)

THE CHEMICAL INDUSTRY MUSEUM
Gossage Building, Mersey Road, Widnes, Cheshire.
Tel: Liverpool 424 2061   ex. 4643/4644

Widnes and Runcorn have played a vital part in the formation of the chemical industry. Indeed, Halton is considered 'the cradle of the chemical industry' in Britain and during the nineteenth century it was the chemical centre of the world. It's fitting, then, that this should be the site chosen for Europe's first chemical industry museum, recording an industry whose history has been largely neglected and whose importance has, perhaps, been underestimated. Displays show all sorts of material relating to the manufacture and use of chemicals including rare process manuals, factory site plans and accident records as well as everyday objects which are products of the industry. The exhibits reveal what it was like to work in the chemical industry – its technical expertise and its dangers. It's salutary to remember that the museum has itself had problems caused by chemicals: it is housed in a building constructed on a chemical-saturated site and acid in the bricks has attacked the newly-painted rooms. But don't worry, the museum isn't bad for your health!

SPECIAL!
Arriving at the top of the Gossage Building, you're treated to an incredible panorama of Runcorn and Widnes. Introductory panels tell you what you can see. The view alone makes a visit to the museum worthwhile.

Open: Tuesday to Saturday, 1000–1630.
Admission fee: yes
Disabled access: good
Picnic facilities
Gifts: on sale
Toilets

HELMSHORE TEXTILE MUSEUMS (incorporating Museum of Lancashire Textile Industry and Higher Mill Museum)
Holcombe Road, Helmshore, Lancashire.
Tel: Rossendale 226459/218838

Nothing has been altered on the upper floor of the mill section of this interesting museum. The mill dates from 1858 and all the machinery you can see is exactly as it was when commercial production stopped. To appreciate the nineteenth-century technology fully it's definitely best to visit when a demonstration is taking place (telephone in advance for details). The person giving the demonstration will probably have worked in the industry and will be able to tell you just what it was like to be employed here – the long hours, the noise, cotton-flights polluting the air. For many years the cotton industry thrived in this region and the two museums on this site tell, in great detail, its story. The historical dimension is crisply presented in the gallery, but it's the exhibits – the machinery which produced material until the 1960s – which really makes Helmshore special. For many years cotton-spinning was carried out on Taylor Lang 714 spindle three-speed self-acting mules. They produced soft, low-count yarn suitable for weft in such clothes as flannelettes, from short staple cotton which was unsuitable for making finer yarns. If you're already lost, but intrigued, visit Helmshore – there's plenty more to learn!

SPECIAL!
The Arkwright Collection of spinning machinery is outstanding (open by prior appointment only). The machinery Arkwright invented was the basis for the textile industry and the processes he developed are more or less the same today. Make sure you see the water-frame – it's the only complete one still in existence.

Open: March, Monday to Friday, 1400–1700. April to June, Monday to Friday, Sunday, 1400–1700. July to September, Monday to Friday, 1000–1700; Sunday, 1400–1700. October, Monday to Friday, Sunday, 1400–1700.
Admission fee: yes
Disabled access: good
Café
Picnic facilities
Gifts: on sale
Toilets

MUSEUM OF LABOUR HISTORY

Former County Sessions House, Islington, Liverpool, Merseyside. Tel: Liverpool 207 0001

First, this is not a museum of the history of the Labour Party. Rather, it aims to portray aspects of working-class life on Merseyside over the last 150 years. It tells the story of ordinary men and women, and the tale is often harrowing. In 1844 over 38,000 people lived in cellar dwellings:

the cellars are 10 to 12 feet square, generally flagged – but frequently having only bare earth for a floor, and sometimes less than six feet in height. There are frequently no windows, so light and air can gain access to the cellars only by the door, the top of which is often not higher than the level of the street.

The crafts of the working class are also presented, like the cooper's art of barrel-making which has been carried out on Merseyside since the fifteenth century. And the Employment Gallery illustrates different types of work from cargo-handling in the docks to mining in St Helens; from spinning tobacco at Ogden's factory at the turn of the century to the making of steam engines.

SPECIAL!
The museum is housed in the former County Session House, a grade II listed building. Its two courts, judges' chambers, barristers' library and jury rooms make atmospheric exhibition spaces. In the oak- and walnut-panelled courtroom you can see a selection of trade-union banners; press a button and the flags will light up!

Open: Monday to Saturday, 1000–1700; Sunday, 1400–1700.

Admission fee: no (donations welcome)
Disabled access: good
Gifts: on sale
Toilets

MANCHESTER JEWISH MUSEUM

190 Cheetham Hill Road, Manchester, Greater Manchester.
Tel: Manchester 834 9879

Walking into this synagogue you'll quickly realize that you've found a wonderful haven off the busy Cheetham Hill Road. The synagogue, opened in 1874, is itself worth attention. It served as a place of worship for Sephardi Jewish immigrants (Sephardim Jews who settled in medieval Spain and Portugal, but who were subsequently expelled in the fifteenth century) who traded in cotton textiles. When, over a century later, the congregation moved to a different place of worship it was decided to turn this Spanish and Portuguese synagogue into a museum. The result is a beautifully restored and fascinating exhibition area. The ground floor retains the essential elements of a synagogue – The Ark (a cupboard lined with satin brocade where the sacred Torah Scrolls are kept), Ten Commandments (a representation of the tablets of stone showing the first two words of each commandment), Ner Tamid (the lamp of perpetual light which is kept burning continuously like that which burns in the Temple in Jerusalem), Bimah (the raised platform from which the Torah is read aloud), and the Torah Scroll (the parchment roll, the most sacred object in the synagogue, on which are hand-written the Five Books of Moses). When you mount the stairs to the Ladies' Gallery (in Orthodox synagogues men and women are seated separately) you'll find that the seats have been removed to make

171

space for the exhibition of documents, articles and photographs which poignantly illustrate Jewish history.

SPECIAL!
The spectacular stained-glass window depicts the seven-branched Menorah and incorporates Psalm 67.

Open: Monday to Thursday, 1030–1600; Sunday, 1030–1700.
Admission fee: yes
Disabled access: ground floor only
Gift shop
Toilets

ORDSALL HALL MUSEUM

Taylorson Street, Salford, Greater Manchester.
Tel: Manchester 872 0251

Bang in the middle of a modern housing estate, Ordsall Hall Museum is a vivid contrast to its surroundings and a remarkable survivor of the march of time; but, after all, it was here first! In fact, Ordsall Hall has been here since 1525, making it one of the finest period houses in the region. Its impressive Great Hall, Star Chamber bedroom, and farmhouse kitchen tell its long story with exhibits from various centuries. The museum also has a section devoted to social history – particularly life in an ordinary Salford home over the last hundred years – with fridges, fires, lamps, mangles and even bars of soap on display. But there's plenty more to see, like the dugout canoe found during the construction of the Manchester Ship Canal, which dates from *c.* 1085.

SPECIAL!
There are two outstanding leatherwork dolls which are worth close inspection, but what these male and female

figures were used for no one knows. Their dress suggests late-seventeenth-century coronation robes. The female doll has her hair loose, a style worn at that time by virgins and queens at their coronations; she also wears a crown. Since James II was not popular it is thought she might be his daughter Mary, who came to the throne with her husband William of Orange during the 'Great Revolution' of 1688.

Open: Monday to Friday, 1000–1230 and 1330–1700; Sunday, 1400–1700.
Admission fee: no
Disabled access: limited
Picnic facilities
Gifts: on sale
Toilets

PILKINGTON GLASS MUSEUM
Prescot Road, St Helens, Mersyside. Tel: St Helens 28882

Pilkingtons claim to be the world's leading glass company, making more different types of glass (a 'concrete of salt and sands or stone') than anyone else. Their museum is, however, a glittering treasure-trove which is little known outside the area. In beautifully-lit showcases, which exhibit glassware to perfection, the museum aims both to illustrate the evolution of glass-making techiques from Ancient Egyptian times to the present and to show some of its many uses. There has, of course, always been a large number of utilitarian uses for glass but over the centuries the craftsmen amused themselves by creating decorative ornaments known as friggers; examples in the museum include fully-rigged ships, tobacco pipes, a fountain surrounded by birds and several walking sticks. The upper floor is devoted to these and other beautiful objects and the processes by which they were made, including a vibrantly colourful crystal collection. The lower floor brings you bang up to date with today's techniques and uses: glass in science and technology, in transport, holograms, periscopes, fibreglass, mirrors and much more.

SPECIAL!
The skill of decoration is an ancient art. Enamelling glass is, for example, a technique which can be dated back to the fifteenth century B.C. The Romans skilfully enamelled glass, but it wasn't until the thirteenth and fourteenth centuries that it became really prized. However, it was the Venetian craftsmen who from about 1500 demonstrated an outstanding ability with this form of decoration. You can see two examples of their work on display.

Open: Monday to Friday, 1000–1700 (March to October, Wednesday until 2100); Saturday and Sunday, 1400–1630.
Admission fee: no
Disabled access: good
Picnic facilities
Gift shop
Toilets

RIBCHESTER DOLLS' HOUSE AND MODEL MUSEUM
Church Street, Ribchester (near Preston), Lancashire.
Tel: Ribchester 520

A small house in a small village is an ideal setting for this private collection of toys. To get to the museum you must climb a steep flight of stairs which gives the feel of ascending to an attic nursery, a very well stocked nursery. Dolls, games, kitchen stoves, dolls' houses, miniature furniture are all on show in a colourful clutter which invites you to look closer. The toys, which date from early Victorian to modern day, provide a voyage of discovery for collectors, enthusiasts and the young at heart!

SPECIAL!
A whole room is, deservedly, devoted to a unique model fairground. It's the work of one man, W.G. Churcher, who spent over ten years painstakingly making these colourful exhibits. It's impressive enough just to see the 'Octopus', 'Big Wheel', 'Giant Swing-boat', 'Steam Yacht' and 'Carousel', but with a 10p coin you can activate their mechanisms and send the whole display into a spectacular frenzy.

Open: Tuesday to Sunday, 1100–1700.
Admission fee: yes
Picnic facilities
Gift shop

SALFORD MUSEUM OF MINING
Buile Hill Park, Eccles Old Road, Salford, Greater Manchester. Tel: Manchester 736 1832

Housed in a building designed by Charles Barry, the Museum of Mining is an eye-catching introduction to the coal industry. It includes a reconstructed coalmine which to some extent manages to conjure up the atmosphere of a working driftmine around the 1930s – the coal-face, pit yard, lamp room, baths and black-smith's shop. It's certainly more than enough to let you know about the dirt and hard work involved, but for more detailed explanations about working life underground at the beginning of the twentieth century you can press a button and hear an interesting and informative commentary. There's also a good gallery which gives artists' impressions of the cramped conditions, pollution, grime and, on a happier note, comradeship. But perhaps most telling of all is the display of coalmining history from the Roman use of coal, its extraction during the Middle Ages, right up to the present day and modern technology. For instance, in 1900 miners were paid a pittance for their labours, about 39p a day (compared with about one pound paid to agricultural workers at the time). The horror of working conditions last century is summed up in a report from 1842, in which Betty Wardle is recorded as saying: 'I have had four children; two of them were born while I worked in the pits . . . I had a child born in the pits, and I brought it up the pit shaft in my skirt'.

SPECIAL!
The horse gin (i.e. horse engine) was a type of winding device used extensively from early times until the mid-nineteenth century. The gin on display dates from the early 1880s and was last used during the 1920s.

Open: Monday to Friday, 1000–1230 and 1330–1700; Sunday, 1400–1700.
Admission fee: no
Picnic facilities
Gifts: on sale
Toilets

SALT MUSEUM

162 London Road, Northwich, Cheshire.
Tel: Northwich 41331

Most of us use salt every day, and it's a measure of its importance that there's been a museum devoted to the history of salt in Northwich for almost a century. In 1889 a small building in Wilton Street housed a collection which included salt samples from around the world – some of which can still be seen in the galleries of the present museum. The rock-salt beds in Cheshire were laid down about 250 million years ago, but they weren't discovered until 1670 by one John Jackson, who was exploring for coal. It's always been difficult to produce salt, but during the nineteenth century it seemed to reach a peak of hardship. The Victorian public was, however, more shocked to hear that women worked in their petticoats alongside men who were stripped to the waist, than to hear of the gruelling labour involved. The salt industry did, in fact, cause major environmental problems in the salt towns. Air was polluted by chimneys built too low to carry away smoke from the coal which was used in huge quantities to heat the salt pans. Acid was formed when brine dripped on to the fires. There was a continuous acrid smell. This excellent museum will certainly make you think before you reach for the salt-cellar!

SPECIAL!
Look out for the salt-worker's clogs – they're totally encrusted with salt crystals.

Open: September to June, Tuesday to Sunday, 1400–1700; July and August, Tuesday to Saturday, 1000–1700.
Admission fee: yes

Gifts: on sale
Toilets

SILK HERITAGE MUSEUM
Paradise Mill, Park Lane, Macclesfield, Cheshire.
Tel: Macclesfield 618228

This is a lovely museum with extremely knowledgeable staff. Indeed, the guide who shows you round will probably have worked all his/her life on the machines displayed. It isn't known how silk first came to Macclesfield (no connection between the town and the Huguenots has been proved) but in the seventeenth century covering buttons with silk thread was a busy industry. Button merchant Charles Roe established the first silk factory in Macclesfield in 1743 and others soon followed; most sent their silk yarns to the weavers in London's Spitalfields. It wasn't until the 1790s that silk-weaving became important in Macclesfield but once established it flourished into the nineteenth century when the practice of 'making up' finished garments was developed and the town specialized in rich woven designs. There's a lot to learn about silk and a tour of this museum on the top floor of an old mill, with its re-created manager's office, card-cutting room and the largest group of Jacquard silk-looms in Europe, is the best place to start.

SPECIAL!
The special item here is, of course, silk. Its brightly-coloured cobwebs, wound tightly ready for weaving, shine brightly and tempt you to treat yourself in the museum shop!

Open: Tuesday to Sunday, 1400–1700.
Admission fee: yes

Disabled access: good
Gifts: on sale
Toilets

STRETTON MILL

Stretton (off A534), near Farndon, Cheshire.
Tel: Farndon 8276

Any idea what a breast-shot wheel or an overshot wheel is? If you have you're probably an enthusiast anyway; if not then make your way to Stretton Mill and find out. There's been a working water-mill at Stretton from the fourteenth century right up until 1959. For a while it lay derelict, then in 1975 a large-scale restoration plan was put into action; the result, an enjoyable focus for a country outing. It's an intimate museum presided over by an enthusiastic guide keen to convey everything he can about 'his' mill. As wheels turn, chains creak and water splashes you'll be treated to a friendly and informative talk on the mechanisms of a mill.

SPECIAL!
Ask to see the shovel made from beech wood which is used to move grain – it looks like an overgrown mustard spoon.

Open: 1 April to 31 October, Tuesday to Sunday, 1400–1800.
Admission fee: yes
Disabled access: limited
Picnic facilities
Gifts: on sale
Toilets

12

SCOTLAND

AUCHINDRAIN OPEN AIR MUSEUM OF COUNTRY LIFE
(on A83), near Inveraray, Strathclyde. Tel: Furnace 235

Auchindrain was a working communal-tenancy farm township from the fifteenth century right up until 1935. the last to survive in Scotland. As was so common in Scotland, several families lived and worked here, almost completely self-sufficient in food, clothing, fuel and shelter. The farm has been beautifully restored (work still continues, a never-ending task!) to give you an idea of the way of life of rural folk in the West Highlands in the eighteenth and nineteenth centuries. Many of the buildings and dwellings have been refurbished in period style and there's an exhibition centre with changing displays. However, what really makes the museum so unusual are the fields where you can see traditional crops growing using the old methods of cultivation – if you don't already know the difference between runrig and lazybed, you soon will!

SPECIAL!
Most of the buildings were built by the tenants themselves using whatever materials came to hand. Displays
show how they were constructed and repaired.

Open: April, May and September, Sunday to Friday,
1100–1600, June to August, daily 1000–1600. Other
times by arrangement.
Admission fee: yes
Disabled access: limited (telephone in advance)
Café
Picnic facilities
Gifts: on sale
Toilets

MUSEUM OF CHILDHOOD
38 High Street (Royal Mile), Edinburgh, Lothian.
Tel: Edinburgh 225 2424 (ex 6636/6652)

This museum, said to be the first ever to be devoted
solely to childhood, was once described as 'the noisiest
museum in the world' and you'll soon see why! Children just can't contain their excitement as they flit from
exhibit to exhibit – dolls, prams, toy animals, musical
instruments, marionettes and tin soldiers, teddy bears
and rocking horses . . . every one has a magic of its
own. The time tunnel is guaranteed to get them gig-
gling at reconstructions of a schoolroom, nursery and
fancy-dress party of a bygone age. But it's not only a
museum for children, it's a nostalgic and most enjoyable
trip back in time for adults too. The museum, housed
in an eighteenth-century tenement block on Edinburgh's historic Royal Mile, was reopened in 1986 after
extensive refurbishment and expansion – and it's now
bigger, livelier (and noisier!) than ever.

SPECIAL!

Children have always been fascinated by conjuring acts. On display is a magic and chemistry outfit dating back to around 1905 complete with all sorts of boxes and test tubes full of strange substances.

Open: Monday to Saturday, 1000–1800 (October to May, 1000–1700); Sundays during the Edinburgh Festival only, 1400–1700.
Admission fee: no
Disabled access: good
Café: nearby
Gifts: on sale

THE GEORGIAN HOUSE

7 Charlotte Square, Edinburgh, Lothian.
Tel: Edinburgh 225 2160

By the mid-eighteenth century Edinburgh had become overcrowded and squalid with the population concentrated in a small area near the castle. To improve conditions, swampland north of Castle Rock was drained and plans drawn up for what is now known as The New Town with wide streets, distinguished squares and elegant Georgian houses. This house at No .7 Charlotte Square has been restored and the lower floors furnished as a New Town house of the period to show what life was like in the Georgian heyday. An audio-visual presentation explains the growth of the New Town and is worth looking at first. Then it's a real feast of style and opulence as you wander around admiring the exquisite furniture – the Hepplewhite table in the dining-room and the gilded seat furniture in the drawing-room; and taking in all the little touches – the Adam detail, the crystal chandelier, even the chamber pot to be used by dining guests! The kitchen is probably the most striking room with its open-range fire, baking oven and hotplate, and cooking dishes and utensils hanging from walls and ceiling. However, you'll find yourself entranced by every room, especially as the staff are so knowledgeable and keen to fill you in on the background – the kitchen, for example, is painted blue because that was the traditional colour for keeping flies away!

Nearby, and worth combining with your visit, is Gladstone's Land (Tel: Edinburgh 226 5856), a seventeenth-century tenement building which, in sharp contrast, shows the living conditions in the Old Town.

SPECIAL!
Look out for the portable water closet which actually flushes!

Open: April to end October, Monday to Saturday, 1000–1700; Sunday, 1400–1700. November, Saturday, 1000–1630; Sunday, 1400–1700 (last admission, half an hour before closing).
Admission fee: yes
Gift shop

GLADSTONE COURT MUSEUM
North Back Road (on A702), Biggar, Strathclyde.
Tel: Biggar 21050

You're in for a real treat – this is a quite incredible museum. Set on the first floor above an extensive gift shop, it's laid out just like a street. You can walk up and down window-shopping or actually wander around the shops and offices, school, bank, village library, photographer's booth and even a telephone exchange, all dating back to around 1850 to 1920. The furnishings and signs, which are typical of a Scottish town at the time, are authentic and the whole experience so lifelike you have to keep reminding yourself you're not dreaming. It's a much-acclaimed museum, but as everyone who has ever visited it will tell you, it's hard to find the words to describe it. Don't miss it, you'll be amazed!

Nearby is the Greenhill Covenanter's House (see below) and it's worth buying a combined ticket which gives you entry to both.

SPECIAL!
Spend some time looking at the advertisements on the walls – some will bring a smile to your face!

Open: Easter to October, Monday to Saturday, 1000–1230 and 1400–1700; Sunday, 1400–1700. Other times by arrangement.
Admission fee: yes
Café
Picnic facilities
Gifts: on sale
Toilets

GREENHILL COVENANTER'S HOUSE
Burn Braes, Biggar, Strathclyde. Tel: Biggar 21050

This old farmhouse has been completely restored and opened as a museum to tell the story of Scotland and the role of the Covenanters from 1603 through to 1707 when the two kingdoms of Scotland and England were united. It's a tale of determined struggle and high values illustrated through an audio-visual display, models, room-sets and relics from local covenanting families including banners, books and Bibles – and the bed where preacher Donald Cargill rested the night before his capture in 1681. History is brought to life through personal stories which highlight the bravery of the Covenanters whose rebellion, in the words of Scottish poet Robbie Burns:

> Cost Scotland blood, cost Scotland tears:
> But it sealed freedom's sacred cause.

You'll find this museum a moving tribute to their courage and achievements.

Just a short walk away is Gladstone Court Museum (page 183).

SPECIAL!
Local diarist Andrew Hay kept a faithful record of the events in Biggar. There's a life-sized model of him sitting with quill in hand in his study.

Open: Easter to October, daily, 1400–1700.
Admission fee: yes
Disabled access: limited
Picnic facilities
Gifts: on sale
Toilets

THE HILL HOUSE

Upper Colquhoun Street, Helensburgh, Strathclyde.
Tel: Helensburgh 3900

There are no guided tours or suggested routes, few explanatory notices or information boards – you're just left alone to wander around the house at your own pace absorbing the highly original domestic architecture of

Glasgow architect Charles Rennie Mackintosh. Hill House was commissioned by the publisher Walter Blackie as a family home and completed in 1904, a masterpiece of design well before its time. The exterior, which overlooks the estuary of the river Clyde, is strictly Scottish vernacular, but the interior is idiosyncratic. What's so striking is the unity of design, characteristic of Mackintosh's work. He gave time and painstaking thought to every detail from the cutlery to the chimney stacks, the light-shades and chairs – and you'll find yourself spending hours just trying to take it all in. The most celebrated room is the elegant White Bedroom with its refreshing feeling of clear, pure light, but every room has its own special charm and subtlety; even the bathroom with the shower designed by Mackintosh is a delight. Whether or not you'd like actually to live there can be the source of days of discussion, but one thing's for certain, you can't help but be overwhelmed by it all. If you're not already well acquainted with the architect then it's worth starting your visit by watching the ten-minute audio-visual display about his life, an inspiration to find out more about the man and his works.

SPECIAL!
Mackintosh is better known for his architecture than his watercolours, but you'll find several here, showing another of his talents.

Open: daily, 1300–1700.
Admission fee: yes
Picnic facilities
Gifts: on sale
Toilets

HUNTERIAN MUSEUM
University Avenue, Glasgow, Strathclyde.
Tel: Glasgow 339 8855 ex 221

The Hunterian is Scotland's oldest public museum, and, as you might expect from a university collection, it's full of fossils, rocks, minerals, archaeology and ethnographic materials. It's named after William Hunter, physician, anatomist and medical teacher who bequeathed his enormous private collection to Glasgow University in 1783. While you're in the university, take the opportunity to see the undercroft of the Bute and Randolph halls, the terrestrial globe (the views from here are splendid), the lion and unicorn staircase – they all help to set the scholastic atmosphere which enhances a visit to the Hunterian Museum.

SPECIAL!
The museum's coin collection, which is based on the original Hunter bequest, is considered to be one of the best in the world and should not be missed.

Open: Monday to Friday, 1000–1700; Saturday, 0930–1300.
Admission fee: no
Disabled access: good
Café
Picnic facilities
Gifts: on sale
Toilets

ISLE OF ARRAN HERITAGE MUSEUM
Rosaburn, Brodick, Isle of Arran, Strathclyde.
Tel: Brodick 2140

This highland island is quite simply stunning; some of the most spectacular rock formations in Britain can be seen here. Granite rock pinnacles rise 3500 feet out of the sea and there's plenty of wildlife to enjoy. A visit to the Isle of Arran Heritage Museum helps you to experience the island to the full. It has a collection of Arran buildings including a typical cottage and a smithy. There are also displays of social history, archaeology and natural history. And if you're in luck, you may also see a demonstration of traditional spinning.

SPECIAL!
Dairy farming has long been practised on Arran and in the Heritage Centre you can see a milk house with all its dairying equipment.

Open: mid-May to mid-September, Monday to Friday, 1030–1330 and 1400–1630, Sunday 1400–1630.
Admission fee: yes
Disabled access: limited
Gifts: on sale
Toilets

LADY STAIR'S HOUSE
Lady Stair's Close, Lawnmarket, Edinburgh, Lothian.
Tel: Edinburgh 225 1131 ex 6593

Hidden away in the corner of pretty Lady Stair's Close off the Royal Mile is this small but intriguing museum devoted to Scotland's three most famous literary gentlemen – Sir Walter Scott, Robert Louis Stevenson and Robert Burns. The contents of the collection are many and varied, with manuscripts, paintings, letters and personal relics including such diverse things as a lock of Scott's hair and the printing press used to print his novels! However, it's the building itself which really gives the museum its character and special charm. It was originally built in 1622 for Sir William Gray, a prominent merchant burgess of the city, and you can't help but think that Scott, Stevenson and Burns would all have approved the choice of this unusual house with its corner stair tower as a resting place for the relics of their lives and works.

SPECIAL!
Beware of the stairs! They're at different heights so that people 'not aware of the house would betray their presence' – an early alarm system.

Open: Monday to Saturday, 1000–1700 (June to September, 1800).
Admission fee: no
Disabled access: limited
Café: nearby
Gifts: on sale
Toilets

LAND O'BURNS CENTRE
opposite Alloway Kirk, Alloway, Strathclyde.
Tel: Ayr 43700

Robert Burns is undoubtedly Scotland's most famous poet, and has associations with many places in Scotland. In the Land O'Burns Centre you can discover where these places of interest are. There's a lively audio-visual display and a fascinating exhibition which outlines the important periods in Burns' life and the major influences on his work. The centre is a good starting point for the Burns Heritage Trail which will take you through Ayr and Dumfries.

While you're in Alloway, there's plenty to see like Alloway Kirk, which features in *Tam O'Shanter*, and the Burns Monument (open April to October; fee) near the picturesque Brig o'Doon.

SPECIAL!
In Alloway you can also visit the auld clay biggin (included in fee to Burns monument) which was built by Burns' father. Here the poet was born on 25 January 1759.

Open: spring and autumn, daily, 1000–1800. Summer, 1000–2100. Winter, 1000–1700.
Admission fee: no, but charge for audio-visual display and exhibition
Disabled access: good
Picnic facilities
Gift shop
Toilets

MUSEUM OF LIGHTING
(Mr Purves' Lighting Emporium), 59 Stephen Street, Edinburgh, Lothian. Tel: Edinburgh 556 4503

This may well rate as one of the smallest, grubbiest and most disorganized museums you'll ever visit. However, it's also friendly, informal and utterly intriguing. Imagine a museum of lighting which is so dimly lit that you fall over items stacked on the floor and knock over precariously balanced objects – that's the Lighting Emporium! This private collection of gas, oil and electric lamps is eccentric to say the least and its enthusiastic owner makes a visit a highly memorable experience. So, be brave and enter this Aladdin's cave of lighting; uncover the owner amidst the dust and chaos, introduce yourself and talk about lighting – it's a topic which is much larger than you might think, so don't expect this visit to be short!

SPECIAL!
Ask about the lamp which was used over a hundred years ago to help deliver a baby – it's there (some-where!) for you to see.

Open: Saturday, 1100–1800 (or any time by appointment).
Admission fee: no

THE DAVID LIVINGSTONE CENTRE
Station Road (off A724), Blantyre, Strathclyde.
Tel: Blantyre 823140

David Livingstone, missionary, doctor and African explorer, was born in the 'single end' of this tenement block in March 1813, the son of a cotton-worker employed at the local mill. Climb the spiral staircase at the side of the building and you'll see what conditions would have been like at the time with twenty-four families living in the block, each with just one room that served as living-room, kitchen and bedroom. The building, set in parkland on the banks of the river Clyde, is now a national memorial to Livingstone with period room-sets, displays of letters and diaries, and artefacts including his medical and geographical instruments. One of the highlights is the darkened room full of tableaux and sound tapes which, at the press of a button, takes you on a journey deep into the heart of Africa – complete with the roar of lions in the background! As well as the exhibits on his life and work there are also two other museums within the complex. The Shuttle Row (Social History) Museum shows industrial life at the time David Livingstone was born with informative displays on agriculture, spinning and coalmining in the area, while the Africa Pavilion describes life in Africa today.

SPECIAL!
Keep a penny aside so you can make the fountain play. The intriguing World Fountain in the museum's gardens traces Livingstone's travels.

Open: Monday to Saturday, 1000–1800; Sunday, 1400–1800 (Africa Pavilion open only April to September).
Admission fee: yes
Disabled access: limited
Café: April to September
Picnic facilities: in beautiful parkland
Gifts: on sale
Toilets

MARY, QUEEN OF SCOTS' HOUSE
Queen Street, Jedburgh, Borders. Tel: Jedburgh 63331

An air of mystery surrounds Mary, Queen of Scots, the tall, dark queen whose eventful life was a catalogue of intrigue, murder and treachery. This museum with its new interpretive centre, sets out to show the truth behind the legend. It's a fascinating display of her life and times, her marriages and the years spent in captivity, with relics including a rare portrait of her future husband, the Earl of Bothwell.

The house, with its beautiful grounds, is part of the Jedburgh Town Trail (pick up a leaflet from the desk or the tourist information centre) which takes you around places of interest in the historic town, such as the twelfth-century abbey and nearby Castle Jail, a Georgian prison which is now a small museum with exhibits about prison life in bygone days.

SPECIAL!
The museum is housed in a sixteenth-century bastel-house where she is reputed to have stayed in 1566.

Open: Easter to October, Monday to Saturday, 1000–1200 and 1300–1700; Sunday, 1300–1700.
Admission fee: yes
Disabled access: limited
Café: nearby
Picnic facilities: in the lovely grounds
Gifts: on sale
Toilets

MENZIES CAMPBELL COLLECTION
(Museum of the Royal College of Surgeons)
18 Nicolson Street, Edinburgh, Lothian.
Tel: Edinburgh 556 6206

If the film *Marathon Man* made you hide your head under a pillow and the thought of going to a dentist makes you feel queasy, then you probably won't fancy visiting the Menzies Campbell Collection, which is a museum of dentistry. But if you don't visit this fascinating, tiny museum you'll be missing a very interesting collection. Although, initially, the objects on display look like instruments of torture, when you inspect them more closely you can't fail to admire the craftsmanship and fine decorative detailing. In 1965 Dr J. Menzies, a distinguished dentist and dental historian, presented his unique collection to the Royal College of Surgeons of Edinburgh on the understanding that it would remain as a 'closed' collection. It's on view today as a mini-museum in its own right within the historical collection of the Royal College. The college collection is also well worth a visit, but with its pickled, bottled and dissected items it's most certainly not for the squeamish!

SPECIAL!
The museum is dominated by a dentist's chair. Large, dark brown and very uninviting, it's sure to make you appreciate its much less intimidating modern-day counterparts!

Open: Monday to Friday, 0900–1700, by appointment only.
Admission fee: no
Disabled access: limited

HUGH MILLER'S COTTAGE
Church Street, Cromarty, Highland. Tel: Cromarty 245

At the tip of the Black Isle – which incidentally is neither an island nor black: it's predominantly green – is the lovely old harbour village of Cromarty. Here, in 1802, Hugh Miller was born. You might not have heard of him but don't let that stop you visiting the cottage where he lived and exploring the beautiful Black Isle. It's impossible to categorize Hugh Miller – he was at various times a stonemason, poet, geologist, church-man and editor – so there's a variety of material on display inside! The rooms downstairs and bedroom upstairs in this tiny, whitewashed, thatched cottage have been furnished in the period style with the help of local craftsmen. The remaining two rooms house static displays and a captioned video programme which describe the life of this remarkable man. Various manu-scripts, early editions of his work, geological drawings and letters from men such as Darwin and Thomas Carlyle are on display. And if you're interested in fossils, you'll be fascinated by the collection on show, many recorded in Miller's own handwriting. Most of the fossils were collected locally, so if you fancy a spot of fossil-hunting yourself, why not explore the nearby 'Fairy Glen' which is just as enchanting as it sounds.

SPECIAL!
As you approach the cottage from the street you'll catch a glimpse of Hugh Miller at the window. Don't worry, there are no ghosts here – just a very lifelike model.

Open: May to September, Monday to Saturday, 1000–1200 and 1300–1700 (June to September, also Sunday, 1400–1700).
Admission fee: yes
Disabled access: limited
Gifts: on sale

OLD BLACKSMITH'S SHOP
Gretna Green (just off A74), Dumfries and Galloway.
Tel: Gretna 38224

Paintings of eloping sweethearts with angry parents in hot pursuit conjure up the scene – this old village smithy was where many a runaway couple have been married by the blacksmith 'priest'. The wedding trade began in the mid-eighteenth century when Lord Hardwicke's Marriage Act put a stop to clandestine marriages in England. The law didn't apply to Scotland, where you need only two witnesses for a couple to declare themselves man and wife and Gretna Green, then the first village over the border, soon cashed in on the laxer Scottish marriage regulations. Although anyone could perform the ceremony – with payment ranging from a couple of guineas to a dram of whisky – the blacksmith's shop, which at the time was the first house in Scotland, naturally got the best deal! Indeed, one 'priest' claimed to have married 7744 people between 1811 and 1847. Anvil weddings were finally made illegal in 1940, but you can still sense the romance and excitement as you wander around the old blacksmith's shop with the original anvil over which the couple traditionally joined hands, photographs, drawings and old marriage certificates, some signed with just a cross. It's best to choose an off-peak time to visit, as it does get rather crowded during the summer season.

SPECIAL
Adjoining is the Coach House with some magnificent horse-drawn coaches ranging from a four-in-hand state landau used by William IV to a Victorian bathchair.

Open: daily (telephone for times)
Admission fee: yes
Disabled access: good
Café and restaurant
Gifts: on sale
Toilets

OLD BYRE HERITAGE CENTRE

Dervaig, Isle of Mull, Strathclyde. Tel: Dervaig 229

Tucked away in what must surely be the prettiest part of this lovely island is the tiny village of Dervaig with its whitewashed houses and round-steepled church. Just a mile south of the village is the Old Byre Heritage Centre, a museum devoted to crofting. It tells the story, through room-sets and tableaux, of a Mull crofter's life at the time of the Highland Clearances (*c.* 1840) and the changes which took place in the following years. There is an audio-visual show and background tapes of music and song with snatches of Gaelic and soft West Highland voices. The whole atmosphere is so lifelike you feel you're being invited to visit the assortment of people, cattle, hens and sheepdogs . . . Before you leave, visit the craft stalls and tea-room on the ground floor to sample a 'Mull Morsel'!

SPECIAL!
As the name suggests, the museum was created from a derelict cow byre – a museum piece in itself! The building was restored with the help of many local craftspeople and volunteers, and the car park is built on a deep peat bog!

Open: summer, Monday to Saturday, 1030–1730; Sunday, 1200–1600.
Admission fee: yes
Disabled access: tea-room on the ground floor only
Café
Picnic facilities
Gift shop
Toilets

PEOPLE'S PALACE MUSEUM

Glasgow Green, Glasgow, Strathclyde.
Tel: Glasgow 554 0223

You can't miss this museum – built of red sandstone, it dominates Glasgow Green, the oldest and probably best-loved of the public parks in the city. And the collections inside do more than justice to the fine exterior. Here you'll find the story of Glasgow and its people from the foundation of the city in 1175–8 through to the present day – including a life-sized model of Billy Connolly! It's impossible to describe all the exhibits, housed on three floors, but they cover everything and anything to do with Glasgow including religion, trades and industries, labour movements, entertainment, sport, arts and crafts and famous personalities. It's all presented in such a lively and interesting way, you'll find yourself wanting to go back again and again – and each time you'll find something new. Adjoining are the Winter Gardens, a lovely place for a cup of tea and also a fascinating place to browse – it's not only full of flowers and plants but some intriguing exhibits, too, such as a parish church bell of 1862 and a series of stained and leaded glass panels illustrating the various fruits and flowers of the Bible.

SPECIAL!
The museum has an extensive collection of women's suffrage memorabilia – the only one in Scotland.

Open: Monday to Saturday, 1000–1700; Sunday, 1400–1700.
Admission fee: no
Café: in the Winter Gardens
Picnic facilities: on Glasgow Green

Gift shop
Toilets

SCOTTISH AGRICULTURAL MUSEUM
Royal Highland Showground, Ingliston, Newbridge, Edinburgh, Lothian. Tel: Edinburgh 333 2674

The museum might be indoors but the theme is very much the outdoor life. The exhibits comprise the best of Scotland's national country life collection with old farming tools, room-sets, models and wonderful photographs showing how the land was worked over the past two hundred years. You're shown how the patterns of farming have changed, the equipment revolutionized and living and working conditions of labourers improved. Your visit begins in a lively fashion with a tape/slide-show introducing you to Scotland's countryside and then just gets more and more interesting – by the end you'll know all about the Lowland ox-teams that ploughed the land, the creels and pack ponies that carried the grain, Meikle's work on developing the threshing-machine, how butter was churned and bread baked, and much, much more. It's one of those museums that leaves you quite exhausted, so you'll probably need a second trip to take it all in.

SPECIAL!
The collection of photographs, some over a hundred years old, gives a very real insight into the way of life of past generations. Take time looking at them.

Open: May to September, Monday to Friday, 1000–1700; Sunday, 1100–1700.
Admission fee: no
Disabled access: good

Café
Picnic facilities
Gifts: on sale
Toilets

THE SCOTTISH FISHERIES MUSEUM

St Ayles, Anstruther Harbour, Anstruther, Fife.
Tel: Anstruther 310628

The sea and fishing are the themes of the collections housed in this wonderful cluster of sixteenth-to-nineteenth-century buildings. And you'll find everything you need to know about the subject here – everything, that is, apart from the fishing boats *Zulu*, *Fifie* and *White Wing*, which are in the harbour itself!

As you step into the cobbled courtyard, you're surrounded by nets hanging up to dry and waiting to be mended together with an assortment of rowing boats, ropes and barrels – all creating a unique atmosphere. Inside, you'll find a large marine aquarium full of weird and wonderful creatures – ask the staff and they'll identify them for you. From here you can wander through rooms chock-a-block with model ships, ships' gear, paintings, maps and charts showing the pattern and history of fishing along the Scottish coast. Upstairs is a poignant reminder of the cruelty of the sea – a room dedicated to the memory of Scottish fishermen who have been lost at sea. Only the relatives and friends of those whose names are recorded on brass plaques around the wall may step inside, but no one can fail to be moved by the memorial.

SPECIAL!
Do visit the room above the net hut in the courtyard. It's been transformed into a traditional fisher's home of the nineteenth century.

Open: April to October, Monday to Saturday, 1000–1750; Sunday, 1400–1700. November to March, closed Tuesday.
Admission fee: yes
Disabled access: limited
Café
Picnic facilities
Gifts: on sale
Toilets

MUSEUM OF SCOTTISH LEAD-MINING
Goldscaur Road, Wanlockhead (on B797), Dumfries and Galloway. Tel: Leadhills 387

Situated in Scotland's highest village, the spectacular mountain scenery surrounding the museum makes a visit even more enjoyable. There are three parts to the lead-mining centre – the indoor museum, the outdoor exhibits and the mine itself. It's a good idea to start inside to get a flavour of what life was like for miners and their families. The displays, which cover 250 years of lead-mining, include all sorts of strange-looking tools and equipment, the reconstruction of a kitchen and a collection of gold, silver and minerals found locally. Outside, one and a half miles of walkway takes you past mine-heads and pumping-engines, including the unique Wanlockhead Beam Engine, and gives you the chance to look at the only surviving smelt-mill in Scotland, a water tunnel that took eleven years to cut and the old 'but-and-ben' cottages. And then finally there's the Loch Nell walk-in mine, which was worked from the early 1700s to 1860. Equipped with safety helmet, you'll be shown around the mine by a guide who'll be happy to answer all your questions. The museum sets out to tell the story of Scottish lead-mining – and can certainly claim to include just about everything.

SPECIAL!
The miners here must have been the best-read anywhere. The Lead Miners' Library, founded in 1756, is full of books enjoyed by the workers.

Open: Easter to end September, daily, museum: 1100–1600, mine: 1300–1530
Admission fee: yes
Picnic facilities
Gifts: on sale
Toilets

SCOTTISH TARTANS MUSEUM
Davidson House, Drummond Street, Comrie, Tayside.
Tel: Comrie 70779

Did you know there are over 1500 Scottish tartans? They're all recorded at the Scottish Tartans Museum. As you'll soon discover, tartans come in all colours and patterns, or setts as they're known. Some can be worn only by royalty; others, of course, belong to the Scottish clans; while some have been created for cities or regiments to mark a special occasion. As well as the hundreds of tartans on display there's also a fascinating exhibition tracing the history of Highland dress from the belted plaids of the sixteenth century through to the eighteenth century when the wearing of Highland dress was outlawed after the Battle of Culloden, and finally the revival in the nineteenth century. Indeed, one of the prized exhibits in the collection is the kilt of John Brown, Queen Victoria's faithful Scottish servant.

Look out too for one of the more bizarre exhibits – a sporran made of human hair!

SPECIAL!
At the back of the museum there's an eighteenth-century weaver's bothy complete with hand-loom. Occasionally there are demonstrations of weaving tartan using hand-spun, naturally dyed wool. You can also wander around the Dye Plant Garden where plants once used to dye the wool are grown.

Open: April to October, Monday to Saturday, 1000–1700; Sunday, 1400–1600. November to March, telephone to check times.
Admission fee: yes
Disabled access: good
Café: nearby
Gifts: on sale
Toilets

SHETLAND COUNTY MUSEUM
Lower Hillhead, Lerwick, Shetland. Tel: Lerwick 5057

There's a wealth of local history inside this modern museum, which has the unique distinction of being the most northerly in the British Isles. As you'd expect from islands whose history has been dominated by the sea, there's a strong maritime element in the collection. Look out for the magnificent ship's figureheads which dominate the main staircase, and the fine display of model ships.

Shetland is also famous for its many archaeological sites which suggest that the islands have been inhabited from at least 2000 B.C. The highlight of the collection is St Ninian's Treasure – a hoard of Celtic silver ornaments and utensils found at St Ninian's Isle in 1958. It's a source of great sorrow to Shetlanders that the original treasure is now in the National Museum of Antiquities of Scotland in Edinburgh, but these silver replicas are still quite magnificent.

Shetland's third claim to fame is, of course, knitting and spinning. Some of the most intricate examples of lace knitting are now so fragile they're kept in darkened cases but if you ask, the staff will be delighted to show them to you.

SPECIAL!
You'll find one of the best marine archaeology collections in Great Britain here. Look out for the material found from the wreck of *El Gran Griffin*, a Spanish Armada ship.

Open: Monday, Wednesday, Friday, 1000–1300, 1430–1700 and 1800–2000; Tuesday and Saturday, 1030–1300 and 1430–1700; Thursday, 1000–1300.
Admission fee: no
Café: nearby
Gifts: on sale

THE TENEMENT HOUSE
145 Buccleuch Street, Garnethill, Glasgow, Strathclyde.
Tel: Glasgow 333 0183

The great, the famous and the notorious have provided historians with a wealth of material to study. Indeed, many museums have been devoted entirely to 'personalities'. But little record has been kept of ordinary people who never made news. There are now folk museums recording social history, but still very little is known about ordinary individuals. And that's what makes the

Tenement House so special. Its occupant, Miss Toward, lived all her days in one part of Glasgow and worked as a typist in a shipping office. She hoarded the letters and postcards people sent her, and kept receipts on her rent, quotations for repairs about the house, notes on jam-making, invitations to church outings, mementoes and photographs. It would seem that Miss Toward never threw anything out! Her tenement home is now open to the public. If you've never been into one of these build-ings before, you'll be surprised to find coal stored beneath the working surface in the kitchen, chairs covered with woven horsehair, stone hot-water bottles – just a few of the ordinary things which belonged to this ordinary woman.

SPECIAL!
There's a kitchen bed for you to see. This was once a universal feature in Glasgow tenement kitchens; indeed there are still some in use in the city today. Space was always limited in a tenement house, so a bed was squeezed into the corner of the kitchen. People took great pride in 'dressing' these beds which would often have floor-to-ceiling curtains. Look out for the bedpole used for making the bed.

Open: April to October, daily, 1400–1700. November to March, Saturday and Sunday, 1400–1600.
Admission fee: yes

THE WEST HIGHLAND MUSEUM
Cameron Square, Fort William, Highland. Tel: Fort William 2169

Tucked away halfway up Fort William's High Street is the West Highland Museum, a real treasure-trove containing everything from tools to tartans. Of particular interest are the relics from the 1745 Jacobite Rising. The whole area has strong connections with the Rising and Bonnie Prince Charlie and a large part of the collection concentrates on this eventful period of Scottish history. The museum also describes West Highland history and folk life – there's a reconstruction of a croft house complete with spinning-wheel, and a lifelike room-set showing the old Governor's Room at Fort William (the original Fort was knocked down to make way for the West Highland Railway).

Spare some time after your visit to admire Ben Nevis, Britain's highest mountain. Fort William lies at the foot of the mountain and the views are spectacular.

SPECIAL!
After the Jacobite defeat at the Battle of Culloden in 1745, Highlanders were forbidden by law to wear Highland dress, carry weapons or retain allegiance to the House of Stuart. The Highlanders, however, devised ingenious ways of showing their loyalty to Bonnie Prince Charlie – like the secret portrait on show in the museum. When you look at the panel all you see are splodges of different-coloured paints but if the panel is used as a tray and a glass put on top, a perfect likeness of the Prince is reflected in the glass!

Open: mid-September to mid-June, Monday to Saturday, 0930–1300 and 1400–1700. Mid-June to mid-September, 0930–2100.
Admission fee: yes
Disabled access: limited
Café: nearby

13
THE SOUTH-EAST

(Kent, East Sussex, West Sussex)

AMBERLEY CHALK PITS MUSEUM
Amberley, near Arundel, West Sussex. Tel: Bury 831370

The guidebook suggests you allow three hours for a visit but you could spend much longer here. The idea of walking around 36 acres of the disused chalk quarries of an old limeworks might not sound particularly appealing – but Amberley is unique. Follow the red arrows on the signboards and you'll be treated to a trip through the industrial and working past of south-east England. You'll see a blacksmith, boat-builder, master printer and other craftspeople at work; a narrow-gauge industrial railway complete with 'Workman's Train' offering visitors a ride; a collection of vintage vehicles; an exhibition of old wirelesses; the massive 'de Wit' lime-kilns; a sewerage pumping-engine and more – there's even a nature trail! Everyone around is enthusiastic and friendly and you can't help but catch the mood.

SPECIAL!
Concrete canoes that can float and concrete bows that are capable of firing arrows – these are just two of the

exhibits in the History of Concrete exhibition telling the story of concrete from 5600 B.C. to the present day.

Open: Easter to end October, Wednesday to Sunday and Bank Holidays, 1000–1800 (last admission, 1700).
Admission fee: yes
Disabled access: limited
Café
Picnic facilities
Gifts: on sale
Toilets

ANNE OF CLEVES HOUSE
Southover High Street, Lewes, East Sussex.
Tel: Lewes 474610

Anne of Cleves, the fourth of Henry VIII's six wives, was married to the King for just six months; the union was then declared void due to non-consummation. By way of alimony Anne was granted a series of manors and houses including this interesting building a few minutes' walk away from Lewes's bustling main streets. You may be disappointed to learn that she never lived in the house and indeed probably never even saw it; however, you won't be disappointed by its present role as a museum. Visitors are allowed to wander quite freely as very little is roped off. There's plenty to take in: the entrance hall contains local pottery – look out for the Sussex pigs candlesticks; the upper bedroom (note the dog-gate at the foot of the stairs) has a couple of delightful cribs dating from *c.* 1700; the Tapestry Room contains four pieces of early-eighteenth-century chinoiserie Soho tapestry woven by John Vanderbank; the Furniture Room is dominated by a joined oak table, *c.* 1700. And if you'd like to know what Lewes was like in days gone by, then take a look at the painting by Dominic Serres. In the Long Gallery you'll find a display case devoted to games from the past while in the Old Kitchen, with its typical Sussex brick floor, you can see all sorts of kitchenware. Finally, it's up a flight of stairs to the Lewes Gallery, which as you might expect is full of local history. The Sussex Archaeological Society, which owns and maintains Anne of Cleves House, stresses that it can also be studied as an architectural structure. A timber-framed building of the 'Wealden' type, it uses a massive amount of wood: beams, rafters, brasing, ties, struts and polished floors. And you'll be left in doubt about the construction of the chimney which seems to crash through the upstairs space. Don't miss the medieval garden, particularly if you've a packed lunch with you; it's full of herbs and toads (take a look, under the sage bushes), and children are free to pick the wild strawberries.

SPECIAL!
Admire the tester bed – no, you don't get a chance to try it out! 'Tester' refers to the roof or ceiling over the bed which in this example (*c.* 1600) is beautifully carved. It would originally have had curtains on its three open sides to provide some privacy and warmth in large, draughty and semi-public rooms.

Open: mid-February to mid-November, Monday to Saturday, 1000–1700; Sunday (April to October only), 1230–1730.
Admission fee: yes
Picnic facilities
Gifts: on sale
Toilets

BUCKLEY'S SHOP MUSEUM
90 High Street, Battle, East Sussex. Tel: Battle 4269

This is a real 'Do you remember . . .?' museum as visitors reminisce about the days when you could get a bunch of bananas for 3d, a top hat cost 3 guineas and sweets were measured out for you. And for those too young to recall the heyday of the corner shop it's a fascinating look back in time. There are well over 1000 exhibits on three floors, mostly beautifully presented within arcades of Edwardian shop-sets. You can windowshop at a jeweller's, a toy shop, pawnbrokers, lace-makers, grocery store, stationers, drapers, chemist and a confectioner/tobacconist. Compare the range of goods (and the prices!) with today; it's quite staggering. There are also room-sets of an Edwardian kitchen, laundry, maid's bedroom and nursery complete with lace-trimmed baby clothes and children's toys. It takes time to absorb it all, and chances are you'll get chatting, so make sure you have an hour or two to spare.

SPECIAL!
Richly decorated cards are on show in the window of B. Gausden, the jewellers, est. 1877. Look out for the elaborate card made by a son for his mother's sixtieth birthday in 1907.

Open: April to October, daily, 1000–1730; November to March, Monday to Wednesday, Friday, Saturday, 1000–1630, Sunday, 1400–1630.
Admission fee: yes
Café: nearby
Gift shop

CHARLESTON FARMHOUSE
Firle (off A27), near Lewes, East Sussex. Tel: Ripe 265

To enjoy Charleston it certainly helps if you're besotted with the Bloomsbury set – the London literary group active during the 1920s and '30s – because, depending on your taste, you'll find this farmhouse either horrendous or captivating. However, whatever your point of view, Charleston is undoubtedly an interesting social record worth visiting. Though there are two ways to visit Charleston (join a tour or wander freely), most people are obliged to trot behind a guide. And it's unfortunate in a house with so much detail that you are not allowed to linger and think about what you're seeing. Nevertheless, the faithful can pay homage to friezes by Duncan Grant and decorative panelling by Vanessa Bell. A leaflet will tell you that this house represents a particular style, now part of art history, and that the style 'found here its finest and most characteristic flowering.' It also notes, 'Charleston is unique' – and that is absolutely true!

SPECIAL!
You are free to wander at your own pace through the pretty flower-filled garden at Charleston and its wooded area which contains stunningly positioned sculptures.

Open: April to October, Wednesday, Thursday, Saturday and Sunday, 1400–1800. (Note: by guided tour only except Sunday.)
Admission fee: yes
Gifts: on sale
Toilets

CHATHAM HISTORIC DOCKYARD
off Dock Road, Chatham, Kent. Tel: Medway 812551

It was here at Chatham that HMS *Victory* was built, and right at the heart of the dockyard is No. 2 Dock where she was laid down in 1759. But *Victory* was just one of the ships to start life from this royal dockyard – the first, *Sunne*, a 56-ton pinnace carrying five guns, was built in 1586; the last, a submarine, *Okanagan*, was launched for the Royal Canadian Navy in 1966. The dockyard closed in 1984 but its long and fascinating history is told through models and interpretive displays in the Visitor Centre, and by artefacts and mementoes collected together in the museum. Both are housed within the vast complex of Georgian and Victorian buildings – the Visitor Centre in the old Galvanizing Shop, and the museum in the Lead and Paint Mill. The exhibits help bring the past of the dockyard to life showing the traditional crafts and skills, the changing designs of the ships of the Royal Navy and the achievements of the yard. But to get the complete picture, take a walk around (you'll be given a map at the Visitor Centre) looking at the different buildings and their uses. Or, better still, join a guided tour (extra fee) and an expert will introduce you to the dockyard, its past glories, trades and traditions.

SPECIAL!
The splendid Commissioner's House, 1703, is the oldest naval building still intact in this country. Its garden is a delight, with glasshouses where two ancient vines still grow and a weeping mulberry known as 'Cromwell's Tree'. You enter by the Old Pay Office where Charles Dickens's father worked as a clerk.

Open: Easter to end October, Wednesday to Sunday and Bank Holidays, 1000–1800. November to March,

212

Wednesday, Saturday and Sunday, 1000–1630 (last admission, 1530).
Admission fee: yes
Disabled access: limited (telephone in advance)
Café: in Assistant Queen's Harbourmaster's House
Picnic facilities
Gifts: on sale
Toilets

CHARLES DICKENS CENTRE
Eastgate House, High Street, Rochester, Kent.
Tel: Medway 44176

You're in Charles Dickens country, for it was around Rochester and Chatham that Dickens spent his early days and many of the characters and places in his novels are based on the people and buildings he knew as a child. The beautiful sixteenth-century Eastgate House, for example, now the home of the Charles Dickens Centre, is the model for both Westgate House in *Pickwick Papers* and the Nun's House in *Edwin Drood*. It contains a colourful collection of talking heads and life-sized models of Dickens's famous characters, complete with their many amusing mannerisms and famous sayings; tableaux with sound and light effects re-creating favourite scenes from his books; and displays illustrating his life and times, the happy memories and sad reflections that shaped his writings. Look out, too, for the first editions of his books and miniature theatre sets. The centre, an enlightening insight into Dickens and his England, makes a good starting point for a trip around other places associated with him; ask at the tourist information centre next door for details.

SPECIAL!

In the garden outside is the Swiss-style chalet that Dickens used as a study. It stood in his garden at Gad's Hill Place, Higham, where he died in 1870.

Open: daily, 1000–1300 and 1400–1700 (last admission, 1230 and 1700).
Admission fee: yes
Disabled access: limited
Café: nearby
Gifts: on sale

FORT AMHERST
Barrier Road, off Dock Road, Chatham, Kent.
Tel: Medway 47747

Fort Amherst is a museum with a difference. It is one of the best examples of a Napoleonic fortress in the country – a whole fourteen acres of fortifications, begun in 1756 to protect the Royal Naval Dockyard (see page 212) and finally completed in 1820. It's now restored to its original state with massive ditches, towering bastions, gun emplacements and a complicated network of underground tunnels. To set the scene, your visit begins in the exhibition and interpretation centre. Then, equipped with all the background knowledge, you're free to wander around the above-ground fortifications or join a guided tour (no need to book) of the tunnels, eerie and haunted, hewn out of the solid chalk by prisoners of war. The tour and various exhibits highlight the working and living conditions at the fortress *c.* 1805 – from the impressive gun battery to the cramped barrack rooms where the men slept two to a bed. A good time to visit is on the first Sunday of every month during the season when the massive cannon is fired.

There are also many special events and displays throughout the summer when scenes from the fort's history are re-enacted (ask for details).

SPECIAL!
One section of the tunnels has been re-created as a wartime communications bunker. Everything is set and working, including the tannoy system, as though it was 19 August 1940, the middle of the heaviest bombing raids.

Open: April to October, Wednesday, Saturday and Sunday (daily in school holidays), 1200–1630. November to March, Sunday, 1200–1630
Admission fee: yes
Disabled access: limited
Café
Picnic facilities: with beautiful views
Gifts: on sale
Toilets

HOUSE OF PIPES
Bramber (on A283), Steyning, West Sussex.
Tel: Steyning 812122

Here, tucked away in the hamlet of Bramber, is the world's only museum of smoking. A strange subject for a museum, you might think – but step inside and you'll be quite astounded by the number and variety of exhibits on show. Indeed, there are seventy-three different types of collection within the museum, all designed to show the effect of smoking on our lives. There's everything from the pipes themselves to lighters, snuff boxes, postcards, packaging, coupons, cutters and matches – you'll even find a set of false teeth! Well, as the extrovert founder Anthony Irving explains, they deserve a place because it's astonishing to see just how badly they get worn down by smoking. The collection, which has been built up by Mr Irving over forty years, comprises 40,000 items from 180 countries covering 1500 years of smoking. It's laid out as a nineteenth-century shopping arcade with the items on display in the shop window fronts and there's always someone there to give you a warm welcome and, if you ask, to show you around.

SPECIAL!
The advertisements which hang from the ceiling make fascinating reading – look out for the one from Craven 'A' dated 1936 which features Mrs Wallace Simpson in her modelling days.

Open: daily, 0930–1830 (evenings by arrangement).
Admission fee: yes
Disabled access: good
Café
Picnic facilities: nearby
Gift shop
Toilets

MECHANICAL MUSIC AND DOLL COLLECTION
Church Road, Portfield, Chichester, West Sussex.
Tel: Chichester 785421

Look up, down and round about – there's something of interest in every corner of this redundant Victorian church hidden down a narrow lane. Penny-farthing bicycles hang from the ceiling, beautifully preserved Victorian dolls add a certain charm, and there's usually the chance to see a magic lantern show. Fascinating though these exhibits are, the main emphasis, however, is on the mechanical musical instruments – barrel organs, fair organs, musical boxes, street pianos, polyphons, phonographs and pianolas. They're all painted and polished and, as you soon discover, in full working order. Visits are by guided tour, lasting around forty-five minutes, when you're shown the instruments and treated to their magical, musical sounds. No need to book, just turn up – tours are at regular intervals.

SPECIAL!
A 21-foot-high marble and stone reredos originally installed in Chichester Cathedral now stands in the museum, a reminder of the past use of the building.

Open: Easter to end September, daily, 1000–1800. October to Easter, Saturday and Sunday, 1000–1700.
Admission fee: yes
Disabled access: good
Gifts: on sale
Toilets

THE REDOUBT FORTRESS
Royal Parade, Eastbourne, East Sussex.
Tel: Eastbourne 33952

This circular ten-gun fortress was built 1804–12 as a defence against the threat of a French invasion during Britain's second war with Napoleon. The threat subsided in 1805, but building continued as part of the policy of fortifying the south-east coast. The fort has been partially restored with a fine collection of gunnery on the battlements and it makes a perfect setting for military tattoos and battle re-enactments during the summer (telephone for details). It's now the home of the Royal Sussex Regiment Collection and the Sussex Combined Services Museum, with exhibits showing their history and achievements. There are also room-sets which show past life in the fort with a re-creation of an officers' mess and conditions in barrack rooms around 1879, and displays on the coastline, Martello towers, the Cinque Ports, and naval events of the past. Especially for children, there's the chance to try on hats, gas masks and uniforms in the 'Artillery Store' with mirrors so you can see how you look!

SPECIAL!
Don't miss the collection of magnificent drums of the Royal Sussex Regiment.

Open: Easter to end October, daily, 0930–1730.
Admission fee: yes
Café
Picnic facilities: on the beach
Gifts: on sale
Toilets

THE ROMAN MOSAIC HOUSE
Longmarket, Canterbury, Kent. Tel: Canterbury 452747

A concentrated bombing raid in 1942 razed many of Canterbury's buildings to the ground, leaving parts of the city open for excavation. One of the great finds was this segment of a Roman town house, with its beautiful mosaic floor and underground heating system. To help you appreciate the work involved in the mosaic pavement, there's a display explaining the tools used and techniques employed. Drawings show how a craftsman would choose a design from a pattern-book, then mark it on the floor and use it as a guide for laying the individually-cut cubes (known as *tesserae*). Much remains of the heating system, known as the hypocaust, and diagrams show how it would have worked; a model of efficiency, the designs form the basis for present-day methods of heating. Also on show are pieces of Roman pottery and other objects, mostly found locally. The custodian will answer your questions and direct you to other Roman sites in Canterbury.

SPECIAL!
A hoard of Roman bronze coins, dating back to 270 A.D., was found in the excavations, and many are on display.

Open: January to March and October to December, Monday to Saturday, 1400–1600. April to September, Monday to Saturday, 1000–1300 and 1400–1600.
Admission fee: yes
Café: nearby
Toilets: nearby

ROYAL ENGINEERS MUSEUM
Brompton Barracks, Prince Arthur Road (B2004),
Chatham, Kent. Tel: Medway 44555 ex 312

The motto of the Royal Engineers is 'Ubique' meaning 'Everywhere' – and as the exhibits in this bright and imaginative museum show, the corps has played an important part in wars and skirmishes all over the world for the last two centuries. This isn't just another military museum – everything is presented in such an exciting way that the tremendous scientific and engineering achievements of the Royal Engineers at war and peace are really brought home to you. There are displays of weapons, equipment, uniforms, models, medals, maps and mementoes which trace the history of military engineering right from 55 B.C. with a model of the bridge Julius Caesar built across the Rhine, one of the first-ever temporary assault bridges. Everything is well labelled, inviting you to find out more. Exhibits of particular interest include the map used by Wellington at the Battle of Waterloo; the only surviving example of a Brennan torpedo; a First World War trench system created as the original plans indicated; and you must meet 'Snob', a mascot in the Crimean War!

SPECIAL!
Major General Charles Gordon, 'Chinese Gordon', was a member of the Royal Engineers. A display illustrates his life and work.

Open: Tuesday to Friday and Bank Holiday Monday, 1000–1700; Sunday, 1130–1700.
Admission fee: yes
Gifts: on sale
Toilets

THE ROYAL NATIONAL LIFEBOAT INSTITUTION MUSEUM

King Edward's Parade, Eastbourne, East Sussex.
Tel: Eastbourne 30717

Part of the poignancy of this small museum is that it's housed in a former boathouse on the seafront – the sound of the sea crashing in the background acts as a permanent reminder of the need for lifeboats and their brave crews. The Old Lifeboat House built in memory of actor William Terris, who became famous for playing seafaring parts, is a perfect home for a collection of just about everything to do with lifeboats and the volunteers who have manned them through the ages. Exhibits range from life-saving equipment, including the old cork lifejackets, to old photographs, descriptions of rescues and a display of ships in bottles. There's also a section on the development of lifeboats and their changing design from the early whalers to modern-day boats. The present-day Lifeboat House is a mile or so (and a beautifully refreshing walk) along the seafront and is often open to the public (ask at the museum for details).

SPECIAL!
Eastbourne's first lifeboat was stationed here in 1822 and the museum has records showing the ships and crews that have been helped since then.

Open: Easter to October, daily, 0900–2100; also Saturday and Sunday throughout the year (telephone to check).
Admission fee: no
Disabled access: limited
Café: nearby
Picnic facilities: nearby
Gifts: on sale
Toilets: nearby

TYRWHITT-DRAKE MUSEUM OF CARRIAGES
Mill Street, Maidstone, Kent. Tel: Maidstone 54497

This fourteenth-century building, once the stables of the Archbishop's Palace, makes the perfect home for a collection of over fifty carriages of all shapes, sizes and descriptions. The museum is full of character and atmosphere; the stairs are lit by carriage lamps and every exhibit has been left in its original state without renovation or repair. There are traders' carts, sedan chairs, horse-drawn carriages and travelling chariots, many of which were used by royalty. Just picture yourself riding in Queen Victoria's carriage with its splendid interior of deep blue brocade! Also on display are liveries, harness and old photographs – in fact, everything you ever needed to know about carriages.

SPECIAL!
Any ideas how sedan chairs got their name? You'll find out in the special exhibition, and also discover how the Duke of Buckingham created an uproar when he was carried in a sedan chair in 1581, the first recorded use in Britain.

Open: January to March and October to December, Monday to Saturday, 1000–1300 and 1400–1700. April to September, Monday to Saturday, 1000–1300 and 1400–1700; Sunday,1400–1700.
Admission fee: yes
Disabled access: limited

WEALD AND DOWNLAND OPEN AIR MUSEUM
Singleton, near Chichester, West Sussex.
Tel: Singleton 348

Set in a country park in lovely Sussex countryside, this open-air museum is a delightful place for an afternoon's walk through the woods, an ideal spot for a peaceful picnic and a colourful venue for folk dancers and entertainers during the summer season. Dotted around the site are over twenty-five historic buildings rescued from around south-east England, including medieval houses, barns, rural craft workshops, agricultural buildings, a sixteenth-century market hall, village school and a seventeenth-century working windmill – all carefully restored and mostly refurbished in period style. There's a building to catch your interest wherever you walk – the Toll Cottage from Beeding, the Cattle Shed from Coldwaltham, the Granary from Littlehampton . . . but be warned, it's easy to get lost so it's worth picking up a map from the ticket desk which outlines a suggested walking tour. Special events are held throughout the year (ask for details).

SPECIAL!
One of the most prized buildings in the collection is 'Bayleaf', an early-fifteenth-century timber-framed hall-house from Chiddingstone. An open fire in the middle of the hall creates a warm and welcoming atmosphere.

Open: Easter to end October, daily, 1100–1700. November to end March, Wednesday, Sunday, 1100–1600.
Admission fee: yes
Disabled access: limited
Café
Picnic facilities
Gifts: on sale
Toilets

WHITBREAD HOP FARM
Beltring, Paddock Wood, Kent. Tel: Maidstone 872068

You can't miss it – just look for the white-coned tops of the Victorian oast-houses! The farm is still working, growing hops for the Whitbread brewery, but the old oast-houses and galleried barns have been turned into a series of museums and craft workshops with play areas and a nature trail. There's a collection of agricultural machinery, carts and harness, and an exhibition of rural crafts, some common, some most unusual. But most fascinating of all are the exhibits on hopping – there's a video telling the story of hops, past and present and a museum full of marvellous old photographs, machines and equipment. You can look around a traditional oast, last used for hopping in 1984, with displays of the various processes and, of course, during the season you can watch the hops being harvested. Set aside a whole day for a visit.

SPECIAL!
This is the training ground and holiday and retirement home for Whitbread shire horses. Find out all about these beautiful horses, and meet them too.

Open: April to October, Tuesday to Sunday and Bank Holiday Monday, 1000–1730 (last admission 1700).
Admission fee: yes
Disabled access: limited (telephone in advance)
Café
Picnic facilities: with play area for children
Gifts: on sale
Toilets

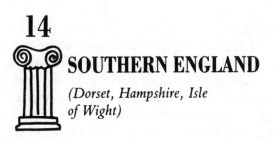

14

SOUTHERN ENGLAND

(Dorset, Hampshire, Isle of Wight)

JANE AUSTEN'S HOUSE

Chawton (off A31), near Alton, Hampshire.
Tel: Alton 83262

This beautiful 300-year-old house was the last home of Jane Austen. The famous novelist lived here with her mother and sister from 1809 until her early death in 1817. In that short time she wrote *Mansfield Park*, *Emma* and *Persuasion* and revised *Sense and Sensibility*, *Pride and Prejudice* and *Northanger Abbey*. The drawing-room, vestibule, dining parlour and upstairs bedroms are all open to the public, furnished with many pieces belonging to Jane – don't miss the table where she did most of her writing. It seems tiny, but apparently Jane was a 'back of an envelope' scribbler, jotting down ideas as they hit her. Many of her hand-written letters are on show, together with personal items, a lock of hair, a patchwork quilt worked by Jane and her mother, illustrations from her books and a display about her various homes. The atmosphere is cosy and friendly with lovely details such as the kettle by the fireplace – a

225

reminder that Jane's main domestic duty was to make the breakfast. By the time you leave, you feel so well acquainted with Jane you can't help but want to read and reread her novels.

SPECIAL!

Jane did her writing in the parlour under semi-secret conditions. The wooden door to this room, known as the 'Creaking Door', acted as a warning that anyone was coming so she could hide her work under the blotter. It's still there but, unfortunately, has been rehung the wrong way round so it no longer creaks!

Open: April to end October, daily, 1100–1630. November, December and March, Wednesday to Sunday, 1100–1630. January and February, Saturday and Sunday, 1100–1630.
Admission fee: yes
Disabled access: limited
Café: opposite
Picnic facilities: in the garden
Gifts: on sale
Toilets

BEMBRIDGE MARITIME MUSEUM

Providence House, Sherborne Street, Bembridge, Isle of Wight. Tel: Isle of Wight 872223/873125

The sound of old sea shanties greeting visitors is just one of the imaginative touches that make this museum on nautical heritage such a pleasant place to browse around. There are six galleries with maritime exhibits dating from the early days of sail to the present-day hovercraft. Displays tell the story of salvage from shipwrecks, highlight the hard life of sailors aboard square riggers, and describe the discovery of HM Submarine *Swordfish*, one of the great mysteries of the Second World War. There's also an important collection of ship models, navigators' instruments and examples of early and amazingly cumbersome diving equipment – the boots alone weigh around 40 lb! The museum is always popular with children (a great way to spend a rainy day on holiday!) and there are quiz sheets available to help them find their way around.

SPECIAL!
Meet the merman, a grotesque-looking creature. It appears quite lifelike, but the merman was a trick played by seamen serving on ships in the Far East.

Open: Easter to October, daily, 1000–1730 (August, until 2100).
Admission fee: yes
Café: nearby
Gift shop
Toilets: nearby

THE BIG FOUR RAILWAY MUSEUM
Dalkeith Steps (rear of 81 Old Christchurch Road), Bournemouth, Dorset. Tel: Bournemouth 22278

As every railway enthusiast will know, the Big Four were the Great Western Railway, the Southern Railway, the London and North Eastern Railway and the London Midland and Scottish Railway – and this museum contains a wealth of memorabilia and models relating to these and other smaller railways. Wherever you look there's something that catches your eye – old signs, whistles, name-plates, crests and cabsides – you can even buy a genuine platform ticket! And don't miss the working model of Pen-y-Darran, designed by Richard Trevithick, which became the first locomotive in the world to pull a load under steam in 1804. The museum is a real magnet for railway buffs, but the exhibits are such a lively reminder of the romance of a past age of travel, it's a treat for everyone.

SPECIAL!
A celebration lunch was held on 7 February 1890 to mark the occasion of the turning of the first sod of the new Derbyshire lines of the Manchester–Sheffield–Lincs Railway Company and the menu is on show – it's a real feast!

Open: Monday to Saturday, 1000–1700.
Admission fee: yes
Gifts: on sale

CALLEVA MUSEUM
Bramley Road (off A340), Silchester, Hampshire.

The Romans settled in Silchester *c.* 40 A.D. Naming it Calleva, meaning 'woody place', they developed some 80 acres into a flourishing administrative centre. Calleva lay in the heart of the civil zone of the Imperial Province of Britain and was part of a network of Roman administrative towns under the overall control of the imperial governor and the procurator for financial affairs in London. You can still see the remains of the town's impressive defensive walls and visit its recently excavated amphitheatre, while in the tiny Calleva Museum (housed in something little bigger than a garden shed and looking remarkably like one) you can learn just how the Romans lived, worked and ruled here some 2000 years ago.

SPECIAL!
Make sure you take note of the drawn reconstruction of Calleva – it gives a good idea of human activity in this area since Neolithic times – then compare it with the diagram of the site today.

Open: daylight hours.
Admission fee: no
Disabled access: limited
Picnic facilities

CHRISTCHURCH TRICYCLE MUSEUM
The Quay, Christchurch, Dorset.

One of the things that did amuse Queen Victoria was her tricycle – apparently she still used to ride it around Osborne House at the grand age of sixty-three! You can hear all about these royal and other tricycling exploits in this unusual museum housed in a restored monastic building. The definition of a tricycle hangs on the wall: 'A rider-propelled vehicle with three wheels', and all around are examples from Victorian times to the modern day. There are also photographs, wall displays and models in period costume: look out for the lady displaying the modesties of Victorian tricycling dress. The museum is centred on tricycles, but you'll find several cycles with more than three wheels here too.

SPECIAL!
The Hen and Chicken's Pentacycle was an ingenious machine. There's one on display, with the model of a postman showing how it was used to deliver parcels.

Open: June to September, daily 1000–1730, Easter, April, May and October, weekends 1000–1730.
Admission fee: yes
Café: nearby
Gifts: on sale
Toilets: nearby

THE MUSEUM OF CLOCKS

Alum Bay (on B3322), Isle of Wight.
Tel: Isle of Wight 754193

The gentle swinging motion of the pendulums, the methodical sound of the tick-tock . . . be prepared, this museum is completely mesmerizing! There are over two hundred clocks and watches from all over the world, and they're all working! But don't be tempted to use them to tell the time, they're all set differently – well, just imagine the commotion if they all struck the hour together: the William Tell Overture resounding from the *c.* 1870 large Black Forest organ clock as two figures appear through the doors; the double strike of the French Vineyard clock, an ancient call for prayer-time; the fourteen chiming bells of the *c.* 1780 English Twelve-Tune Bracket clock; and, of course, the shrill cuckoo of the wooden *c.* 1880–1900 Black Forest Cuckoo clock – and that's just a few of the horological sights and sounds in the collection! The time-pieces are all clearly labelled with explanations of their origins and working mechanisms – there are church clocks, mystery clocks, a perpetual motion clock, a rolling ball clock, the forerunner of the digital watch and lots more. Many are rare, some are highly ornate, others give novelty value – but all are different and absolutely intriguing.

SPECIAL!
The Chinese Fire Dragon Boat clock, *c.* 1800, is an early form of alarm clock. An incense stick used to be

lit at one end then, as it burned along, metal balls fell
into the boat, making a clatter and waking you up!

Open: July to September, Sunday to Friday,
1100–1700.
Admission fee: yes
Disabled access: good
Gifts: on sale
Toilets: nearby

D-DAY MUSEUM

Clarence Esplanade, Portsmouth, Hampshire.
Tel: Portsmouth 827261

This museum is relatively new – it was opened in 1984
as part of the fortieth anniversary celebrations of D-
Day – and is the only one of its kind completely devoted
to the Normandy Landings. The highlight is undoubtedly the Overlord Embroidery, an exquisite piece of
needlework over 80 metres long, which tells the story
of the invasion. Follow it round the room – some of the
figures appear to move as you do. However, there's
also an exciting audio-visual show which describes life
in the war years, invites you behind the scenes of the
landings and encourages you to share the experience of
being on a landing-craft on the last run in to the beach.
And there's an overwhelming number of maps, diagrams, models, military equipment and field-guns, plus
some of the actual vehicles that took part in the action.
If you're not old enough to remember D-Day yourself,
it's a good idea to visit with someone who does – it
makes the exhibition even more powerful.

SPECIAL!
The mighty Sherman tank might be rather war-battered
but it's still in perfect working order.

Open: daily, 1030–1730.
Admission fee: yes
Disabled access: good
Picnic facilities: nearby
Gifts: on sale
Toilets

THE DINOSAUR MUSEUM

Icen Way, Dorchester, Dorset. Tel: Dorchester 69880

Just what does the skin of a dinosaur feel like? Cold and scaly? Hot and clammy? You can find out for yourself by touching a replica skin in this unique museum which tells you virtually all there is to know about dinosaurs and their relatives – from the formation of fossils to the daily diet of a Diplodocus and the excavations of dinosaur remains. The subject matter might be old – indeed, dinosaurs became extinct around 65 million years ago – but there's nothing antiquated about the displays: actual-size reproductions, computerized, mechanical and electronic exhibits and a special viewing gallery with an audio-visual show. It's all so vivid, you almost feel as though the great creatures are following you around!

SPECIAL!
It's believed that the first dinosaurs were walking on earth some 200 million years ago. Casts of actual dinosaur footprints, discovered in Swanage in 1981, are here in the museum. It's awesome to think these date back some 130 million years to the early Cretaceous period.

Open: daily, 0930–1730.
Admission fee: yes

Disabled access: limited
Café: called 'The Hungry Dinosaur' and serving up dinosaurian delights!
Gifts: on sale
Toilets

THE LILLIPUT MUSEUM OF ANTIQUE DOLLS AND TOYS

High Street, Brading, Isle of Wight. Tel: Isle of Wight 407231

Everyone who has ever loved a doll will love this delightful museum full of beautiful dolls, some with houses, and old toys. With well over 2000 exhibits, the earliest of which is a stone Ushabti grave figure of 2000 B.C., it's considered to be one of the most comprehensive and finest private collections in the country. Its importance is obvious, but the real charm of the museum is that all the dolls and toys have been acquired from the original owner or a descendant, so the individual story behind each is known. As you walk around you'll find every exhibit is clearly labelled and it makes fascinating reading – there's the nesting doll presented by Mr Khrushchev, ex-Premier of Russia; a wax doll dressed in a remnant of Queen Caroline's wedding gown; the first Action Man; and a Vauxhall pedal-car, complete with petrol and oil cans on the running board. The owner, Margaret Munday-Whitaker, has become a leading expert on dolls and doll-collecting and if you contact her in advance she'll be happy to show you around her much-loved collection personally.

SPECIAL!
The Crab Claw Doll of 1885 with hands, feet, nose and chin of crab claws is thought to be unique. She's

carrying a small bag complete with a note: 'With best wishes from my missus and she hopes the goose is not tough – December 1885'. The doll belonged to a fisherwoman in Perth, Scotland, and was given to the museum by a relative.

Open: mid-March to mid-January, daily; summer, 1000–1000; winter, 1000–1700.
Admission fee: yes
Disabled access: good
Café: nearby
Gift shop: doll collectors' items on sale
Toilets: nearby

OATES MEMORIAL MUSEUM AND THE GILBERT WHITE MUSEUM

'The Wakes', Selborne, near Alton, Hampshire.
Tel: Selborne 275

It's the five-acre garden that most people come to see – and, indeed, it really is worth a special visit. It was here at his country home, 'The Wakes', that the Reverend Gilbert White, eighteenth-century clergyman-naturalist and author of *The Natural History and Antiquities of Selborne*, lived for most of his life. White kept detailed notes on his garden over forty-two years – his successes and failures, books studied, methods used – making it one of the best-documented gardens of the time. It's a charming and peaceful haven of natural history made doubly interesting if you follow the key plan highlighting the various plants, trees and landscaped features.

Inside 'The Wakes' there are two museums – the ground floor is devoted to the life and works of Gilbert White, natural history and the beautiful village of

Selborne. The staircase and upstairs rooms are set aside for exhibits on two members of the Oates family – Frank Oates, nineteenth-century naturalist and explorer in Africa; and his nephew Captain Lawrence Oates who accompanied Scott on the Antarctic expedition, 1910–12. Exhibits and displays in the Oates Memorial Museum are a tribute to the bravery and lasting achievements of these two men.

Have a look around the village, too – the Gilbert White Memorial Window is in the Norman church opposite the museum and shouldn't be missed. It depicts St Francis preaching to the birds, many of which were mentioned by White in his writings. The Romany Folklore Museum and Workshop (see p. 236) is a short walk away.

SPECIAL!
Captain Oates died on his thirty-second birthday in March 1912, suffering from frostbite and gangrene. A display highlights the tragedy of his last words as he walked out of the tent into a blizzard, saying to his companions: 'I am just going outside. I may be some time.'

Open: March to October, Tuesday to Sunday, 1200–1730 (last admission, 1700).
Admission fee: yes
Café: nearby
Gifts: on sale (including footpath leaflets showing walks around Selborne)
Toilets

POOLE POTTERY MUSEUM
The Quay, Poole, Dorset. Tel: Poole 672866

This small museum attached to the Poole Pottery is cleverly positioned so visitors have to walk through the showroom and shop to reach it! But once you've made your way past the shelves full of colourful pottery pieces on sale, you'll find the museum collection with an audio-visual show. The exhibits and displays highlight the history, techniques and leading people involved in the manufacture of pottery here on the quay since 1870. It gives you some idea of the craftsmanship and processes involved, but you'll get a fuller picture if you combine a visit with a guided tour of the factory. To book a tour telephone in advance (fee).

SPECIAL!
One case is full of pottery made to commemorate royal weddings and engagements.

Open: Monday to Saturday, 0900–1700.
Admission fee: no
Disabled access: good
Café
Picnic facilities: along the quayside
Gift shop
Toilets

ROMANY FOLKLORE MUSEUM AND WORKSHOP
High Street, Selborne, near Alton, Hampshire.
Tel: Selborne 486

Set up and run by a true Romany, you can be assured that every part of this museum of Gypsy life is authentic. The owner, now a waggon-builder, restorer and decorator, was on the road until 1974 and still lives in his caravan in the garden, cooking meals over an open fire. He hadn't intended to start a museum but visitors to his workshops were so intrigued that he decided to answer everyone's questions by gathering together a collection of Gypsy bygones. Many of the items on display belonged to himself, his family or friends and others have been donated or bought – but all are original, from the rod tents to the peg-bags. Every aspect of Gypsy life is covered such as early history, language, music, dress, crafts and living accommodation – and outside there are several full-size living caravans, including an old Brush Waggon, the only one in the country, all in various states of restoration. The owner, whom you can watch at work in the yard, will probably find a few minutes to charm you with some of the old Gypsy stories and superstitions. (The Oates Memorial Museum and the Gilbert White Museum is a short walk away.)

SPECIAL!
The Romany horse-dealer's suit was one of the last to be made. Notice the size of the poacher's pocket!

Open: daily, 1030–1730.
Admission fee: yes
Disabled access: limited
Café: nearby
Gifts: on sale (on a Romany theme)

THE ROYAL MARINES MUSEUM

Royal Marines Eastney (entrance through main gate of Barracks), Southsea, Hampshire. Tel: Portsmouth 819385

Best behaviour please! Sergeant-Major Bertie Leman is keeping a careful eye on you, and he warns that smoking, spitting and 'nicking' of objects are strictly forbidden! At the press of a button, the lifelike figure of Bertie welcomes you to the museum and leaves you quite exhausted by describing all there is to see. But don't worry, just follow the arrows on the floor and you won't miss anything. The exhibits describe the eventful history of the Royal Marines from 1664 to the present day with medals, uniforms, models, drums and trumpets, photographs, historic portraits, silver, and special displays highlighting the stories of the courage of individual men and women. It's all housed in the original Victorian RM Artillery Officers' Mess – soak up the architectural beauty as you enjoy the collection.

SPECIAL!
The medal collection is one of the finest in the world, with all ten Royal Marines Victoria Crosses and over 6000 other awards for valour.

Open: daily, 1000–1630.
Admission fee: no
Disabled access: limited
Café: May to September
Picnic facilities
Gifts: on sale
Toilets

ROYAL NATIONAL LIFEBOAT INSTITUTE MUSEUM
RNLI Headquarters, West Quay Road, Poole, Dorset.
Tel: Poole 671133

Since the RNLI was founded in 1824, it has saved over 112,000 lives from drowning at sea. The small museum, based at their headquarters, explains the history of this voluntary organization and gives credit to the bravery of the lifeboat crew who turn out at all hours and in all weathers to answer distress calls. Exhibits include models, photographs, drawings and other memorabilia showing the changing design of lifeboats and equipment and describing some of the many rescues over past years. Of particular note is the display centred on the short but brave life of Grace Darling (1815–42), heroine of the sea. Read the story of how, in September 1838, she helped her father, a lighthouse keeper, launch a boat and fight the cruel seas to rescue survivors of the wrecked Forfarshire steamboat. The museum is open throughout the year but on two days every July the RNLI holds open days here (telephone for details). You can see around the Operations Room and workshops, watch demonstration launchings and exercises and actually go on board a lifeboat and meet the crew.

SPECIAL!
If you ever thought tying a knot was simple, think again! There's a showcase full of different knots: a Crow's Foot, an Eye Splice, a Spike Hitch.

Open: Monday to Friday, 0930–1630.
Admission fee: no
Disabled access: good
Gifts: on sale (proceeds to the RNLI)
Toilets

THE ROYAL NAVAL MUSEUM
HM Naval Base, Portsmouth, Hampshire.
Tel: Portsmouth 733060

Portsmouth's historic dockyard is probably best known as the home of three famous warships, the *Mary Rose*, HMS *Victory* and *The Warrior*, but situated alongside is this museum devoted to the Royal Navy. Its aim, to relate the complete history of the navy from Tudor times to the South Atlantic campaign of 1982, is ambitious and surprisingly successful. Housed in a series of Georgian storehouses, exhibits include figureheads, ship models, medals and uniforms. A special section is set aside as a tribute to Admiral Lord Nelson with displays and personal relics describing his life and times, and, of course, his famous victories. And to give you the full impact of the part the Royal Navy played in the Battle of Trafalgar, there's a huge panorama of the battle complete with commentary and deafening sound effects. Permanent exhibitions are on themes such as 'Victorian Heyday 1861–1905' and 'The Modern Navy', and there are also temporary exhibitions throughout the year.

SPECIAL!
You can't miss the State Barge – it's large, ornate and right in the middle of the Victory Collection! Its last outing was in 1806 when it carried the body of Lord Nelson from Greenwich Hospital to Whitehall Stairs before the ceremonial interment at St Paul's Cathedral.

Open: daily, 1030–1700 (except Christmas week).
Admission fee: yes
Disabled access: limited
Café

Gift shop
Toilets

ROYAL NAVY SUBMARINE MUSEUM
Gosport (signposted via Haslar Bridge), Hampshire.
Tel: Gosport 529217

There's no mistaking this museum – the huge silhouette
of HM Submarine *Alliance* seems to fill the skyline for
miles around. Nor is there any doubt about the proce-
dure once you arrive, it's all very well ordered. A visit
begins in the Briefing Room with a ten-minute audio-
visual display giving you the background to submarines, their development, and how they dive, stay
down and attack. And then it's a guided tour around
HMS *Alliance*, now fully restored to her service condition. You're shown around all the compartments and
into the control and engine rooms – the dangers being
stressed at every point. The conditions for the sixty or
so seamen aboard were, to say the least, cramped, with
low ceilings and very little room to move about. (You
get the full flavour of just how uncomfortable it would
have been, so if you suffer from claustrophobia, don't
even attempt the tour.) The guide brings it all to life,
peppering the technical and operational details with
fascinating titbits. (Early petrol-engined submarines
carried three white mice as part of their crew, with an
allowance of one shilling a day for food! The mice,
sensitive to gasoline, would signal a leak by squeaking.)
The tour lasts around an hour and a half and then you're
free to wander around the museum and other displays.
You'll probably want to make straight for the navy's
first submarine No.1, known as 'Holland 1', launched
in October 1901, which is now open for visitors to look
around, but do save time for the museum, which traces

the development of submarines and underwater warfare from the earliest days to the present nuclear age. There are pictures, artefacts, Jolly Roger flags and models of British submarines since 1901.

SPECIAL!
The first submarine to make an attack was in 1776 at New York harbour. The story of HMS *Turtle* versus HMS *Eagle* is really exciting; don't miss it!

Open: daily, 1000–1630 (last tour); (November to March, 1530).
Admission fee: yes
Disabled access: limited
Café: selling Pussars Rum!
Picnic facilities: on the harbour
Gifts: on sale
Toilets

RUSSELL-COTES ART GALLERY AND MUSEUM
East Cliff, Bournemouth, Dorset. Tel: Bournemouth 21009

Stepping inside the door of this museum housed in a Victorian mansion is just like walking back to a past age of grandeur and dignity. A calm immediately descends as you start appreciating the outstanding beauty of the paintings, ceramics, furniture and period rooms. It's a collection to take slowly and quietly, savouring every object on display. The mansion, which stands in secluded grounds still kept in the Victorian style, was originally East Cliff Hall, built in 1894 as a home for Sir Merton and Lady Russell-Cotes, highly influential citizens. They filled it with their collections of fine and applied art, most with a strong oriental theme, brought back from their travels abroad. The hall and contents were given to Bournemouth in 1908, the condition being that Sir Merton and his wife could continue to live there. Sir Merton died in 1921 but the collection remains virtually unchanged. It would take a whole book to give credit to the many items on display, so take a look for yourself!

SPECIAL!
The view over the Bournemouth Bay from the boudoir is quite spectacular. This dainty little room is where Lady Russell-Cotes would entertain. Look at the plaque on the wall listing her royal visitors.

Open: Monday to Saturday, 1000–1730.
Admission fee: yes
Disabled access: limited
Café
Gifts: on sale
Toilets

THE MUSEUM OF SMUGGLING HISTORY
Botanic Gardens, Ventnor, Isle of Wight.
Tel: Isle of Wight 853677

Some of the smuggling tricks used through the ages have to be seen to be believed – tea in hollowed stones, a barrel of brandy in a top hat, the 'Mona Lisa' in a false-bottomed suitcase, diamonds in a cigar, rings in a garter and opium in oranges. These and other smuggling methods are on show (often by X-ray camera) in this museum which traces the history of smuggling. The story begins around 700 years ago in the days of pirates, 'owlers' windows and auctions by candlelight and continues right up to the present, explaining the rather startling facts and showing the dangerous lengths to which people will go. It's all underground, situated in huge vaults, with exhibits and models showing the hideaways and secret signals of the early days, the punishments and the personalities.

SPECIAL!
Who'd have thought spaceman Alan Shepherd was a smuggler? A life-sized model shows him standing on the moon holding a golf ball – smuggled without the knowledge of Mission Control!

Open: Easter to end September, daily, 1000–1730.
Admission fee: yes
Café: nearby
Picnic facilities: in the Botanic Gardens
Gifts: on sale
Toilets

SOUTHAMPTON HALL OF AVIATION
Albert Road South, Southampton, Hampshire.
Tel: Southampton 635830

Visions of those magnificent men in their flying machines come to mind as you wander around this purpose-built aviation museum. Aircraft, real and model, fill the hall – many hanging dramatically from the ceiling! The Solent was one of the leading areas for the experimentation and development of aircraft, and the exhibits, which include not only the flying machines themselves but also photographs, paintings and engines, trace the history of twenty-six aircraft companies. Among the most notable is Supermarine, where Reginald Joseph Mitchell, designer of the legendary Spitfire, was employed. A display shows the development of the Spitfire between 1939 and 1948 and gives details of thirty of the main versions. To complete the picture, you can see a Spitfire at close hand – a Vickers Super-marine Spitfire F Mk 24, 1946. Mitchell also designed the trophy-winning aircraft S6B and displays highlight the tremendous flying feats that were involved in the race to claim this celebrated trophy.

SPECIAL!
The four-engined Sandringham Flying Boat, which weighs a massive 21 tons, dominates the hall. You're allowed to explore on board. If you'd like to be shown around the flight deck by an expert, just ask at the desk.

Open: Tuesday to Saturday, 1000–1700; Sunday, 1200–1700.
Admission fee: yes
Disabled access: limited
Café
Gifts: on sale
Toilets

THE TOLPUDDLE MARTYRS MUSEUM
TUC Memorial Cottages (on A35), Tolpuddle, Dorset.
Tel: Puddletown 237

In February 1834, six agricultural labourers from this small Dorset village were arrested on a charge of taking part in an 'illegal oath' ceremony while forming a trade union. The men – George Loveless, James Loveless, Thomas Standfield, John Standfield, James Brine and James Hammett – were sentenced to seven years' trans-portation to the penal colonies of New South Wales and Van Dieman's Land. It caused such a public outcry that eventually the men were pardoned and were allowed to return to England three years later. They became known as the Tolpuddle Martyrs. These six cottages were built in 1934 in memory of the part they played in the struggle for the rights of trade unionists, and are now the home of local labourers and their families. One room has been set aside as a museum with photographs and artefacts describing their arrest, trial and transportation and also telling the history of the trade-union movement.

SPECIAL!
In many ways the museum spreads across the whole village, and it's well worth picking up a leaflet which shows the position of historical sites nearby such as Thomas Standfield's Cottage and James Hammett's grave, all within easy walking distance.

Open: daily, 0900–1800.
Admission fee: no (donations appreciated)
Café: in village
Gifts: on sale

THE WAREHAM BEARS

18 Church Street, Wareham, Dorset. Tel: Wareham 6671

You've heard of the teddy bears' picnic – well, now there's a teddy bears' museum! There are around seventy bears all 'living' in a cellar here in Wareham – and each has a very distinct character of its own. There's the naughty Miss Annabel de Trot who likes being out late, Mr and Mrs Gilbert the gardeners, Miss Pizzi Carter, a very tidy bear with an ear for music, Elizabeth Wilhelm who makes all the other bears' clothes, and Walker who prefers not to wear any! All these miniature bears are beautifully presented in mini-stage sets, complete with accessories, showing life in and around their house. If you can just forget the outside world for an hour or so and lose yourself in the land of make-believe then you'll find a warm welcome at Wareham.

SPECIAL!
Scrum is one of the newest members of the community – all the way from America. He's playing No. 4 in the Rugger Ground scene for the Bearbearians against the All Blues!

Open: mid-March to mid-September, Monday to Friday, 1000–1630; Saturday, 1000–1300.
Admission fee: yes
Café: nearby
Picnic facilities: nearby
Gift shop: with teddy bears, postcards and bear-related goods!
Toilets

15

THE THAMES AND THE CHILTERNS

(Bedfordshire, Berkshire, Hertfordshire, Oxfordshire)

BRITISH TELECOM MUSEUM

35 Speedwell Street, Oxford, Oxfordshire.
Tel: Oxford 246601

Though a small and intimate museum, with some 150 different styles of old telephone on display, its extensive reserve collection makes this the largest museum of its kind. Both connoisseurs and children are sure to enjoy a visit; for the expert there's the first telephone to have its own handpiece – a beautiful Victorian object dating from 1892 – while for the youngster there's a switchboard to operate and an old 'Press button A' coinbox to make a call from. But it's the enthusiast who'll get the most from the collection, so give it a go – it's a lot of fun.

SPECIAL!
Look out for the wartime telephones – there's even one fitted inside a gas mask!

Open: Monday to Friday, 1000–1200 and 1400–1600 by appointment only; write to the curator.

Admission fee: no
Disabled access: good
Picnic facilities: river Thames towpath nearby
Toilets

THE BUNYAN MEETING HOUSE AND MUSEUM

Mill Street (entrance in Castle Lane), Bedford,
Bedfordshire.
Tel: Bedford 58075

John Bunyan (1628–88), celebrated author of *Pilgrim's Progress*, lived most of his life in and around Bedford and this museum is a tribute to his achievements. Housed in the buildings of the Bunyan Meeting House, the church which Bunyan founded in 1672, it contains all his surviving personal relics and traces his life from the days when he had few equals in 'cursing, swearing, lying and blaspheming the Holy name of God' through his conversion, his talent for preaching and writing, and the years spent in prison for his beliefs. Among the many items on display are letters, manuscripts, paintings and mementoes such as the flute he carved from his prison stool and the jug his daughter would fill with soup for him. The Meeting House itself is still open for public services. Take a look at the exquisite bronze doors – the ten panels show scenes from the *Pilgrim's Progress*. You can pick up a free leaflet, 'John Bunyan's Bedford', from the museum which suggests a trail around the area. (Nearby is the Cecil Higgins Art Gallery and Museum, page 254.)

SPECIAL!
The museum boasts the world's largest collection of translations of *Pilgrim's Progress* – in 169 languages!

Open: April to end September, Tuesday to Saturday, 1400–1600.

Admission fee: yes
Café: nearby
Picnic facilities: nearby
Gifts: on sale

COGGES FARM MUSEUM
Church Lane, Cogges, near Witney, Oxfordshire.
Tel: Witney 72602

The Manor House at Cogges Farm dates from the thirteenth century. Its fully furnished dining-room, drawing-room and working kitchen have been brought to life by careful attention to detail – spectacles beside an open book, fresh fruit in a bowl, a clock ticking, an open ink pot beside the farm accounts ledger, bloomers pegged out on the washing line. In the garden herbs flourish and colourful borders provide fresh flowers for cutting. By following the 'History Trail' around the farm buildings and the surrounding land, you can see the story of human settlement here, dating back 5000 years. There's also a 'Natural History Trail' signposted by small information panels which indicate what flora and fauna you can see. The farmyard is particularly good fun for children because apart from the granary traphouse, the stable block, dairy and waggoners' hut, there are also pigsties where they can watch pigs and sometimes piglets.

SPECIAL!
Pay a visit to Cogges parish church, which is separated from the farm by a drystone wall. This pretty church was once part of an extensive medieval priory.

Open: Easter to first week in November, Tuesday to Sunday, 1030–1730 (closed 1630 in October and November).

Admission fee: yes
Disabled access: limited
Café
Picnic facilities
Gifts: on sale
Toilets

FRANK COOPER MUSEUM
84 High Street, Oxford, Oxfordshire. Tel: Oxford 245125

Tiny but tasty! If you feel your breakfast table isn't complete without a pot of marmalade, you're sure to enjoy a visit to the Frank Cooper Museum. It's very small, so don't go out of your way to visit, but if you're in Oxford call in and learn the story of 'Oxford' marmalade. Pots of this famous spread have travelled the world, going with Captain Scott to the South Pole and up Everest with Sir Edmund Hillary and Sherpa Tensing.

SPECIAL!
In 1874 Sarah Cooper, using an old family recipe, made 76 lb of marmalade on her kitchen range. Sarah's recipe book is on display, so if you can read her writing you'll be able to make her recipes!

Open: Monday to Saturday, 1000–1800; Sunday, 1200–1700 (summer only).
Admission fee: no
Disabled access: limited
Gift shop

MUSEUM OF ENGLISH RURAL LIFE

University of Reading (off A327), Whiteknights, PO Box 229, Reading, Berkshire. Tel: Reading 875123 ex 475

The well-thought-out displays of agricultural tools, domestic equipment and implements related to rural industry make the Museum of Rural Life a joy to visit. Items are grouped together with a sense of design as well as practical purpose and, best of all, they're neither hidden behind glass nor cordoned off with ropes. There's a really superb collection of waggons which have been restored and studied – each showing clear regional stylistic differences. It's certainly worth seeking out this fascinating collection on the edge of Reading University campus, and if you're particularly interested in a specific aspect of English rural life you can also write for permission to see items in its extensive reserve collection.

SPECIAL!
This is the home of the biggest corn dolly you're ever likely to set eyes on! This 6 foot 6 inch straw effigy of King Alfred was made in 1961 by a master-thatcher to demonstrate his ancient craft.

Open: Tuesday to Saturday, 1000–1300 and 1400–1630.
Admission fee: no
Disabled access: good
Gifts: on sale
Toilets

FIRST GARDEN CITY HERITAGE MUSEUM

296 Norton Way South, Letchworth Garden City, Hertfordshire. Tel: Letchworth 683149

Rapid industrialization during the nineteenth century led to overcrowded towns and cities. Slums quickly developed and a few liberal-minded industrialists attempted to provide better environments for their workers. Progressive planning, good housing and pleasant environmental conditions were pioneered in Letchworth, the world's first garden city (the estate was formally opened in October 1903). Here in the museum you can trace the background to the Garden City Movement both by studying the large reserve collection and by looking at the displays which cover the reasons why Letchworth was the chosen site and its social history. It's housed in the former drawing office of the architects Barry Parker and Raymond Unwin, who were both ardent campaigners for better housing; the building retains some of its original furniture which was designed by Parker. Parker and Unwin had a great influence on house design and many of the houses in Letchworth reflect their interest in the Arts and Crafts Movement.

SPECIAL!
The Three Magnets is the most famous of all planning diagrams. It argues succinctly for the benefits provided by a combination of town and country. At the centre of the diagram is the question, 'The People, Where Will They Go?'.

Open: Monday to Friday, 1400–1630; Saturday, 1000–1300 and 1400–1600.
Admission fee: no
Disabled access: good

Picnic facilities
Gifts: on sale
Toilets

CECIL HIGGINS ART GALLERY
Castle Close, Bedford, Bedfordshire.
Tel: Bedford 211222

Set in beautiful grounds just a stone's throw from the river Ouse, this art gallery and museum is best known for its outstanding collections of English and continental ceramics and glass, especially from the eighteenth century, and for the particularly fine displays of English watercolours and drawings, costume and lace. Once the pride and joy of art connoisseur Cecil Higgins (1856–1941), who lived in the adjoining house, these collections attract visitors from near and far. However, the museum is also a fascinating showcase of Victoriana. Higgins's home, known as the Victorian House, has been furnished throughout with period furniture and all the trimmings of the Victorian domestic life. To get the full benefit of the room-sets, pick up a picture guide at the entrance which takes you through the various items in each room pointing out their use – the foot-warmer and candle-snuffer in the library, for example, and the straight-backed sofa in the drawing-room, ideal for ladies in tight corsets! There are plenty of attendants on duty, so feel free to ask questions.

While you're in Castle Close, it's worth looking around the Bedford Museum (Tel: Bedford 53323) which is next door. It has displays on local history including a large collection of agricultural tools and sections on archaeology, geology and the natural history of the area. Look out for the model of Bedford Castle, which was demolished in the siege of 1224.

254

(Also nearby is The Bunyan Meeting House and Museum, page 249.)

SPECIAL!
A dolls' house, an exact replica of Oakley House, Bedfordshire, was designed and fitted out by two local children *c.* 1921 – the detailing is beautiful.

Open: Tuesday to Friday, 1230–1700; Saturday, 1100–1700; Sunday, 1400–1700.
Admission fee: yes
Disabled access: limited
Café: nearby
Picnic facilities: in the grounds
Gifts: on sale
Toilets

KINGSBURY WATER MILL
St Michael's Street, St Albans, Hertfordshire.
Tel: St Albans 53502

On the bank of the river Ver, just half a mile upstream from picturesque St Albans and a short walk from the remains of the Roman city of Verulamium, Kingsbury Mill is an attractive landmark. Its site was chosen with care, probably during Elizabethan times, as being near corn-growing areas and as having sufficient fall of water to power its water wheel. You can see milling machinery from the original mill and a good selection of old dairying and farming implements as well as the fascinating water wheel itself.

SPECIAL!
Outside the museum, on the grass, there's what's known locally as the 'Hertfordshire Pudding Stone', which is thought to be 60 million years old.

Open: Wednesday to Saturday, 1100–1700; Sunday, 1200–1700.
Admission fee: yes
Café
Picnic facilities
Gifts: on sale
Toilets

MUSEUM OF OXFORD

St Aldates, Oxford, Oxfordshire. Tel: Oxford 815559

Oxford is an historic town so packed with things to see and do that it's all too easy to find yourself plodding from one place of interest to the next wondering when it will come to an end; that's definitely *not* the way to see this city of 'dreaming spires'. So, to get things into proportion, make for the Museum of Oxford. A local museum, it tells the city's story from Saxon times when it was just a small settlement, through its flourishing medieval period, the development of the university colleges, and up to the present day. However, if you can, avoid the summer months when this relatively small space becomes overwhelmed with enthusiastic visitors.

SPECIAL!
Look out for the whip carried by the driver of the Royal Mail coach. In fact it's a pistol in disguise and was used by coachmen to defend themselves against highwaymen.

Open: Tuesday to Saturday, 1000–1700.
Admission fee: yes
Gifts: on sale

OXFORD UNIVERSITY MUSEUM
Parks Road, Oxford, Oxfordshire. Tel: Oxford 272950

Like many of Oxford's collections, the University Museum is housed in splendid architectural surroundings worth visiting in their own right. The result of a highly publicized competition held in 1853 and won by Dublin architect Benjamin Woodward, it's an outstanding example of Victorian Gothic. Opened in 1860, its Gothic-style architecture was championed by critic John Ruskin and by such university students as William Morris (see William Morris Gallery, page 124) and Edward Burne-Jones. In *Reminiscences of Oxford* Reverend W. Tuckwell described the building of the museum:

> The lovely museum rose before us like an exhalation; its every detail, down to panels and footboards, gas-burners and door-handles, an object lesson in art, stamped with Woodward picturesque inventiveness and refinement. Not before had ironwork been so plastically trained as by Skidmore in the chestnut boughs and foliage which sustained the transparent roof; the shafts of the interior arcades representing in their sequence the succession of British rocks . . .

Well, that should be enough to make you want to visit! Indeed, hours and hours can be spent studying the exhibits – zoology, entomology, geology and mineralogy – or simply soaking up the atmosphere. Everything from the spectacularly huge skeleton of an African elephant to the intricate patterns of a live beehive can be found in this undeniably dramatic setting.

SPECIAL!
Look out for the 'Red Lady' – she's highly controversial. Fact or fiction, her story is certainly interesting; you'll find her at the foot of the south-west staircase.

Open: Monday to Saturday, 1200–1700.
Admission fee: no
Gifts: on sale
Toilets

PITT RIVERS MUSEUM
South Parks Road, Oxford, Oxfordshire.
Tel: Oxford 270927

An extraordinary museum packed with extraordinary things; Pitt Rivers brims over with objects which are guaranteed to fascinate and even frighten. Masks, musical instruments and objects for magical rituals, jewellery, weapons, artefacts and even a huge totem pole. As a museum devoted to ethnology the Pitt Rivers is outstanding – you're sure to want to visit again and again. Every display case and every corner reveals some unusual item – a collection of lace bobbins, a set of peasant chairs from Norway which have children's milk teeth set into them, a Maori feather box . . . making it a definite 'must' among museums.

SPECIAL!
There's a display case labelled 'Treatment of Dead Enemies: Head Hunters'. In it you can see tattooed skulls, shrivelled scalps and shrunken heads.

Open: Monday to Saturday, 1400–1600.
Admission fee: no
Disabled access: by prior arrangement
Gifts: on sale
Toilets

THE SHUTTLEWORTH COLLECTION
Old Warden Aerodrome, Biggleswade, Bedfordshire.
Tel: Biggleswade 288

The setting is beautiful – right in the heart of the Bedfordshire countryside – and the collection is unique. The thirty historic aeroplanes of the Shuttleworth Collection, spanning the progress of aviation from the 1909 Blériot to the 1941 Spitfire, are all airworthy, and that's quite an achievement. To prove their flying ability the planes are put through their paces at special flying display days during the summer season (telephone for details). It's on these flying days that the grass aerodrome really comes to life – the enthusiasm of the spectators is so catching, you can't help but share the excitement. However, if you want to get a close look at the collection, it's best to choose a quieter time. There's a wonderfully hushed atmosphere as you wander around the planes, including the First World War fighters and de Havilland sporting stars, and enjoy the range of memorabilia – it's just like taking a step back in time. There's also a garage full of motor vehicles dating from 1898 and the Panhard Levassor, all in working order and motored out on occasions. Whether you're a real enthusiast or just want a good day out, the Shuttleworth Collection is well worth a visit.

SPECIAL!
It takes time and skill to keep the planes and vehicles in tiptop condition, and you can see the restorers at work in Hangar No. 1. They're experts and will be happy to answer your questions about restoration and repair.

Open: daily (except for Christmas week), 1030–1730 (1630 November to March). Last admission, one hour before closing.

Admission fee: yes
Disabled access: good
Café
Picnic facilities
Gift shop
Toilets

THE TOWER OF ST MICHAEL AT THE NORTH GATE

Cornmarket, Oxford, Oxfordshire. Tel: Oxford 240940

Definitely one for the fit! Up steps, steps and more steps, it's a long climb to the top of St Michael's Tower, a beautiful old tower which, pre-dating the *Domesday Book* (1086), is Oxford's oldest building. Once on the roof you'll be rewarded with splendid views over the city and out to the countryside beyond. You should be able to spot Keble College, John Radcliffe Hospital, Sheldonian Theatre, Bodleian Library, Christchurch Cathedral, Tom Tower, Carfax Tower, Boars Hill, Nuffield College, Cumnor Hill and St Mary Magdalen College. The climb is exhausting, but on the way up you can stop to admire the bells. The church has a peal of six; the largest weighs over half a ton and was cast in the Woodstock Foundry in 1668. However, the bells no longer ring a full circle because of possible damage by vibration to the tower. You can also take a breather about halfway up where the old church clock mechanism sits on a platform – for a small charge you can activate its chimes. You'll have gathered by now that St Michael's is worth visiting as much for its historical interest and bird's-eye view as for its collection, but do take a look at the museum. Minute, exquisite and devoted mainly to priceless church silver and ancient church accounts dating back to 1404, the museum is, after all, the reason for your visit!

SPECIAL!
On show is the moneybox which prisoners in the
Bocardo hung on a cord outside the prison in the hope
of getting a coin or two from passers-by.

Open: Monday to Saturday, 1000 (1100 during the
winter)–1700; Sunday, 1400–1600 (closed during
services).
Admission fee: yes
Café: Wednesday and Saturday only
Picnic facilities
Gifts: on sale
Toilets

THE VERULAMIUM MUSEUM
St Michael's Street, St Albans, Hertfordshire.
Tel: St Albans 54659

St Albans was once the third largest 'municipium' or
city in Roman Britain. It was known as Verulamium
and was situated on the banks of the river Ver on the
outskirts of present-day St Albans. You can discover
more about the Roman city in the Verulamium
Museum, which has a wide range of finds from local
excavations including fine mosaics, pottery, painted
plaster and details from everyday life, such as a jet
counter, a shale pin, tacks and studs. Interpretive displays are well presented and informative; perhaps particularly useful is the large model of the Roman city
showing how it may have looked in the third century
A.D. Starting from the museum you can make a tour of
the site of Verulamium taking in the theatre (fee to
enter), basilica, hypocaust, 'London' Gate, city wall and
bastion.

SPECIAL!
All too easy to miss, in a small display case beside the entrance door, is a beautiful bronze statue of Venus.

Open: April to November, Monday to Saturday, 1000–1730; Sunday, 1400–1730. December to March, Monday to Saturday, 1000–1600; Sunday, 1400–1600.
Admission fee: yes
Disabled access: good
Picnic facilities
Gifts: on sale
Toilets

16

WALES

BEAUMARIS GAOL
Steeple Lane, Beaumaris, Isle of Anglesey, Gwynedd.

Spooky and spine-chilling, dark and dismal – you won't forget a visit to this Victorian gaol. As you walk around the building with its punishment cells, workrooms and exercise yards, you have to keep reminding yourself that this is no film set – these miserable conditions were a grim reality for prisoners in the nineteenth century. Particularly haunting is the condemned man's cell and the last walk to the gibbet, but every part has a strange fascination all its own – the laundry, with washing on the line, where women prisoners did the washing; the kitchen, showing the different (and most unappetizing) foods given to each class of prisoner; and the examples of typical cells, including the drunk's cell, complete with everything but the mice and rats! Displays show the punishments thought to fit the crime and there's also an exhibition of documents on prison life at the time. Ask at the desk for details of the Law and Order Trail through the town. (Nearby is the Museum of

Childhood, page 265.)

SPECIAL!
The gruesome treadmill, which worked the gaol's
water-pump, is the only one in Britain still in position.
The prisoners used to tread the mill, six working, six
resting at intervals of ten to fifteen minutes, for six
hours a day.

Open: May to September, daily, 1100–1800.
Admission fee: yes
Disabled access: limited
Café: nearby
Gifts: on sale

BIG PIT MINING MUSEUM
Blaenavon (off A465), Blaenavon, Gwent.
Tel: Blaenavon 790311

Get yourself kitted out with a safety helmet, cap lamp,
belt and battery and let an ex-miner take you on a
thrilling ride down the 300-foot-deep shaft to the pit
bottom. The tour above and below ground lasts around
an hour, but you'll wish it was longer! Big Pit was
closed as a working pit in February 1980 after a hundred
years of coal production and what makes it so special
for the visitor is that you're shown around by the
miners who actually worked here. They're so full of
entertaining tales and stories, you get a really good idea
of exactly what the conditions were like. But the
museum is much more than just a trip underground;
you can also see what went on above the surface – with
workshops, stables, haulage engines, a winding engine,
forge and miner's cottage, and don't forget the pithead
baths where the miners could wash off the dirt of the

day. An exhibition of photographs and artefacts describes the past of the pit and daily life in a mining community. You'll want to see everything, so leave yourself a whole day free to explore the Big Pit – you'll need it. And remember, it's a real mine, not a reconstruction, so do wear warm and sensible clothing.

SPECIAL!
You'll ride down to the underground workings in a pit cage – a relatively civilized way of travelling when you look at photographs from the past. How would you fancy clinging on to a chain!

Open: March to November, daily, 1000–1700 (last tour, 1530).
Admission fee: yes
Disabled access: limited (give advance notice of visit)
Café: in the workers' old cafeteria
Picnic facilities
Gifts: on sale
Toilets

MUSEUM OF CHILDHOOD
1 Castle Street, Beaumaris, Isle of Anglesey, Gwynedd.
Tel: Beaumaris 810448

This museum, standing in the shadow of the thirteenth-century castle, is a real Aladdin's Cave of children's playthings over the past 150 years. The nine rooms and corridors are overflowing with around 1400 exhibits – some unique, many rare but all full of that magical charm of childhood. The rooms are divided into different themes: Room 1 has a collection of music boxes, magic lanterns and other audio and visual items, several of which are played hourly; Room 3 is full of trains, cars, toy figures and clockwork toys; while Room 6 is home for an amazing cross-section of dolls and educational toys and games. Other rooms contain displays of money boxes, pottery, glass, paintings, furniture, samplers, rocking-horses, early cycles and even 1930s arcade machines from Brighton pier. There really is something here for everyone – but you'll probably need two visits to take it all in. Nearby is a museum on a quite different theme but well worth visiting, Beaumaris Gaol (page 263).

SPECIAL!
Watch the pennies drop: the museum has one of the country's largest collections of money boxes, both mechanical and still banks. Some are quite ingenious!

Open: Monday to Saturday, 1000–1730; Sunday, 1100–1700.
Admission fee: yes
Disabled access: limited
Café: nearby
Picnic facilities
Gift shop
Toilets: nearby

FFESTINIOG RAILWAY MUSEUM
Harbour Station, Porthmadog, Gwynedd.
Tel: Porthmadog 2384

There's no better place for a railway museum than at a railway station – and that's exactly where you'll find the Ffestiniog Railway Museum. Visitors usually come here for a ride (admission fee) on the famous Ffestiniog Narrow Gauge Railway, now restored to its past steaming glory, rather than to look at the museum, but the exhibits are well worth a trip in their own right. Housed in the former goods shed, the museum illustrates the proud history of the railway from its opening in 1836 as a link between the quarries and the port, through its pioneering days as the world's first passenger-carrying narrow-gauge line, its eventual decline and finally the restoration by dedicated volunteers. You'll find photographs, models and mementoes – and to bring the whole thing to life, there are the trains steaming in and out of the station. (Nearby is the Gwynedd Maritime Museum, page 271.)

SPECIAL!
The line used working horses until 1863. Displays show how it operated.

Open: daily, 0900–1700.
Admission fee: no
Disabled access: good
Café
Picnic facilities: on the harbour
Gifts: on sale
Toilets

THE GEOLOGICAL MUSEUM OF NORTH WALES
North Wales Visitor Centre, Bwlchgwyn (off A525), Wrexham, Clwyd. Tel: Wrexham 757573

Before you go inside, take a look at the Rock Garden by the side of the museum buildings. It's full of rock types – metamorphic, sedimentary and igneous – gathered from all parts of North Wales, and acts as a good starting point for a visit to this museum devoted to geology. Displays indoors include 'A Walk Through Time', a time tunnel showing the evolution of North

267

Wales over 600 million years; 'Industrial Geology' with exhibits on industries such as coalmining, cement-making, quarrying; and the always popular dinosaurs and fossils. The museum obviously has a particular appeal for geologists, but with sparkling gems, enormous geological specimens and imaginative showcases, it helps explain a complicated subject in a lively way – geology is more than just a load of old rocks!

SPECIAL!
The Mineral Exchange Exhibition is fascinating. Here you'll find minerals, many extremely rare, from various countries which have taken part in an exchange scheme masterminded by the museum.

Open: Monday to Friday, 1000–1600. May to September, also Saturday and Sunday, 1100–1630 (other times by appointment).
Admission fee: yes
Disabled access: limited
Café: opposite
Picnic facilities: with lovely views
Gifts: on sale
Toilets

LLOYD GEORGE MEMORIAL MUSEUM
Criccieth (on A497), Gwynedd. Tel: Criccieth 2654

'As a man of action, resource and creative energy, he stood, when at his zenith, without a rival' – that was Winston Churchill's tribute to David Lloyd George (1863–1945), the 'Great Commoner' and 'Founder of the Welfare State'. This small museum in his boyhood village is a tribute to Lloyd George, his many political campaigns, reforms and achievements. Displays highlight the progress of his career and exhibits include Deeds of Freedom, caskets, photographs, a family tree, documents and cartoons depicting the major events of his life. Just a short walk away is a memorial on the banks of the Dwyfor which marks the spot where the great statesman was buried in March 1945.

SPECIAL!
Richard Lloyd, whom young David knew as 'Uncle Lloyd', had a great influence on his nephew. There's a portrait of this distinguished-looking Nonconformist pastor who helped foster Lloyd George's passionate concern for social justice.

Open: Easter to end September, Monday to Friday, 1000–1700 (also July and August, Saturday and Sunday, 1400–1600).
Admission fee: yes
Disabled access: good
Café: nearby
Picnic facilities
Gifts: on sale
Toilets: nearby

THE GRANGE CAVERN MILITARY MUSEUM
Holywell (off A55), Clywd. Tel: Holywell 713455

If this museum wasn't so well signposted you'd probably miss it – Grange Cavern, a former limestone quarry set 60–100 feet below the surface, provides perfect camouflage, and has been used as such in recent years. Indeed, 11,000 tons of bombs were stored here during the Second World War, including the Barnes Wallis bouncing bombs. It's no longer used either for quarrying limestone or as a bomb store, but the floodlit cavern is now a unique and atmospheric home for an enormous display of military vehicles and exhibits. There are over seventy vehicles here, both wheeled and tracked – all well labelled so you can picture their past lives – but pride of place goes to the Long Range Desert Group Chevrolet vehicle, the only known one of its kind to survive the Second World War. Left exactly in the condition it was found in the deserts of Egypt, its remarkable story is told by an audio-visual show. There's also a reconstruction of an Anderson air-raid shelter and a chillingly authentic replica of a battle trench from the First World War complete with the sound of bombs blasting in the background. The Inner Museum has exhibits including maps, models, uniforms, mortars, grenades and shells dating back to the eighteenth century.

SPECIAL!
Forget the military exhibits for a few minutes and concentrate on the geology within the cavern – you'll find many fine examples of seashells and fossils.

Open: May to September, daily, 0900–1800. October to April, daily, 1000–1700. February to March, weekends, 1000–1700 (last ticket, one hour before closing).
Admission fee: yes
Disabled access: good
Café: in the NAAFI
Picnic facilities
Gifts: on sale
Toilets

GWYNEDD MARITIME MUSEUM
The Harbour, Porthmadog, Gwynedd.

The main exhibit and highlight is the *Garlandstone*, a 120-ton sailing ketch built in 1909, which has a long and eventful history. She's moored outside and you're welcome to climb on board and look around. Try to imagine her days as a coastal trader with cargoes including coal from the Forest of Dean, corn and flour from Ireland and granite from Pembrokeshire. The museum itself is situated on one of the old wharves of the harbour, the exhibits housed within the last remaining slate house. There are models, photographs and prints, a collection of shipwright's tools and tremendous tales of record-breaking sea passages, all illustrating the maritime history of Porthmadog, once an important slate exporting centre. Although the emphasis is on the harbour life of the town, there are displays showing the maritime past of the whole of Great Britain, making for an entertaining and informative visit. A few minutes' walk away is the Ffestiniog Railway Museum (page 266).

SPECIAL!
What's an old piece of wood doing in pride of position? Read the story attached – apparently it's from the wreck of a locally-made ship found in the Falklands.

Open: April to September, daily, 1000–1800.
Admission fee: yes
Disabled access: good
Picnic facilities: on the harbour
Gifts: on sale

TOM NORTON'S COLLECTION OF OLD CYCLES AND TRICYCLES

Automobile Palace, Temple Street, Llandrindod Wells, Powys. Tel: Llandrindod Wells 2214

Don't expect a conventional museum building – this unusual collection of historic cycles is housed in the sales area of a working garage. And as space is at a premium they're mostly attached to the ceiling, so make sure your neck muscles are well primed before your visit! The cycles and tricycles – many rare and valuable – date from 1869 to 1938 and are all extremely well documented with fascinating stories and details in the illustrated catalogue. Ignore the comings and goings in the garage and concentrate on the exhibits – you'll gain a new insight into the history of cycling and even pick up a few tips on riding a boneshaker!

SPECIAL!
Any volunteers? The owner of the collection is looking for a willing lady to take the 'Quadrant' Tandem Tricycle (*c.* 1879) out on the road. One look at this ingenious machine is enough to put you off!

Open: Monday to Saturday, 0800–1700.
Admission fee: no
Disabled access: good
Café: nearby
Picnic facilities: nearby
Toilets

ROBERT OWEN MEMORIAL MUSEUM
Broad Street, Newtown, Powys. Tel: Newtown 26345

Robert Owen, inspirer of the Co-operative movement and pioneer of modern British socialism, was born in Newtown in 1771. He left the town at the age of ten but it had always been his wish that 'I will lay my bones whence I derived them' and in 1858 he returned to his birthplace to die. Owen is buried in St Mary's Churchyard and this museum acts as the town's memorial to him. With an introductory audio-visual display, manuscripts, books, photographic displays and many personal artefacts, it takes you through his life from his childhood days (he was an exceptional boy who read *Pilgrim's Progress* at ten years old) through his years as a model employer, his achievements in New Lanark, his energetic campaigns for social and factory reforms, and finally his last years. It's the story of a remarkable man with a strong social conscience.

SPECIAL!
The Robert Owen obelisk stands as a memorial in Kensal Green Cemetery, London. There's a large photograph of it in the museum. The epitaph is worth reading.

Open: Monday to Friday, 0945–1145 and 1400–1530; Saturday, 1000–1130 (telephone to check as times vary).
Admission fee: no
Café: nearby
Gifts: on sale

PORTMEIRION
Penrhyndeudraeth (off A487), Gwynedd.
Tel: Porthmadog 770228

You're about to enter a completely different world – an Italianate-style village, the dreamchild of architect Sir Clough Williams-Ellis, built between 1926 and 1978. This unique open-air museum on the shores of Traeth Bach is, in Sir Clough's own words, a 'home for fallen buildings' and among the many brought here to rest are a Bath house colonnade, a Romanesque baroque bell tower and a town hall. As you walk around, remember that this is what the creator believed to be the ideal village in the ideal setting. Ask yourself whether he achieved his aim of providing proof that given enough loving care a beautiful site could be developed without spoiling it. Whether you like it or loathe it, there's no denying that Portmeirion is a talking point – you'll be discussing it for hours afterwards! And if you're really interested, you can stay here for more than a day – within the village, there's a luxury residential hotel and several holiday cottages as well as restaurants and specialist shops.

SPECIAL!
With the mountains of Snowdonia in the background, the village made a dramatic setting for the television series 'The Prisoner', and a special information centre describes the filming and various locations used.

Open: April to end October, daily, 0930–1730.
Admission fee: yes
Disabled access: limited
Café
Picnic facilities: the village marks the entry to a wild

garden with 20 miles of paths through woodlands bordered by sandy beaches
Gifts: on sale
Toilets

ROCK PARK SPA
Llandrindod Wells, Powys. Tel: Llandrindod Wells 4307

In its fashionable heyday visitors would flock to Rock Park Spa to take the waters and hopefully cure themselves of all manner of ailments. The 18-acre woodland park is now beautifully landscaped and both the Pump Room and Bath House have been reopened. The Bath House contains exhibits and illustrations describing the history and growth of this and other Welsh spas. Some of the contraptions used on the patients seem more like torture than treatment although the reports of the results are quite amazing. It's largely pictorial but exhibits include an old bath chair and bath, curious-looking bottles, strange recipes and a painful-looking needle-spray shower, prescribed as a general tonic. The adjoining Pump Room is decorated and furnished in Edwardian style and for the strong-willed there are pumps serving three different natural mineral waters.

SPECIAL!
The visitors' book from the Lake Hotel shows two important guests to the spa in 1912: the Prince and Princess of Munster, Germany, reputed to be the Kaiser and his family.

Open: May to September, daily, 1000–1800 (telephone to check winter opening).
Admission fee: no
Disabled access: good

Café: in Pump Room, serving traditional Welsh teas
Picnic facilities
Toilets

W.H. SMITH MUSEUM
High Street, Newton, Powys. Tel: Newton 26280

This is a W.H. Smith shop and museum rolled into one
– and both are equally charming. The shop, which is
open for business as usual, has been perfectly restored
to its original state when it first opened in 1927,
complete with beautiful oak fittings, the former Ladies'
Bookstall, and two hand-painted lanterns hanging outside. On the first floor is the museum which traces the
history of W.H. Smith, Newsagents and Booksellers,
from its beginnings in 1792 when Henry Walton Smith
opened a tiny newsvendor's shop in Little Grosvenor
Street, London. The old photographs are fascinating –
so too are many other exhibits including a replica of a
horse-pulled delivery cart; a remarkable scale model of
a 1920s shop; hanging signs; handbooks for salesmen;
pieces of furniture, including the all-important umbrella
stand; and a display showing the daily round of a
newsboy in 1930. It's unique, don't miss it!

SPECIAL!
The rooms where the museum is now were once the
shop's circulating-library department. Photographs
show the rise and fall of the W.H. Smith library scheme.

Open: Monday to Saturday, 0930–1730 (early closing
Thursday).
Admission fee: no
Disabled access: limited
Café: nearby
Gifts: on sale
Toilets: nearby

SYGUN COPPER MINE
Beddgelert (on A4898), Caernarfon, Gwynedd.
Tel: Beddgelert 595

Mining for copper at Mynydd Sygun stopped in 1903. The mine was left untouched until 1983 when it was rediscovered – a perfectly preserved monument to the skill of local miners. It was restored and opened in 1986 as a living museum. Visits to the mine are by guided tour, thirty to forty breathtaking minutes of real fascination as you're taken underground to see first-hand the working conditions of the miners, hear a commentary about mining techniques and stop to admire the magnificent stalactite and stalagmite formations glistening in the torchlight. Then as you emerge from the deep, dark tunnel you'll be rewarded with splendid views of the Gwynant valley deep in the heart of Snowdonia, an absolute must for every photographer. It's cold (around 9°C all year) down the mine and wet underfoot, so come prepared – but don't worry about a hat, you'll be provided with a miner's helmet! Guided tours leave from the Visitor Centre at regular intervals and it's worth having a good look around the photographs, working models, artefacts and audio-visual presentation in the centre before going underground.

SPECIAL!
Copper was the first metal used by man because it could be so easily crafted into armaments and utensils. Exhibits in the Visitor Centre show some early weapons made with copper.

Open: Easter to end October, daily, 1000–1800 (last tour, 1715).
Admission fee: yes
Disabled access: Visitor Centre only

Picnic facilities: with superb views
Gifts: on sale
Toilets

WELSH FOLK MUSEUM
St Fagans, Cardiff, South Glamorgan. Tel: Cardiff 569441

Where do you begin to start explaining this amazing museum? Even the staunchest of museum sceptics couldn't fail to enjoy the Welsh Folk Museum, around a hundred acres of beautiful parkland with centuries-old buildings reconstructed stone by stone from every corner of Wales, plus exhibitions and craft workshops all devoted to telling the story of the wealth of Welsh culture and tradition through the ages. There are even flocks of sheep and Welsh black cattle in the background! It can be rather difficult to find your way around the site, so to make the most of it, buy a map from the bookshop and plan your route first. A central feature, and one not to be missed, is St Fagans Castle, an Elizabethan Manor House built within the curtain wall of a medieval castle and surrounded by eight acres of formal gardens, terraces and fish ponds. It has been restored and refurbished in seventeenth-century style and stands in grand and formal contrast to the farmhouses, cottages and working buildings dotted around. Look out for Penrhiw Chapel, which still seems to reverberate with hymns and preaching; the farmhouse complete with a butter churn and butter-working table in the kitchen; the circular pigsty; old cockpit; toll house; Victorian school; and the woollen mill where you can see fleece being transformed into flannel. All the buildings are furnished with traditional furniture, and imaginative touches really bring them to life – there's Tricer bread on the table in the quarry house, for example, and old lesson books in the school. An attendant is on duty in each building to answer any questions. The exhibition galleries are laid out in a lively way and complement the open-air section of the museum perfectly. Special events and demonstrations are held throughout the year; ask for details.

SPECIAL!
Music is very much a part of Welsh culture, so naturally there's an impressive display of musical instruments including the medieval Welsh 'crwth' and 'pibgorn'.

Open: Monday to Saturday, 1000–1700; Sunday, 1430–1700.
Admission fee: yes
Disabled access: good
Café
Picnic facilities
Gift shop: crafts made by museum craftspeople are on sale
Toilets

WELSH MINERS MUSEUM
Afan Argoed Country Park (on A4107), Cynonville, Port Talbot, West Glamorgan. Tel: Cymmer 850564

This is the story of the history of mining told by the men who worked underground and their families – a chance to look at the working and living conditions through the eyes of the miners themselves. As you enter, you're shown inside a typical miner's cottage of the 1920s. Press the button for background music (miners' ballads, of course!). Other displays include early mining equipment set in realistic scenes, vivid photographs, and descriptions of the terrible disasters and dangers. A special section highlights the tragedy of children working the mines. And to provide you with a personal explanation, the voice of a miner describes the hardship and struggle of the daily, dirty grind and gives you an introduction to the various mining techniques. It's a real revelation, a no-nonsense insight into the world of the valley communities, and a museum with such an impact you feel almost moved to tears.

SPECIAL!
The scene from a miner's kitchen is beautifully detailed – look at the broth simmering in the iron saucepan and the wooden bathtub by the fire.

Open: April to October, daily, 1030–1800. November to March, Saturday and Sunday only, 1030–1700.
Admission fee: yes
Café
Picnic facilities: in Afan Argoed Country Park
Gifts: on sale
Toilets

WELSH SLATE MUSEUM
Padarn Country Park (on A4086), Llanberis, Gwynedd.
Tel: Llanberis 870630

It's almost as though time has stood still since everyone downed tools when the Dinorwig slate quarry closed in 1969. Even the canteen, 'Y Caban', looks as if the workmen have left in a hurry – mugs and playing cards are scattered across the tables. There's a strange, deserted atmosphere, a feeling that somehow you shouldn't be there. But don't worry, you're not trespassing – the workshops, machinery and plant of the Dinorwig quarry, one of the two largest in Wales, have been preserved as a museum to show life and labour in the quarrying communities. You can see most of the original machinery, including machines for sawing, splitting and trimming slate; the foundry with its tall furnace and pattern-makers' loft; a collection of quarry rolling stock including the working steam locomotive 'Una'; and the huge water wheel which used to drive the workshops' machines. A blacksmith is often at work in the smithy and there are regular displays of the quarryman's craft. There's little explanation – display boards would spoil the atmosphere – but to help you find your way around the site and understand more about the daily work at the quarry, there's a film and interpretive gallery. You can also join a guided tour through the Dinorwig quarry (admission fee); ask at the desk for details.

SPECIAL!
The giant water wheel, built in 1870 and measuring 50 feet 5 inches in diameter, is a remarkably impressive sight. Follow its workings to see the extent of the machinery it powered.

Open: Easter to end April, daily, 0930–1730. May to September, daily, 0930–1830 (last ticket, 1800).
Admission fee: yes
Disabled access: good
Café: in nearby Railway Lake Terminus
Picnic facilities: around the Padarn Country Park
Gifts: on sale
Toilets: nearby

WOLVESNEWTON FOLK MUSEUM
Wolvesnewton, near Llangwm (off B4235), Gwent.
Tel: Wolvesnewton 231

First, a little about the museum buildings, which are made from stone quarried from the hill they're standing on. They were designed in the late eighteenth century as a Model Farm; the highly practical crucible layout is quite ingenious, a unique example of agricultural architecture. Inside, the folk collections are just as unusual. Exhibits include old agricultural machinery, horse-drawn vehicles, toys, wartime souvenirs and Doulton pottery – all in varying states of repair. There are also craft workshops and craft displays, but the real appeal of the museum is the Victoriana housed in the pig room! By the time you've had a giggle at the naughty postcards, marvelled at the medicinal treatments of the day and questioned the mechanics of such complicated contraptions as the knife-grinding machine, one thing's for sure, you'll enjoy a slice of Victorian apple-cake served in the café! Most of the museum is under cover, so don't be put off by the weather.

SPECIAL!
You could spend hours looking at the tiny details in the Victorian bedroom – the wash-stand, rag rugs, patchwork quilt and, of course, the portrait of Queen Victoria hanging on the wall.

Open: April to end September, daily, 1100–1800. October and November, Saturday and Sunday, 1100–1800.
Admission fee: yes
Disabled access: good
Café: serving home-baked food
Gifts: on sale (extensive range)
Toilets

17

THE WEST COUNTRY
(Avon, Devon, Somerset)

AMERICAN MUSEUM
Claverton Manor (near Bath University), Bath, Avon.
Tel: Bath 60503

The strenuous organization which lies behind this, the
first American museum outside the United States, is
immediately obvious and it's impressive. Two hundred
years of American history is told through a series of
furnished rooms. In each room a knowledgeable attendant waits to tell you all she knows – ask a question and
watch her face light up as she launches into her favourite
topic (the attendants are genuinely interested in 'their'
rooms and spend the winter months genning up). The
quality of the exhibits is excellent and the contrasts and
contradictions of early American life well illustrated.
You can see the life of colonial New England during
the 1680s, a 1770s cosy kitchen tavern (where you may
be lucky enough to be offered some home baking), an
early-nineteenth-century country-style bedroom and an
elegant Greek Revival dining-room which is typical of
New York at the time of the Civil War. There are also

galleries devoted to the religious community of Shakers, the American Indian and the Spanish colonists of New Mexico. Worth particular study is the textile room with its large collection of quilts and coverlets. Materials were scarce and women made use of every scrap to produce these colourful patterned coverings. Their efforts gave rise to a certain type of social gathering known as a 'quilting bee': friends would gather around a frame and work together, perhaps on a cover for a bride-to-be, then, work over, they'd have supper and finally round off the evening with a dance.

SPECIAL!
In the beautiful gardens of Claverton Manor seek out the Fairfax memorial: the final act in a romantic drama, the story of George Washington and Sally Fairfax. When Washington was seventeen he fell in love with his neighbour's new nineteen-year-old bride. Correspondence between them continued throughout their lives. Sally sent Washington flowers and shrubs for his garden in America and when Mount Vernon Garden was being planted at Claverton cuttings from those very plants were sent back to England. The ivy was planted beneath the memorial to Sally Fairfax reuniting them 'by this stone and these flowers'. Or as George Washington said, 'In silence . . . joy'.

Open: Thursday to Sunday, 1400–1700; Monday, 1100–1700.
Admission fee: yes
Disabled access: limited (approx. a third of the rooms only but no admission fee)
Café
Gift shop
Toilets

BATH INDUSTRIAL HERITAGE CENTRE

Camden Works Museum, Julian Road, Bath, Avon.
Tel: Bath 318348

Hidden behind Bath's fashionable Georgian terraces, there's another much less well known lifestyle to be discovered. Bath Industrial Heritage Centre provides some fascinating answers to the question: how did ordinary people in Bath live and work during the Victorian and Georgian ages? The building itself is interesting; built in 1777 as a real tennis court (you can still see some court markings), it was later used as a malt house, charity school, pin factory and engineering works. The museum is, however, an authentic reconstruction of the entire works of J.B. Bowler – Victorian brass founder, general engineer and manufacturer of aerated water! His firm was in business for some ninety-seven years and during that time it seems virtually nothing was thrown away – the Bowlers were true collectors! Hand-tools, working gas-lamps, bottles, letters, large pieces of machinery (ask to see them in operation) and tiny details from everyday life – they're all here, evocatively recording what Bath was like for a small provincial family business in Victorian times.

SPECIAL!
Take a good look at 'Davis and Son'. It's an early form of illuminated shop sign made from iron tubing with holes through which gas was fed. It was then a case of striking a match and standing well back!

Open: March to November, daily, 1400–1700. December to February, Saturday and Sunday, 1400–1700.
Admission fee: yes
Disabled access: limited (telephone in advance)

Gift shop
Toilets

BATH POSTAL MUSEUM
8 Broad Street, Bath, Avon. Tel: Bath 60333

From comic songs to clay tablets and from pigeons to postmen – the story of the post certainly spans a huge period of time. In fact, there's been some form of postal system for over 4000 years and at the Bath Postal Museum you can discover some of the innovations which have made letters part of our everyday life. You can even try your hand at some postal service use the Victorian franking-machine or have a go at making the perforations between stamps. In the mid-nineteenth century each postage stamp was cut from a sheet with scissors! But in 1854 the first machines which could punch lines of perforations appeared and the post service hasn't looked back since!

SPECIAL!
Assyrian clay tablets are the earliest form of letter. You can see one still in its original clay casing. It dates from 2000 B.C.

Open: Monday to Saturday, 1100–1700; Sunday, 1400–1700.
Admission fee: yes
Café
Gift shop
Toilets

COBBATON COMBAT VEHICLES MUSEUM

Cobbaton, Chittlehampton, Umberleigh, near Barnstaple, Devon. Tel: Chittleham 414

The owner of Cobbaton Combat Vehicles Museum regards the items in his collection as mobile war memorials; rather than glorifying war they mark its horror, reality, hardships, comradeship and achievement. It's a museum which undoubtedly means different things to different people; for veterans, the old fighting machines bring back vivid and often sad memories; for youngsters they're cumbersome objects to be stared at with awe. The collection recalls the years 1939–45 with vehicles and equipment of the Allied forces, particularly Canadian (the Canadians lost more young men per head of population than any other of the Allies). It also shows something of life in wartime Britain with Home Guard, ARP wardens, gas masks, ration books, an Anderson shelter and a realistically re-created bomb-damaged room. Appropriate music and news bulletins play from period wirelesses, setting an atmosphere far removed from the corrugated iron bunker in which the museum is housed. Providing a more up-to-date note, there's a small display of relics from the Falklands, including a piece of earth!

SPECIAL!
Two or even three hours can easily slip by at Cobbaton without you realizing it. However, one exhibit which never slips by is the Churchill MK VII. Named after Sir Winston Churchill, this heavily armoured infantry tank is a 44-ton monster.

Open: Easter to October, daily, 1000–1800.
Admission fee: yes

Disabled access: good
Gift shop
Toilets

COMBE MARTIN MOTORCYCLE COLLECTION

Cross Street, Combe Martin, Devon. Tel: Combe Martin 2346

Looking like someone's garage – a garage which most definitely belongs to a motorcycle enthusiast – this private collection is a 'must' for the motorbike addict and an interesting place to browse. Displayed against a background of old petrol pumps, signs, garage equipment, helmets and old boots, there are at any one time up to forty-five bikes on show. And there are always plenty of eager father-and-son duos giving them close attention! If you spot a 1928 Norton (model 18 500 cc), a very dirty, scruffy-looking item indeed, don't make any suggestions about cleaning it up a bit. In its early days the Norton was raced at Brooklands and has since passed through the years without ever being cleaned. Its present owner threatens to remove it from display if anyone attempts a clean-up – he wants it kept just the way it is: dust, grease, dirt and all!

SPECIAL!
George Bernard Shaw gave Lawrence of Arabia a motorbike as a gift – a Brough Superior (1929). You can identify it easily by the Arab-costumed model standing next to it!

Open: end May to mid-September, daily, 1000–1800.
Admission fee: yes
Disabled access: good
Gift shop

MUSEUM OF COSTUME

Assembly Rooms, Bennett Street, Bath, Avon.
Tel: Bath 61111

Styles have changed over the centuries and, judging from some of the costumes on display, so has the human shape! Fashionable dress for men, women and children, from as early as the sixteenth century, is well presented in this captivating museum. In the Panorama Room, period scenes provide evocative settings for costumes from 1820 to 1960, while other displays show royal and ceremonial clothes, babies' clothes and underwear. There's more to costume than just clothes, but if you're not convinced of this, take a look at the case of accessories: it's full of shawls, shoes and scarves, brooches and belts, fans and feathers, jewellery, bags, bracelets, buttons and buckles, parasols and powder puffs.

SPECIAL!
Modern fashion hasn't been forgotten. It's represented by the work of leading twentieth-century British and European designers and is augmented by an annual selection of the 'Dress of the Year'.

Open: March to October, Monday to Saturday, 0930–1800; Sunday, 1000–1800. November to February, Monday to Saturday, 1000–1700; Sunday, 1100–1700.
Admission fee: yes
Disabled access: good
Gifts: on sale
Toilets

EXETER MARITIME MUSEUM
The Quay, Exeter, Devon. Tel: Exeter 58075

The setting for a museum containing some 100 to 150 boats couldn't be better – the quay of the river Exe. Its warehouses, cellars and canal basin provide a wonderfully atmospheric environment for these large and very beautiful exhibits. The museum is situated on both banks of the Exe and the picturesque hand-pulled ferry which links the two sites adds to the excitement of a visit. There's lots to see and to feel – this is a 'please touch' museum! You are invited to push and pull, clamber and climb, and in general do all the things you will automatically want to do; like feeling the weight of Britain's most primitive craft, the curragh (still used in Ireland and Wales), or running your hand along the smooth joints of the sophisticated proa which is planked and sewn together (there's not a nail or screw in it!). Both light *and* smooth is the birchbark canoe built by the Algonquin Indians – its hull is made from a single piece of bark turned inside out. In contrast there's the enormously heavy Danish steam tug, *St Canute*, which still raises steam from time to time and which is always enormously popular with children. Many of the boats are regularly sailed, including the magnificent *Jolie Brise*, three times winner of the Fastnet race, and the elegant dhow from Bahrain. There are some extraordinary exhibits like the white swan boat, but there are no gimmicks. An excellent introduction to the boats on display and their use is the museum brochure written by David Goddard; but, best of all, board a few and enjoy yourself!

SPECIAL!
Most spectacular of all the crafts on display is perhaps the Hong Kong fishing junk *Keying II*. More than

simply a fishing boat, this is a floating home. As such it must keep out frequent torrential rain (making it a good bet for an outdoor exhibit in Britain!), provide shelter, be warm in winter and cool in summer. It must be stable to allow cooking and reasonably safe for children. The huge bulk of the junk will quickly appear to shrink when you imagine husband, wife, grandparents, children, grandchildren, aunts, uncles, dogs, cats, chickens and ducks all crammed in.

Open: daily, 1000–1700; July and August, 1000–1800.
Admission fee: yes
Disabled access: limited
Café
Picnic facilities: everywhere. You can even eat your sandwiches on board the junk if you want!
Gift shop
Toilets

FLEET AIR ARM MUSEUM

Royal Navy Air Station (off A303), Yeovilton, Somerset.
Tel: Ilchester 840565

You'll need an absolute minimum of two hours to visit this major international aviation museum. It's one of only two museums in the world devoted to naval aviation, so it provides an opportunity to see exhibits you won't see anywhere else. The museum both preserves naval aircraft and artefacts and tells the stories of individual aviators; the result is interesting and informative. You can, for example, see the first British-built Concorde in the supersonic exhibition, while the Falklands section contains four captured Argentine aircraft and a British Wasp helicopter.

291

SPECIAL!

The museum has taken some pains to show the important role women play in the Royal Navy. There's a special WRENS display showing their efforts during the Second World War. A dispatch rider makes her way through the rubble of bombed Britain while other WRENS test the radio and engine of an aircraft.

Open: March to October, daily, 1000–1730. November to February, daily, 1000–1630.
Admission fee: yes
Disabled access: good
Café
Picnic facilities
Gift shop
Toilets

HELE MILL

Hele Bay, Ilfracombe, Devon. Tel: Ilfracombe 63162

Restoration of this now fully working water-mill took five years and when you look at the before-and-after photographs on display you can see why. New millstones had to be made and machinery found and installed, as well as the straightforward restoration of the building. The mill's story is that of three millers, Bill Briggs, Luther Solway and a third whose name is never mentioned as it is said to upset his ghost! It's believed that one night the unfortunate miller, working late and alone, caught his coat in the moving cog mechanism and was slowly mangled to death. If you've never been to a working mill, this is a good one to visit as it's an informal place where you're free to browse at your own pace with plenty of labels to help you understand what's happening and what's on display.

SPECIAL!
In 1927 mechanization to some extent took over from water-power when a diesel engine was installed. It's capable of driving machinery far beyond the capabilities of the ancient water wheel.

Open: Easter to end October, Monday to Friday, 1000–1700; Sunday, 1400–1700.
Admission fee: yes
Gifts: on sale
Toilets

HERSCHEL HOUSE AND MUSEUM
19 New King Street, Bath, Avon. Tel: Bath 336 228

A Mecca for anyone interested in astronomy, this unimposing house in Georgian Bath is where William Herschel discovered the planet Uranus, thereby doubling the size of the known solar system. Exhibits include Herschel's family history, his telescopes, lenses, musical instruments, optical mirrors and even concert programmes. Perhaps more important, there are books, letters and documents relating to Herschel's discoveries in astronomy and thermology. You can stand in his workshop with its furnace and lathe, and imagine him casting spectacular metal mirrors.

SPECIAL!
Wander out into the garden; it was in this tiny space in March 1781 that Herschel set up his telescope and discovered Uranus.

Open: March to October, daily, 1400–1700. November to February, Sundays only, 1400–1700.
Admission fee: yes
Toilets

MORWELLHAM QUAY

Near Tavistock (off A390), Devon. Tel: Tavistock 832766

When someone dressed in the costume of the 1860s greets you, you know you've arrived at Morwellham. Period costume is just one of the many touches which help to bring the exhibits in this large open-air museum alive. There are quay workers, a smithy, servant girls, shop assistants and a host of other workers looking after the cottages, dockyard, shire horses, laboratory and hydroelectric power station. You can watch barrels being made in the cooper's shed and have your photograph taken wearing top hat and tails or bonnet and long skirt. The village of Morwellham was, just over a hundred years ago, perhaps the most important copper ore exporting centre in Europe. It's seen shipping come and go on the river Tamar for over seven hundred years. Today it thrives as a picturesque, nostalgic and informative place for the whole family to spend an enjoyable day out.

SPECIAL!
The trip into a real copper-mine is something you'll never forget. As the small train which trundles you underground comes to a halt, and the lights in the tunnel go out, you get an idea of working conditions in this once highly productive mine.

Open: daily, 1000–1800 (October to March, closes at dusk).

Admission fee: yes
Disabled access: very limited
Café: closed October to March
Picnic facilities
Gifts: on sale
Toilets

THE SHOE MUSEUM
High Street, Street, Somerset. Tel: Street 43131

Shoes and boots of all descriptions – pointed and rounded, tied with bows and fastened with buckles, made of canvas, leather, silk, wood and even grass – are all shown here in this small museum housed in the oldest part of the factory of shoe manufacturers C. and J. Clark. With exhibits dating back to Roman times, there are shoes that fitted famous feet, Georgian shoe buckles, fashion plates, photographs and documents plus hand-tools and shoe-making machinery – including the 'Knox' Chopper, 'Lockett' Crimper and 'Besto' Bottom Filler! It's all absolutely fascinating. It's worth noting that there are many shops in Street selling shoes at factory prices – a good way of rounding off your visit.

SPECIAL!
Too big for his boots? William Legge (*c.* 1870–1910), better known as Bill Cant (he was from Canterbury!), was 7 feet 4 inches high and weighed 32 stone. His boots, especially made for him by a village shoe-maker, are on display – they're size 19!

Open: Easter Monday to October, Monday to Saturday, 1000–1645 (winter months by appointment).
Admission fee: no
Café: nearby
Gifts: on sale

SPARKFORD MOTOR MUSEUM
Sparkford (off A359), near Yeovil, Somerset.
Tel: North Cadbury 40804

Every car in the museum not only gleams from bonnet to wheel trim, it also works. Almost every day a motor is started up and a vehicle taken for a spin locally because it's the museum's view that to preserve motoring heritage cars must be kept in full working order – what's more, it's great fun for the curator! This is an enthusiast's museum, so if you'd like to inspect something a little more closely – perhaps you'd like to peer into the engine of the powerful TVR Tuscan – just ask and all will be revealed. If you'd like to learn more, attend a lecture (telephone for details) which not only covers all the technical information you could ever wish to know, but will also fill you in on all sorts of snippets to do with motoring history, like Emily Pankhurst's demands for a lady's motorbike – you can see the uncomfortable result on display.

SPECIAL!
The world's first convertible car was a Daimler which quite clearly originated from a stage-coach design. One problem though – it took two and a half hours to convert!

Open: daily, 0930–1730.
Admission fee: yes
Disabled access: good
Picnic facilities
Gift shop
Toilets

18 YORKSHIRE AND HUMBERSIDE

(Humberside, North Yorkshire, South Yorkshire, West Yorkshire)

ABBEY HOUSE MUSEUM
Kirkstall Road, Leeds, West Yorkshire. Tel: Leeds 755821

Atmosphere just oozes from this twelfth-century building which was originally the Great Gatehouse of Kirkstall Abbey. Later the home of a family of Leeds ironmasters and today an attractive folk museum, Abbey House is a lovely place to visit. It has a fine collection of toys, dolls and costumes and some fascinating slot-machines which you can operate with old pennies.

SPECIAL!
The main attraction of the museum are undoubtedly the reconstructed full-size Victorian streets. These folds, courts, gates and yards contain shops, cottages and workshops most of which were once to be found in Leeds. They have been painstakingly rebuilt and their interiors carefully and accurately furnished. You can visit the grocer's and the tin-tack maker's, press your

297

nose to the pipe-maker's shop window and pay a call to the 'Hark to Rover Inn'!

Open: April to September, Tuesday to Saturday, 1000–1800; Sunday, 1400–1800. October to March, Tuesday to Saturday, 1000–1700; Sunday, 1400–1700.
Admission fee: yes
Disabled access: limited
Toilets

ABBEYDALE INDUSTRIAL HAMLET
Abbeydale Road South (on A621), Sheffield, South Yorkshire. Tel: Sheffield 367731

The Abbeydale Industrial Hamlet dates back to the eighteenth century when it was a thriving scytheworks. By the early 1900s the demand for scythes, sickles and reaping-hooks had declined and production stopped in 1933. However, much has now been restored and an Interpretation Centre in the former warehouse explains the works. Exhibits not to miss include the Tilt Forge of 1785 where scythe blades were forged under hammers powered by a huge water wheel, 18 feet in diameter; a grinding hull of 1817; the crucible steel furnace of the type developed by Huntsman in 1742 – the forerunner of the production of steel for which Sheffield is famous; and the hand-forges where crucibles were often made by foot! You can also see the Counting House and Manager's House furnished in period style and a workman's cottage of the 1840s. The best time to visit is when they're holding one of their special events (telephone for details) – the various workshops are a buzz of activity.

SPECIAL!
The enormous piece of machinery near the entrance is
the Jessop Tilt Hammers dating from the early nineteenth century – water-powered hammers used to forge
scythes.

Open: Monday to Saturday, 1000–1700; Sunday, 1100-
1700.
Admission fee: yes
Disabled access: limited
Café: in the original Counting House
Picnic facilities
Gifts: on sale
Toilets

ARMLEY MILLS

*Leeds Industrial Museum, Canal Road, Armley, Leeds,
West Yorkshire. Tel: Leeds 637861*

Armley Mills makes an impressive boast: it claims to
have once been the world's largest woollen mill. It
occupies a site in West Riding where the river Aire
makes a sweeping curve, creating a natural fall of water
which was successfully harnessed to provide power for
the mill. The museum's collection reflects the mill's
important manufacturing heritage from the nineteenth
century onwards together with other major industries
which flourished in the north of England during the last
century. Leeds, for instance, was a great leather-tanning
town, supplying leatherworks to the Midlands, Europe
and North America. The museum's collection of leather
equipment ranges from the drums and paddles used in
tanning to examples of the sewing-machines which
produced some 100,000 pairs of shoes and boots every
year. Then there was the printing industry – the earliest

presses on display include a cast-iron Columbian press with eagle and serpent decoration which was used by the printer of the local newspaper. In addition, you can see a good selection of water, steam and petrol engines, machine tools, cranes, locomotives and, of course, the spinning-mules which brought such wealth to the textile industry.

SPECIAL!
You may be surprised to find the Armley Palace Picture Hall (*c*. 1912) reconstructed in the museum. But this area has been associated with the cinema since as early as 1888 when Louis Le Prince first took moving pictures from Leeds bridge.

Open: April to September, Tuesday to Saturday, 1000–1800; Sunday, 1400–1800. October to March, Tuesday to Saturday, 1000–1700; Sunday, 1400–1700.
Admission fee: yes
Disabled access: limited
Toilets

MUSEUM OF ARMY TRANSPORT
Flemingate, Beverley, Humberside. Tel: Hull 860445

The subtitle of this museum is 'The Royal Corps of Transport Collection of Army Road, Rail, Sea and Air Transport', and its policy is to collect, restore and display artefacts used by the British Army for the conveyance of men, equipment and supplies. However, the museum is far from being a solemn place to visit. A large sign in one section invites you to 'explore', and that's just what children do, with great enthusiasm. It's fun to clamber over an armoured vehicle – you might like to have a go even if you're not so young! The museum has over seventy vehicles on display and it strives to show how they would have looked when in use – some in a mobile field workshop, others in a desert scene. The whole museum site covers some two acres and includes the waggon used by Lord Roberts in the Boer War, a Rolls-Royce used by Field Marshal Montgomery in the Second World War and an armoured rail tractor used in the First World War. There's certainly plenty to see!

SPECIAL!
Outside the museum stands the 'Blackburn Beverley' transport aircraft. Built by the Blackburn aircraft company, it took its name from the attractive nearby market town of Beverley (well worth spending an hour or two exploring). You can board the aeroplane and see a mini-museum which records the history of air supply from 1916 to the Falklands War. Without doubt, this is a 'hit' with children.

Open: daily, 1000–1700.
Admission fee: yes
Disabled access: telephone in advance
Café
Gift shop
Toilets

BECK ISLE MUSEUM
Pickering, North Yorkshire. Tel: Pickering 73653

Pickering is dominated by impressive Pickering Castle, but tucked away beside attractive Pickering Beck – a pretty trout stream spanned by a partially medieval bridge – is Beck Isle Museum. Inside this handsome stone-built Regency house you can trace social and domestic life over the last two centuries. Victorian memorabilia abound alongside the everyday items of nineteenth-century life in this small slice of Yorkshire. Milking utensils, photographic equipment, a cobbler's workbench are all here to see. Environments have been created for some of the exhibits: a Victorian bar room for the beer engine, barrels, jars and bottles; a gentleman's outfitter's for the stock of collars and soft buttons. And there's more outdoors with a blacksmith's shop, wheelwright's, tack room and the popular wishing well.

SPECIAL!
On display there's a lovely red bed-quilt which dates from 1888. Each of its small squares was embroidered by a child. You can't help but wonder what happened to Martha Holliday, Sarah Mitchell and Mary Barker, to name but a few of the many young girls who recorded their names.

Open: April to October, Monday to Saturday, 1030–1230 and 1400–1730; Sunday (August only), 1030–1230 and 1400–1900.
Admission fee: yes
Disabled access: limited
Picnic facilities
Gifts: on sale

THE BRONTË PARSONAGE MUSEUM
Haworth, Keighley, West Yorkshire. Tel: Haworth 42323

Tourists have been making the trip to the pretty Yorkshire village of Haworth for a long time – Charlotte Brontë was famous in her own lifetime and the earliest American visitors were arriving in 1850. The sextant was paid two shillings and sixpence (12½p) to point her out in church! If you're a keen Brontës fan making a 'pilgrimage' to the parsonage where they lived, you won't be disappointed. The house has been lovingly cared for and the items have been intelligently displayed. Most of the furniture and many of the objects around the parsonage once belonged to the Brontës, including the sofa on which Emily died and the surprisingly tiny table around which the sisters paced as they discussed their books. Outside, the garden has been replanted (except for two corsica pines which Charlotte planted herself) with early-Victorian plants – re-creating a cottage garden with herbs, shrubs and flowers which the Brontës would recognize.

SPECIAL!

The Brontë children played together inventing adventures for their toy soldiers and recording them in tiny books – the smallest is an inch and a half long. They deal with the mythical country of Angria and are filled with fighting, noble deaths, struggles for power, loves, hates and agonies. These imaginative manuscripts proved a real apprenticeship for the literature of their later years.

Open: October to March, daily, 1100–1630. April to September, 1100–1730 (try to visit out of season).
Admission fee: yes
Café: plenty in the village
Picnic facilities: the moor is a few minutes' walk
Gift shop

CALDERDALE INDUSTRIAL MUSEUM
Piece Hall, Halifax, West Yorkshire. Tel: Halifax 59031

Entering this industrial museum you quite literally 'clock in', by putting your entrance ticket into a factory clocking-in machine. The museum tells the story of the mills which once thrived in Calderdale and the lives of the people who worked in them. Some of Halifax's streets have been reconstructed – complete with authentic sounds and smells! Wool is obviously the major industry represented here, with working machinery, regular demonstrations (don't be afraid to ask to see things in action) and an original Spinning Jenny. Other industries haven't been forgotten – look out for the sweet-wrapping machines. Ropes, cork, leather, carpets, knitting, mining and quarrying have also all been associated with Calderdale over the last two centuries and they're all remembered in this interesting museum.

SPECIAL!
The building which houses the Calderdale Industrial Museum must rate as one of the most special pieces of commercial, historic architecture in Britain – the Piece Hall. A 'piece' was a length of woollen or worsted cloth and the Piece Hall is the Manufacturers' Hall where traders displayed and sold their wares. Opened on New Year's Day 1779, the hall is a magnificent building, a massive rectangular structure which surrounds a courtyard of 10,000 square yards. The four sides are each three storeys high, providing a total of 315 rooms each approximately 12 feet by 8 feet with its own classical-style door.

Open: Tuesday to Saturday, 1000–1700; Sunday, 1400–1700.
Admission fee: yes

Disabled access: good
Picnic facilities: in the Piece Hall square
Gifts: on sale
Toilets

PENNY ARCADIA

Ritz Cinema, Market Place, Pocklington, Humberside.
Tel: Pocklington 303420

This isn't just a museum, it's an experience! In the bowels of the Ritz Cinema in Pocklington, there's a treasure-trove of amusement machines. Before you see the collection, you're treated to an unusual and entertaining show. It takes place on the cinema stage and, suffice it to say, it's memorable! Then, when the show is over, the stage opens up and stairs appear festooned with fairground lights; you're invited to step beneath into the unique world of Penny Arcadia. Here there's the chance to see 'What the Butler Saw', make the acquaintance of a magician who levitates a lady from a coach and experience 'Chinese Torture'. This underworld of slot machines includes an army of one-armed bandits. There are mechanical music-boxes, singing birds, and fortune-tellers abound – Madam Sandra, the Gypsy and the Chinese crystal-gazer to introduce but a few. And there are competitive games like the rock-ola world series baseball game. If you're in the area, visit this museum – you'll never forget it!

SPECIAL!
Ten pence in the 'Robot Organ' at the entrance to Penny Arcadia secures you a personal performance of robotic music as three burly life-sized individuals jolt into action.

Open: May to September, daily, 1230–1700. June to August, daily, 1000–1700.
Admission fee: yes
Gifts: on sale
Toilets

NATIONAL MUSEUM OF PHOTOGRAPHY, FILM AND TELEVISION

Prince's View, Bradford, West Yorkshire.
Tel: Bradford 727 488

Have you ever wondered why movies move? Well, in this large and exciting museum you can find out. If you're an expert, you might already know how photography is used to see stress, how it makes visible the invisible and how holograms work, but expert or amateur, you're sure to find something of interest here. The exhibitions show photography as documentary record, as an extension of human vision and as an art form from the old camera obscura to the ultramodern satellite. There's a section showing photography as news, like the cameraman on the moon and the dramatic stills from the Falklands crisis, and a section on portrait studios with Lord Lichfield 'there every day – in person – to tell you about it'. Two floors of displays explore 'The Story Of British Television', charting the progress of the medium from the end of the nineteenth century to the present day, while 'Television Behind the Screen' provides a glimpse behind the scenes on the making of television programmes. In addition to the permanent displays there are special temporary exhibitions which, as the museum has huge resources to call upon, are often very interesting. Finally, you can experience IMAX – the biggest cinema screen in Britain!

SPECIAL!
Visit the Channel 4 Video Box – it's your chance to air
your opinions about television!

Open: Tuesday to Sunday, 1100–1800.
Admission fee: no
Disabled access: good
Café
Gift shop
Toilets

RYEDALE FOLK MUSEUM
Hutton-Le-Hole, Moors National Park, North Yorkshire.
Tel: Lastingham 367

A visit to Ryedale Folk Museum will bring you into the
heart of stunning Yorkshire countryside. Hutton-Le-
Hole boasts a babbling brook, ancient stone houses and
an undulating village green – all of which make an
attractive setting for this fascinating museum. From the
outside it would seem to be tiny, but that's a clever
deception which preserves the atmosphere of the village. In fact, hidden behind the entrance there's an
extensive open-air collection covering some two and a
half acres. You can visit a blacksmith's shop, craft
workshops, a crook cottage, manor house, crofter's
cottage and barn. There's certainly plenty to see and
enjoy in the museum, but make sure you leave some
time to explore the whole area – it's breathtaking!

SPECIAL!
The reconstructed glass furnace is unique. This type of
furnace was introduced into Britain during Elizabethan
times by French and Flemish glassworkers at the time
of the Huguenot persecutions.

Open: last weekend in March to end October, Monday to Sunday, 1100–1800 (last admission, 1715).
Admission fee: yes
Disabled access: good
Picnic facilities
Gift shop
Toilets

SHIBDEN HALL
Godley Lane, Halifax, West Yorkshire.
Tel: Halifax 52246

Shibden Hall is surrounded by Halifax, but you'd never know! This attractive fifteenth-century half-timbered manor house is set in its own beautiful parkland. It's packed with things to see – but none of them is labelled, so it's a case of enjoying what you can and not worrying too much about its date, use or history. Every room reflects a different period in the house's life which includes its earliest owners, the Lister family, whose portraits still stare down from the walls. Everywhere you look there's wood; the walls are panelled, the floors are made from huge planks, there's carved furniture and large exposed beams. If you're interested in crafts, ring before visiting as craft workshops are often held at Shibden.

SPECIAL!
Outside the manor you'll find a Pennine barn – it has a distinctive stone-flagged floor and slabbed roof.

Open: April to September, Monday to Saturday, 1000–1800; Sunday, 1400–1700. February, Sunday, 1400–1700. March, October and November, Monday to Saturday, 1000–1700; Sunday, 1400–1700.

Admission fee: yes
Disabled access: limited
Café
Picnic facilities
Gifts: on sale
Toilets

SPRINGHEAD PUMPING STATION

Springhead Avenue (off Willerby Road), Hull, Humberside.
Tel: Hull 28591

By prior arrangement you can visit Springhead Pumping Station and its waterworks museum – certainly an intriguing place. Touring the station it's hard to imagine a more unlikely place for a museum – this is very much an operational waterworks. However, after you've been shown the present plant with its borehole pumps, boosters and diesel alternators, you can take a look round the waterworks' historical collection. There are old wooden pipes excavated from the streets of Hull alongside sections of their modern counterparts; drawings and photographs of the old pumping station and its later modernization. If you happen to be knowledgeable in this field you'll undoubtedly enjoy your visit, but the simply curious can easily spend an interesting hour or so learning about the history of fresh water supply.

SPECIAL!
The main exhibit is a single-acting Cornish beam engine. A giant, painted a daunting pink colour, the engine was used until 1910 to pump some 6.75 million gallons of water every day.

Open: Monday to Friday (by appointment only).
Admission fee: yes
Toilets

MUSEUM OF VICTORIAN REED ORGANS AND HARMONIUMS

Victoria Hall, Saltaire, near Bradford, West Yorkshire.
Tel: Bradford 585601

If you're an organ enthusiast you'll spend hours and hours in this small museum. In it you can see over forty reed organs including a unique ornately carved exhibition organ and a Holt 3 manual and pedal reed organ built for Dr Conway of Ely Cathedral. But you can do more than just look; if you have the skill you can take the opportunity to play one of these magnificent instruments. If you can't play you can still listen because this museum of Victorian reed organs and harmoniums is visited by guided tour and the owner will certainly give you a tune or two!

SPECIAL!
The town of Saltaire is well worth visiting; in fact it could be considered something of a museum in its own right. Sir Titus Salt (1803–76) set out to demonstrate that industry and good living conditions were compatible – the result is Saltaire. Built between 1851 and 1871, it provided everything Salt believed essential for a decent life: work, health, education, leisure, moral instruction. And it's all still there for you to explore. Take a look at the Mill Works which in its heyday employed 3000 people; the Congregational church which has been described as 'the most beautiful Free Church in the North of England'; the canal, river and railway which together provided excellent links with

Bradford, Leeds and Manchester; residential areas like Albert Terrace with its attractive cottages and pretty almshouses; Victoria Square – the lions on its four corners are said to have been originally for Trafalgar Square; and, finally, the statue of Sir Titus, majestic in its parkland setting.

Open: Wednesday to Monday, 1100–1600.
Picnic facilities: in nearby park
Gifts: on sale
Toilets

WILLIAM WILBERFORCE MUSEUM
Wilberforce House, 23–25 High Street, Hull, Humberside.
Tel: Hull 222755

Great efforts have been made in the dockland area of Hull to improve the facilities and attract visitors. The local authority has even carefully reconstructed a section of cobbled road in front of Wilberforce House. William Wilberforce was born in Hull on 24 August 1759 in this waterfront house in High Street. The house, which is the oldest surviving example of the prosperous merchants' houses which once curtained the dockside warehouses, is now a museum devoted to this man who campaigned tirelessly for the abolition of slavery.

SPECIAL!
Dummy figures people the rooms of Wilberforce House. No, they're not an example of the curators trying to give you some scale! They were, it's said, made to decorate public gardens in the late eighteenth century.

Open: Monday to Saturday, 1000–1700; Sunday, 1430–1630.
Admission fee: no
Picnic facilities
Gifts: on sale
Toilets

REGIONAL TOURIST BOARDS

Cumbria Tourist Board
Ashleigh
Holly Road
Windermere
Cumbria LA23 2AQ
Tel: Windermere 4444

East Anglia Tourist Board
Toppesfield Hall
Hadleigh
Suffolk 1P7 5DN
Tel: Hadleigh 822922

East Midlands Tourist Board
Exchequergate
Lincoln
Lincolnshire LN2 1PZ
Tel: Lincoln 531521/3

Guernsey Tourist Board
Crown Pier
St Peter Port
Guernsey
Tel: St Peter Port 23552

Heart of England Tourist Board
2-4 Trinity Street
Worcester

Worcestershire WR1 2PW
Tel: Worcester 613132

Isle of Man Tourist Board
13 Victoria Street
Douglas
Isle of Man
Tel: Douglas 4323 (winter);
Douglas 4328/9
(May–September)

Jersey Tourist Board
Weighbridge
St Helier
Jersey
Tel: St Helier 24779

London Tourist Board and
Convention Bureau
26 Grosvenor Gardens
London SW1W 0DU
Tel: 01-730 3488

Northern Ireland Tourist Board
River House
48 High Street
Belfast
Northern Ireland
Tel: Belfast 231221 or 246609

Northumbria Tourist Board
Aykley Heads
Durham DH1 5UX
Tel: Durham 46905

North West Tourist Board
The Last Drop Village
Bromley Cross
Bolton
Lancashire BL7 9PZ
Tel: Bolton 591511

Scottish Tourist Board
23 Ravelston Terrace
Edinburgh EH4 3EU
Tel: Edinburgh 332 2433

South East England Tourist
Board
1 Warwick Park
Tunbridge Wells
Kent TN2 5TA
Tel: Tunbridge Wells 40766

Southern Tourist Board
Town Hall Centre
Leigh Road
Eastleigh

Hampshire S05 4DE
Tel: Eastleigh 616027

Thames and Chilterns Tourist
Board
8 The Market Place
Abingdon
Oxfordshire OX14 3UD
Tel: Abingdon 22711

Welsh Tourist Board
Brunel House
2 Fitzalan Road
Cardiff CF2 1UY
Tel: Cardiff 499909

West Country Tourist Board
Trinity Court
37 Southernhay East
Exeter
Devon EX1 1QS
Tel: Exeter 76351

Yorkshire and Humberside
Tourist Board
312 Tadcaster Road
York YO2 2HF
Tel: York 707961

INDEXES

Abbeydale Industrial Hamlet, 298–9
Abbey House Museum, 297–8
Acton Scott Working Farm, 67–9
Amberley Chalk Pits Museum, 207–8
American Museum, 283–4
Annalong Cornmill, 134–5
Anne of Cleves House, 208–9
Apsley House, 112–13
Armagh County Museum, 135–6
Armley Mills, 299–300
Army Transport, Museum of, 300–301
A.T.J. Museum, The, 24–5
Auchindrain Open Air Museum of Country Life, 180–81
Austen, Jane, House of, 225–6
Avoncroft Museum of Buildings, 69–70

Ballycopeland Windmill, 136–7
Bass Museum of Brewing, The, 70–71
Bath Industrial Heritage Centre, 285–6
Bath Postal Museum, 286
Battle of Britain Memorial Flight, 44–5
Battle of Flowers Museum, 105–6
Beamish North of England Open Air Museum, 149–50
Beatrix Potter Museum, 90
Beaumaris Gaol, 263–4
Beck Isle Museum, 301–2
Bede Monastery Museum, 151–2
Bell Foundry Museum, 45–6
Bembridge Maritime Museum, 226–7
Berwick Barracks, 152–4
Big Four Railway Museum, The, 227–8
Big Pit Mining Museum, 264–5
Blists Hill Open Air Museum, 71–2
Booth, William Memorial Complex, 46–7
Border Regiment and King's Own Border Regiment, The Museum of, 11–12
Borough Museum and Art

315

Gallery, Berwick Barracks, 152

Bowes Museum, The, 154–5

Brantwood, 12–13

Brewhouse Yard Museum, 47–8

British Telecom Museum, 248–9

Brontë Parsonage Museum, The, 302–3

Buckley's Shop Museum, 210

Bunyan Meeting House and Museum, The, 249–50

'By Beat of Drum', Berwick Barracks, 153

Calderdale Industrial Museum, 304–5

Calleva Museum, 228–9

Cambridge and County Folk Museum, 25–6

Captain Cook Birthplace Museum, The, 155–6

Castle Cornet, 62–3

Catherine Cookson Exhibition, 156–7

Cecil Higgins Art Gallery, 254–5

Charles Dickens Centre, 213–14

Charleston Farmhouse, 211

Chartered Insurance Institute's Museum, 113–14

Chatham Historic Dockyard, 212–13

Chatterley Whitfield Mining Museum, 72–3

Cheltenham Art Gallery and Museum, 73–4

Chemical Industry Museum, The, 167–8

Childhood, Museum of, Beaumaris, 265–6

Childhood, Museum of, Edinburgh, 181–2

Christchurch Mansion, 26–7

Christchurch Tricycle Museum, 229–30

Church Farm Museum, 48–9

Cider, Museum of, 74–5

Clive House Museum, 76

Clocks, The Museum of, 230–31

Coalport China Works Museum, 76–7

Cobbaton Combat Vehicles Museum, 287–8

Cogges Farm Museum, 250–51

Colchester Castle, 27–8

Combe Martin Motorcycle Collection, 288

Commandery, The, 77–8

Cook, Captain, Birthplace Museum, 155–6

Cookson, Catherine, Exhibition, 156–7

Cooper, Frank, Museum, 251

Corinium Museum, 78–9

Costume, Museum of, 289

Cotswold Woollen Weavers, 80

Cregneash Village Folk Museum, 96–7

Cromwell Museum, 28–9

Cumberland Pencil Museum, 14–15

David Livingstone Centre, The, 191–2

D-Day Museum, 231–2

Dental Museum, 114–15

Dickens, Charles, Centre, 213–14

Dinosaur Museum, 232–3

Dr Johnson's House, 119

Doll and Toy Museum, The, 15

Dyson Perrin's Museum, 81

East Midlands Aeropark, 50–51

Easton Farm Park, 29–30

Elizabeth Castle, 106–7

English Rural Life, Museum of, 252

Exeter Maritime Museum, 290–91

Fermanagh County Museum, 137

316

Ffestiniog Railway Museum, 266–7

First Garden City Heritage Museum, 253–4

Fleet Air Arm Museum, 291–2

Folk Museum, (Guernsey), 63–4

Forge Mill Needle Museum, 82

Fort Amherst, 214–15

Fort Grey Maritime Museum, 64–5

Frank Cooper Museum, 251

Freud Museum, 115–16

Gainsborough Old Hall, 52–3

Garden History, Museum of, 116–17

Geological Museum of North Wales, The, 267–8

Georgian House, The, 182–3

German Underground Hospital, 107–8

Giant's Causeway Centre, 138–9

Gladstone Court Museum, 183–4

Gladstone Pottery Museum, 83–4

Glanford Shell Museum, 31

Grandad's Photography Museum, 32

Grange Cavern Military Museum, The, 269–70

Greenhill Covenanter's House, 184–5

Green's Mill and Science Centre, 53–4

Grimes Graves, 33

Grocery Shop Bygones, Museum of, 34

Grove Rural Life Museum, The, 97–8

Guernsey Museum and Art Gallery, 65–6

Gwynedd Maritime Museum, 271

Hancock Museum, The, 157–8

Hele Mill, 292–3

Helmshore Textile Museums (incorporating Museum of Lancashire Textile Industry and Higher Mill Museum), 168–9

Herschel House and Museum, 293–4

Higgins, Cecil, Art Gallery, 254–4

Hill House, The, 185–6

House of Pipes, 215–16

Hugh Miller's Cottage, 194–5

Hunday National Tractor and Farm Museum, 158–9

Hunterian Museum, 187

Iron, Museum of, 84–5

Iron Bridge and Tollhouse, The, 85

Ironbridge Gorge Visitor Centre, 86–7

Island Fortress Occupation Museum, The, 109–10

Isle of Arran Heritage Museum, 188

Isle of Man Railway Museum, 99

Jackfield Tile Museum, 87

Jane Austen's House, 225–6

Jarrold, John, Printing Museum, 36

Jersey Museum, 110–11

Jewish Museum, 118

John George Joicey Museum, 159–60

John Jarrold Printing Museum, 36

Johnson, Dr, House of, 119

Joicey, John George, Museum, 159–60

Keats' House, 120

Kendal Museum of Lakeland Life and Industry, 16

Keswick Railway Museum, 17

Kew Bridge Engines Trust, 121–2

Kingsbury Water Mill, 255–6
King's Own Scottish Borderers
  Regimental Museum,
  Berwick Barracks, 153

Labour History, Museum of,
  170–71
Lady Stair's House, 188–9
Lady Waterford Hall, 165
La Hougue Bie Museum, 108–9
Lakeland Motor Museum,
  18–19
Land O'Burns Centre, 189–90
Laxey Wheel, The (The Lady
  Isabella), 99–101
Lighting, Museum of, 190–91
Lilliput Museum of Antique
  Dolls and Toys, 233–4
Linley Sambourne House,
  122–3
Lisburn Museum, 139–40
Livingstone, David, Centre,
  191–2
Lloyd George Memorial
  Museum, 268–9
London Taxi Museum, 123–4

Manchester Jewish Museum,
  171–2
Manx Museum, The, 101
Maryport Maritime Museum,
  19–20
Mary, Queen of Scots' House,
  192–3
Mechanical Music and Doll
  Collection, 216–17
Menzies Campbell Collection,
  193–4
Midland Motor Museum, 88
Miller, Hugh, Cottage of,
  194–5
Monkwearmouth Station
  Museum, 160–61
Morpeth Chantry Bagpipe
  Museum, 161–2
Morris, William, Gallery,
  124–5
Morwellham Quay, 294–5

Murray Motorcycle Museum,
  102
Musical Museum, The, 125–6
Mustard Shop Museum, The,
  37

National Cycle Museum, 49–50
National Horseracing Museum,
  35–6
Nautical Museum of
  Photography, Film and
  Television, 306–7
National Tramway Museum,
  59–60
Nautical Museum, 103
Newry and Mourne Museum,
  140–41
Norfolk Shire Horse Centre,
  The, 38–9
Norton, Tom, Collection of
  Old Cycles and Tricycles,
  272

Oakham Castle, 54–5
Oates Memorial Museum and
  the Gilbert White Museum,
  234–5
Old Blacksmith's Shop, 195–6
Old Byre Heritage Centre, 197
Old Merchant's House and
  Row 111 Houses, 39–40
Old Royal Observatory, 126–7
Opie, Robert, Collection,
  89–90
Ordsall Hall Museum, 172–3
Owen, Robert, Memorial
  Museum, 273
Oxford, Museum of, 256
Oxford University Museum,
  257–8

Peak District Mining Museum,
  55–6
Penny Arcadia, 305–6
People's Palace Museum, 198–9
Pilkington Glass Museum,
  173–4
Pitt Rivers Museum, 258

Poole Pottery Museum, 236–7
Port Erin Seashell Museum, 104
Portmeirion, 274–5
Potter, Beatrix, Museum, 90
Preston Hall Museum, 162–3

Redhouse Cone Museum, 91
Red House Stables Working
    Carriage Museum, 56–7
Redoubt Fortress, The, 217–18
Regimental Museum of the
    Royal Inniskilling Fusiliers,
    141
Regimental Museum of the
    Royal Irish Fusiliers, 142
Ribchester Dolls' House and
    Model Museum, 174–5
Robert Opie Collection, The,
    89–90
Robert Owen Memorial
    Museum, 273
Rock Park Spa, 275–6
Roman Army Museum, The,
    164
Roman Mosaic House, The,
    218–19
Royal Crown Derby Porcelain
    Co. Museum, 57–8
Royal Engineers Museum,
    219–20
Royal Inniskilling Fusiliers,
    Regimental Museum of the,
    141
Royal Irish Fusiliers,
    Regimental Museum of the,
    142
Royal Marines Museum, The,
    238–9
Royal National Lifeboat
    Institute Museum (Poole),
    239
Royal National Lifeboat
    Institution Museum
    (Eastbourne), 220–21
Royal Naval Museum, The,
    240–41
Royal Navy Submarine
    Museum, 241–2

Russell-Cotes Art Gallery and
    Museum, 242–3
Rutland Cottage Music
    Museum, 58
Ryedale Folk Museum, 307–8

St Bride's Crypt Museum, 128
Saint Patrick Heritage Centre
    and Down Museum, 143
Salford Museum of Mining,
    175–6
Salt Museum, 177–8
Scottish Agricultural Museum,
    199–200
Scottish Fisheries Museum,
    The, 200–201
Scottish Lead-mining, Museum
    of, 201–2
Scottish Tartans Museum,
    202–3
Scott Polar Research Institute,
    The, 40–41
Shetland County Museum,
    203–4
Shibden Hall, 308–9
Shirehall Museum, The, 41–2
Shoe Museum, The, 295
Shuttleworth Collection, The,
    259–60
Silk Heritage Museum, 178–9
Sir John Soane's Museum,
    129–30
Smith, W. H., Museum, 276
Smuggling History, The
    Museum of, 243–4
Soane, Sir John, Museum,
    129–30
Southampton Hall of Aviation,
    244–5
Sparkford Motor Museum, 296
Springhead Pumping Station,
    309–10
Stoke-on-Trent City Museum
    and Art Gallery, 91–2
Stott Park Bobbin Mill, 20
Stretton Mill, 179
Sygun Copper Mine, 277–8

Tenement House, The, 204–5
Theatre Museum, 130–31
Thomas Webb Museum, 93–4
Thursford Collection, The, 42–3
Tolpuddle Martyrs Museum, The, 245–6
Tom Norton's Collection of Old Cycles and Tricycles, 272
Tower of St Michael at the North Gate, The, 260–61
Transport Museum, 144
Tudor House Museum, 92–3
Tyrwhitt-Drake Museum of Carriages, 221–2

Ulster-American Folk Park, 145–6
Ulster Folk and Transport Museum, 146–8
Ulster Museum, 148

Verulamium Museum, The, 261–2
Victorian Reed Organs and Harmoniums, Museum of, 310–11

Wallace Collection, 131–2
Wareham Bears, The, 246–7

Waterways Museum, The, 60–61
Weald and Downland Open Air Museum, 222–3
Webb, Thomas, Museum, 93–4
Wedgwood Museum, 94–5
Welsh Folk Museum, 278
Welsh Miners Museum, 279–80
Welsh Slate Museum, 280–81
West Highland Museum, The, 205–6
Whitbread Hop Farm, 223–4
W. H. Smith Museum, 276
Wilberforce, William, Museum, 311–12
William Booth Memorial Complex, 46–7
William Morris Gallery, 124–5
William Wilberforce Museum, 311–12
Wimbledon Lawn Tennis Museum, 132–3
Windermere Steamboat Museum, 21–2
Wine and Spirit Museum and Pottery, 166
Wolvesnewton Folk Museum, 282
Wordsworth Museum, 22–3

Agriculture:
  Abbeydale Industrial Hamlet, 298–9
  Acton Scott Working Farm Museum, 67–9
  Auchindrain Open Air Museum of Country Life, 180–81
  Ballycopeland Windmill, 136–7
  Beamish North of England Open Air Museum, 149–50
  Cambridge and County Folk Museum, 25–6
  Church Farm Museum, 48–9
  Cogges Farm Museum, 250–51
  Cregneash Village Folk Museum, 96–7
  Easton Farm Park, 29–30
  English Rural Life, Museum of, 252
  Hunday National Tractor and Farm Museum, 158–9
  Isle of Arran Heritage Museum, 188
  Norfolk Shire Horse Centre, The, 38–9
  Red House Stables Working Carriage Museum, 56–7
  Scottish Agriculture Museum, 199–200
  Weald and Downland Open Air Museum, 222–3
  Whitbread Hop Farm, 223–4

Archaeology and Prehistory:
  Armagh County Museum, 135–6
  Bede Monastery Museum, 151–2
  Calleva Museum, 228–9
  Colchester Castle, 27–8
  Corinium Museum, 78–9
  Dinosaur Museum, The, 232–3
  Fermanagh County Museum, 137
  Geological Museum of North Wales, The, 267–8
  Grimes Graves, 33
  Hugh Miller's Cottage, 194–5
  La Hougue Bie Museum, 108–9
  Manx Museum, The, 101

321

Oxford University Museum, 257–8

Roman Army Museum, The, 164

Roman Mosaic House, The 218–19

St Bride's Crypt Museum, 128

Shetland County Museum, 203–4

Stoke-on-Trent City Museum and Art Gallery, 91–2

Verulamium Museum, The, 261–2

Architectural Interest:
Anne of Cleves House, 208–9
Auchindrain Open Air Museum of Country Life, 180–81
Avoncroft Museum of Building, 69–70
Beamish North of England Open Air Museum, 149–50
Border Regiment and King's Own Border Regiment, The Museum of, 11–12
Brantwood, 12–13
Chatham Historic Dockyard, 212–13
Christchurch Mansion, 26–7
Cregneash Village Folk Museum, 96–7
First Garden City Heritage Museum, 253–4
Fort Amherst, 214–15
Gainsborough Old Hall, 52–3
Hill House, The, 185–6
John George Joicey Museum, 159–60
Lady Stair's House, 188–9
Manchester Jewish Museum, 171–2
Morwellham Quay, 294–5
Newry and Mourne Museum, 140–41
Oakham Castle, 54–5

Old Merchant's House and Row 111 Houses, The, 39–40
Oxford University Museum, 257–8
Portmeirion, 274–5
Russell-Cotes Art Gallery and Museum, 242–3
Ryedale Folk Museum, 307–8
St Bride's Crypt Museum, 128
Saint Patrick Heritage Centre and Down Museum, 143
Shirehall Museum, The, 41–2
Sir John Soane's Museum, 129–30
Tower of St Michael at the North Gate, The, 260–61
Tudor House Museum, 92–3
Ulster-American Folk Park, 145–6
Weald and Downland Open Air Museum, 222–3
Welsh Folk Museum, 278–9
W. H. Smith Museum, 276
William Wilberforce Museum, 311–12
Wolvesnewton Folk Museum, 282

Armed Services:
Apsley House, 112–13
Armagh County Museum, 135–6
Army Transport, Museum of, 300–301
Battle of Britain Memorial Flight, 44–5
Berwick Barracks, 152–4
Borough Museum and Art Gallery, 152
'By Beat of Drum', 153
King's Own Scottish Borderers Regimental Museum, 153
Border Regiment and King's Own Border Regiment, The Museum of, 11–12

Castle Cornet, 62–3
Chatham Historic Dockyard, 212–13
Cobbaton Combat Vehicles Museum, 287–8
Commandery, The, 77–8
D-Day Museum, 231–2
Elizabeth Castle, 106–7
Fleet Air Arm Museum, 291–2
Fort Amherst, 214–15
German Underground Hospital, 107–8
Grange Cavern Military Museum, The, 269–70
Island Fortress Occupation Museum, The, 109–10
John George Joicey Museum, 159–60
Redoubt Fortress, The, 217–18
Regimental Museum of the Royal Inniskilling Fusiliers, 141
Regimental Museum of the Royal Irish Fusiliers, 142
Roman Army Museum, The, 164
Royal Engineers Museum , 219–20
Royal Marines Museum, The, 238–9
Royal Naval Museum, The, 240–41
Royal Navy Submarine Museum, 241–2

Art, see Fine Arts

Aviation, see Transport

Ceramics and Glass:
Bede Monastery Museum, 151–2
Bowes Museum, The, 154–5
Cecil Higgins Art Gallery, 254–5
Clive House Museum, 76

Coalport China Works Museum, 76–7
Dyson Perrins Museum, 81
Glandford Shell Museum, 31
Jackfield Tile Museum, 87
Pilkington Glass Museum, 173–4
Poole Pottery Museum, 236–7
Redhouse Cone Museum, 91
Royal Crown Derby Porcelain Co. Museum, 57–8
Stoke-on-Trent City Museum and Art Gallery, 91–2
Thomas Webb Museum, 93–4
Wedgwood Museum, 94–5

Children's Interest:
Beatrix Potter Museum, 90
Brewhouse Yard Museum, 47–8
Childhood, Museum of (Beaumaris), 265
Childhood, Museum of (Edinburgh), 181–2
Doll and Toy Museum, The, 15
Lilliput Museum of Antique Dolls and Toys, The, 233–4
Mechanical Music and Doll Collection, 216–17
Ribchester Dolls' House and Model Museum, 174–5
Tudor House Museum, 92–3
Wareham Bears, The, 246–7

China, see Ceramics and Glass

Cinematography and Photography:
Grandad's Photography Museum, 32
National Museum of

Photography, Film and
Television, 306–7

Clocks and Watches:
Clocks, The Museum of,
230–31

Coins and Medals:
Castle Cornet, 62–3
Hunterian Museum, 187

Costume and Accessories:
Armagh County Museum,
135–6
Castle Cornet, 62–3
Christchurch Tricycle
Museum, 229–30
Costume, Museum of, 289
Gainsborough Old Hall, 52–3
National Horseracing
Museum, 35–6
Romany Folklore Museum
and Workshop, 236–7
Scottish Agriculture
Museum, 199–200
Shoe Museum, The, 295
Wimbledon Lawn Tennis
Museum, 132–3

Craft:
Amberley Chalk Pits
Museum, 207–8
American Museum, 283–4
Battle of Flowers Museum,
105–6
Bell Foundry Museum, 45–6
Cambridge and County Folk
Museum, 25–6
Cheltenham Art Gallery and
Museum, 73–4
D-Day Museum, 231–2
Exeter Maritime Museum,
290–91
Isle of Arran Heritage
Museum, 188
John Jarrold Printing
Museum, 36
Lisburn Museum, 139–40

Manx Museum, The, 101
Morwellham Quay, 294–5
People's Palace Museum,
198–9
Poole Pottery Museum,
236–7
Preston Hall Museum, 162–3
Royal Crown Derby
Porcelain Co. Museum,
57–8
Shibden Hall, 308–9
Ulster Folk and Transport
Museum, 146–8
Wareham Bears, The, 246–7
Welsh Folk Museum, 278–9
Welsh Slate Museum, 280–81
West Highland Museum,
The, 205–6
Whitbread Hop Farm, 223–4
William Morris Gallery,
124–5
Wine and Spirit Museum and
Pottery, 166
Wolvesnewton Folk
Museum, 282

Cycles, see Transport

Ethnographic:
Pitt Rivers Museum, 258

Farming, see Agriculture

Fine Arts:
Apsley House, 112–13
Berwick Barracks, 152–4
Borough Museum and Art
Gallery, 152
'By Beat of Drum', 153
King's Own Scottish
Borderers Regimental
Museum, 153
Bowes Museum, The, 154–5
Brantwood, 12–13
Cecil Higgins Art Gallery,
254–5
Christchurch Mansion, 26–7
Freud Museum, 115–16

Lady Waterford Hall, 165
Preston Hall Museum, 162–3
Russell-Cotes Art Gallery and
   Museum, 242–3
Stoke-on-Trent City
   Museum and Art Gallery,
   91–2
Wallace Collection, 131–2
Wedgwood Museum, 94–5

Folk Collections:
   Abbey House Museum,
      297–8
   American Museum, 283–4
   Armagh County Museum,
      135–6
   Beamish North of England
      Open Air Museum, 149–50
   Beck Isle Museum, 301–2
   Brewhouse Yard Museum,
      47–8
   Cambridge and County Folk
      Museum, 25–6
   Church Farm Museum, 48–9
   Cogges Farm Museum,
      250–51
   Cregneash Village Folk
      Museum, 96–7
   Easton Farm Park, 29–30
   Fermanagh County Museum,
      137
   Folk Museum (Guernsey),
      63–4
   Grocery Shop Bygones,
      Museum of, 34
   Grove Rural Life Museum,
      The, 97–8
   Hunday National Tractor and
      Farm Museum, 158–9
   Isle of Arran Heritage
      Museum, 188
   Jewish Museum, 118
   Kendal Museum of Lakeland
      Life and Industry, 16
   La Hougue Bie Museum,
      108–9
   Manx Museum, The, 101
   Morwellham Quay, 294–5

Norfolk Shire Horse Centre,
   The, 38–9
Ryedale Folk Museum, 307–8
Scottish Agriculture
   Museum, 199–200
Shibden Hall, 308–9
Ulster-American Folk Park,
   145–6
Ulster Folk and Transport
   Museum, 146–8
Weald and Downland Open
   Air Museum , 222–3
Welsh Folk Museum, 278–9
West Highland Museum,
   The, 205–6
Wolvesnewton Folk
   Museum, 282

Food and Drink:
   Annalong Cornmill, 134–5
   Bass Museum of Brewing,
      The, 70–71
   Cider, Museum of, 74–5
   Frank Cooper Museum, 251
   Green's Mill and Science
      Centre, 53–4
   Grocery Shop Bygones,
      Museum of, 34
   Hele Mill, 292–3
   Mustard Shop Museum, The,
      37
   Whitbread Hop Farm, 223–4
   Wine and Spirit Museum and
      Pottery, 166

Furniture and Woodwork:
   American Museum, 283–4
   Anne of Cleves House, 208–9
   Bowes Museum, The, 154–5
   Cecil Higgins Art Gallery,
      254–5
   Cheltenham Art Gallery and
      Museum, 73–4
   Christchurch Mansion, 26–7
   Gainsborough Old Hall, 52–3
   Georgian House, The, 182–3
   John George Joicey Museum,
      159–60

Tudor House Museum, 92–3
Wallace Collection, 131–2
William Morris Gallery,
  124–5

General:
  Armagh County Museum,
    135–6
  A.T.J. Museum, The, 24–5
  Bowes Museum, The, 154–5
  Christchurch Mansion, 26–7
  Corinium Museum, 78–9
  Fermanagh County Museum,
    137
  Guernsey Museum and Art
    Gallery, 65–6
  Hunterian Museum, 187
  Manx Museum, The, 101
  Newry and Mourne
    Museum, 140–41
  Ordsall Hall Museum, 172–3
  Penny Arcadia, 305–6
  People's Palace Museum,
    198–9
  Preston Hall Museum, 162–3
  Russell-Cotes Art Gallery and
    Museum, 242–3
  Shetland County Museum,
    203–4
  Stoke-on-Trent City
    Museum and Art Gallery,
    91–2
  Ulster Museum, 148
  Wallace Collection, 131–2
  West Highland Museum,
    The, 205–6
  Wolvesnewton Folk
    Museum, 282

Geology:
  Giant's Causeway Centre,
    138–9
  Glandford Shell Museum, 31
  Stoke-on-Trent City
    Museum and Art Gallery,
    91–2

Glass, see Ceramics and Glass

Horses, see Agriculture

Industry, see Science and
  Industry

Lighting:
  Lighting, Museum of,
    190–91

Manuscripts:
  Beatrix Potter Museum, 90
  Brontë Parsonage Museum,
    The, 302–3
  Dr Johnson's House, 119
  First Garden City Heritage
    Museum, 253–4
  Hugh Miller's Cottage,
    194–5
  Lady Stair's House, 188–9
  Land O'Burns Centre,
    189–90
  Manchester Jewish Museum,
    171–2
  Wordsworth Museum, 22–3

Maritime, see Shipping

Medical:
  Dental Museum, 114–15
  Freud Museum, 115–16
  Menzies Campbell
    Collection, 193–4
  Rock Park Spa, 275–6

Motoring, see Transport

Music and Musical Instruments:
  Mechanical Music and Doll
    Collection, 216–17
  Morpeth Chantry Bagpipe
    Museum, 161–2
  Musical Museum, The,
    125–6
  Rutland Cottage Music
    Museum, 58–9
  Thursford Collection, The,
    42–3
  Victorian Reed Organs and

Harmoniums, Museum of,
310–11

Natural History:
Captain Cook Birthplace
Museum, The, 155–6
Cogges Farm Museum,
250–51
David Livingstone Centre,
The, 191–2
Garden History, Museum of,
116–17
Geological Museum of North
Wales, The, 267–8
Hancock Museum, The,
157–8
Oates Memorial Museum and
the Gilbert White Museum,
234–5
Oxford University Museum,
257–8
Port Erin Seashell Museum,
104
Scott Polar Research
Institute, The, 40–41
Stoke-on-Trent City
Museum and Art Gallery,
91–2

Personality:
Apsley House, 112–13
Beatrix Potter Museum, 90
Bede Monastery Museum,
151–2
Bowes Museum, The, 154–5
Brantwood, 12–13
Brontë Parsonage Museum,
The, 302–3
Bunyan Meeting House and
Museum, The, 249–50
Captain Cook Birthplace
Museum, The, 155–6
Catherine Cookson
Exhibition, 156–7
Charles Dickens Centre,
213–14
Charleston Farmhouse, 211
Cromwell Museum, 28–9

David Livingstone Centre,
The, 191–2
Dr Johnson's House, 119
Freud Museum, 115–6
Garden History, Museum of,
116–17
Greenhill Covenanter's
House, 184–5
Green's Mill and Science
Centre, 53–4
Herschel House and
Museum, 293–4
Hill House, The, 185–6
Hugh Miller's Cottage,
194–5
Jane Austen's House, 225–6
Jersey Museum, 110–11
Keats' House, 120
Lady Stair's House, 188–9
Lady Waterford Hall, 165
Land O'Burns Centre,
189–90
Linley Sambourne House,
122–3
Lloyd George Memorial
Museum, 268–9
Mary, Queen of Scots'
House, 192–3
Monkwearmouth Station
Museum, 160–61
Mustard Shop Museum, The,
37
Oates Memorial Museum and
the Gilbert White Museum,
234–5
People's Palace Museum,
198–9
Robert Owen Memorial
Museum, 273
Romany Folklore Museum
and Workshop, 236–7
Royal Engineers Museum,
219–20
Royal National Lifeboat
Institute Museum (Poole),
239
Royal National Lifeboat

Institution Museum, The
  (Eastbourne), 220–21
Royal Naval Museum, The,
  240–41
Russell–Cotes Art Gallery and
  Museum, 242–3
Saint Patrick Heritage Centre
  and Down Museum, 143
Scott Polar Research
  Institute, The, 40–41
Sir John Soane's Museum,
  129–30
Tenement House, The, 204–5
Tolpuddle Martyrs Museum,
  The, 245–6
W. H. Smith Museum, 276
William Booth Memorial
  Complex, 46–7
William Morris Gallery,
  124–5
William Wilberforce
  Museum, 311–12
Wimbledon Lawn Tennis
  Museum, 132–3
Wordsworth Museum, 22–3

Philately:
  Bath Postal Museum, 286

Photography, see
  Cinematography and
  Photography

Prehistory, see Archaeology
  and Prehistory

Railways, see Transport

Science and Industry:
  Abbeydale Industrial Hamlet,
    298–9
  Amberley Chalk Pits
    Museum, 207–8
  Annalong Cornmill, 134–5
  Armley Mills, 299–300
  Ballycopeland Windmill,
    136–7

Bath Industrial Heritage
  Centre, 285–6
Beamish North of England
  Open Air Museum, 149–50
Bell Foundry Museum, 45–6
Big Pit Mining Museum,
  264–5
Blists Hill Open Air
  Museum, 71–2
British Telecom Museum,
  248–9
Calderdale Industrial
  Museum, 304–5
Chatterley Whitfield Mining
  Museum, 72–3
Chemical Industry Museum,
  The, 167–8
Cumberland Pencil Museum,
  14–15
Forge Mill Needle Museum,
  82
Gladstone Pottery Museum,
  83–4
Green's Mill and Science
  Centre, 53–4
Hele Mill, 292–3
Helmshore Textile Museums
  (incorporating Museum of
  Lancashire Textile Industry
  and Higher Mill Museum),
  168–9
Herschel House and
  Museum, 293–4
Iron, Museum of, 84–5
Iron Bridge and Tollhouse,
  The, 85
Ironbridge Gorge Visitor
  Centre, 86–7
John Jarrold Printing
  Museum, 36
Kew Bridge Engines Trust,
  121–2
Kingsbury Water Mill, 255–6
Laxey Wheel, The (The Lady
  Isabella), 99–101
Lisburn Museum, 139–40
Morwellham Quay, 294–5

Old Royal Observatory,
126–7
Peak District Mining
Museum, 55–6
Pilkington Glass Museum,
173–4
Redhouse Cone Museum, 91
Robert Opie Collection, The,
89–90
Salford Museum of Mining,
175–6
Salt Museum, 177–8
Scottish Lead-mining,
Museum of, 201–2
Springhead Pumping Station,
309–10
Stott Park Bobbin Mill, 20
Stretton Mill, 179
Sygun Copper Mine, 277–8
Welsh Miners Museum,
279–80
Welsh Slate Museum, 280–81

Shipping:
Bembridge Maritime
Museum, 226–7
Captain Cook Birthplace
Museum, The, 155–6
Chatham Historic Dockyard,
212–13
Exeter Maritime Museum,
290–91
Fort Grey Maritime
Museum, 64–5
Gwynedd Maritime
Museum, 271
Maryport Maritime Museum,
19–20
Nautical Museum, 103
Royal National Lifeboat
Institute Museum (Poole),
239
Royal National Lifeboat
Institution Museum
(Eastbourne), 220–21
Royal Navy Submarine
Museum, 241–2

Scottish Fisheries Museum,
The, 200–201
Shetland County Museum,
203–4
Windermere Steamboat
Museum, 21–2

Silver:
Tower of St Michael at the
North Gate, The, 260–61

Social History:
Abbey House Museum,
297–8
Acton Scott Working Farm
Museum, 67–9
American Museum, 283–4
Bath Industrial Heritage
Centre, 285–6
Beamish North of England
Open Air Museum, 149–50
Beaumaris Gaol, 263–4
Beck Isle Museum, 301–2
Blists Hill Open Air
Museum, 71–2
Buckley's Shop Museum, 210
Bunyan Meeting House and
Museum, The, 249–50
Calderdale Industrial
Museum, 304–5
Chartered Insurance
Institute's Museum,
113–14
Chatterley Whitfield Mining
Museum, 72–3
Christchurch Mansion, 26–7
Cobbaton Combat Vehicles
Museum, 287–8
David Livingstone Centre,
The, 191–2
English Rural Life, Museum
of, 252
First Garden City Heritage
Museum, 253–4
Folk Museum (Guernsey),
63–4
Forge Mill Needle Museum,
82

Gainsborough Old Hall, 52–3
Georgian House, The, 182–3
German Underground
  Hospital, 107–8
Giant's Causeway Centre,
  138–9
Gladstone Court Museum,
  183–4
Gladstone Pottery Museum,
  83–4
Greenhill Covenanter's
  House, 184–5
Grove Rural Life Museum,
  The, 97–8
House of Pipes, 215–16
Ironbridge Gorge Visitor
  Centre, 86–7
Island Fortress Occupation
  Museum, The, 109–10
Isle of Arran Heritage
  Museum, 188
Jersey Museum, 110–11
John George Joicey Museum,
  159–60
Kendal Museum of Lakeland
  Life and Industry, 16
Labour History, Museum of,
  170–71
Laxey Wheel, The (The Lady
  Isabella), 99–101
Linley Sambourne House,
  122–3
Lloyd George Memorial
  Museum, 268–9
Manchester Jewish Museum,
  171–2
Morwellham Quay, 294–5
Newry and Mourne
  Museum, 140–41
Old Blacksmith's Shop,
  195–6
Old Byre Heritage Centre,
  197
Old Merchant's House and
  Row 111 Houses, The,
  39–40
Ordsall Hall Museum, 172–3
Oxford, Museum of, 256

People's Palace Museum,
  198–9
Preston Hall Museum, 162–3
Robert Opie Collection, The,
  89–90
Robert Owen Memorial
  Museum, 273
Romany Folklore Museum
  and Workshop, 236–7
St Bride's Crypt Museum,
  128
Salford Museum of Mining,
  175–6
Shirehall Museum, The, 41–2
Smuggling History, The
  Museum of, 243–4
Stott Park Bobbin Mill, 20
Tenement House, The, 204–5
Tolpuddle Martyrs Museum,
  The, 245–6
Ulster-American Folk Park,
  145–6
Verulamium Museum, The,
  261–2
Welsh Folk Museum, 278–9
West Highland Museum,
  The, 205–6
William Wilberforce
  Museum, 311–12

Sport:
  National Horseracing
    Museum, 35–6
  People's Palace Museum,
    198–9
  Wimbledon Lawn Tennis
    Museum, 132–3

Tapestry and Textiles:
  American Museum, 283–4
  Anne of Cleves House, 208–9
  Armley Mills, 299–300
  Cotswold Woollen Weavers,
    80
  D-Day Museum, 231–2
  Helmshore Textile Museums
    (incorporating Museum of
    Lancashire Textile Industry

and Higher Mill Museum),
168–9
Scottish Tartans Museum,
202–3
Shetland County Museum,
203–4
Silk Heritage Museum, 178–9

Theatre:
Theatre Museum, 130–31

Transport:
Amberley Chalk Pits
Museum, 207–8
Army Transport, Museum
of, 300–301
A.T.J. Museum, The, 24–5
Battle of Britain Memorial
Flight, 44–5
Beamish North of England
Open Air Museum, 149–50
Big Four Railway Museum,
The, 227–8
Christchurch Tricycle
Museum, 229–30
Cobbaton Combat Vehicles
Museum, 287–8
Combe Martin Motorcycle
Collection, 288
East Midlands Aeropark,
50–51
Ffestiniog Railway Museum,
266–7
Grange Cavern Military
Museum, The, 269–70
Hunday National Tractor and
Farm Museum, 158–9
Isle of Man Railway
Museum, 99
Keswick Railway Museum,
17
La Hougue Bie Museum,
108–9

Lakeland Motor Museum, 18
London Taxi Museum,
123–4
Midland Motor Museum, 88
Monkwearmouth Station
Museum, 160–61
Murray Motorcycle
Museum, 102
National Cycle Museum,
49–50
National Tramway Museum,
59–60
Oakham Castle, 54–5
Old Blacksmith's Shop,
195–6
Red House Stables Working
Carriage Museum, 56–7
Shuttleworth Collection,
The, 259–60
Southampton Hall of
Aviation, 244–5
Sparkford Motor Museum,
296
Thursford Collection, The,
42–3
Tom Norton's Collection of
Old Cycles and Tricycles,
272
Transport Museum, 144
Tyrwhitt-Drake Museum of
Carriages, 221–2
Ulster Folk and Transport
Museum, 146–8
Waterways Museum, The,
60–61
Wolvesnewton Folk
Museum, 282

Watches, see Clocks and
Watches

Woodwork, see Furniture and
Woodwork

331

Guides now available in paperback from Grafton Books

Brian J Bailey
Lakeland Walks and Legends (illustrated) £1.50 ☐

Mary Cathcart Borer
London Walks and Legends (illustrated) £1.95 ☐

Mary Peplow & Debra Shipley
London for Free £2.50 ☐

Janice Anderson & Edmund Swinglehurst
Scottish Walks and Legends:
  The Lowlands and East Scotland (illustrated) £1.50 ☐
  Western Scotland and The Highlands (illustrated) £1.50 ☐

David Daiches
Edinburgh (illustrated) £1.95 ☐
Glasgow (illustrated) £3.95 ☐

Peter Somerville-Large
Dublin (illustrated) £2.25 ☐

Frank Delaney
James Joyce's Odyssey (illustrated) £2.95 ☐

Paul Johnson
The National Trust Book of British Castles (illustrated) £4.95 ☐

Nigel Nicolson
The National Trust Book of Great Houses (illustrated) £4.95 ☐

Tom Weir
Weir's Way (illustrated) £2.95 ☐

To order direct from the publisher just tick the titles you want
and fill in the order form.   **HB1181**

Regional books in paperback from Grafton
Books

Chris Barber
Mysterious Wales (illustrated)   £2.50 ☐

Brian J. Bailey
Lakeland Walks and Legends (illustrated)   £1.50 ☐

Tom Weir
Weir's Way (illustrated)   £2.95 ☐

David Daiches
Edinburgh (illustrated)   £1.95 ☐
Glasgow (illustrated)   £3.95 ☐

Peter Somerville-Large
Dublin (illustrated)   £2.25 ☐

Frank Delaney
James Joyce's Odyssey (illustrated)   £2.95 ☐

Mary Cathcart Borer
London Walks and Legends (illustrated)   £1.95 ☐

Mary Peplow and Debra Shipley
London for Free   £2.50 ☐

To order direct from the publisher just tick the titles you want
and fill in the order form.   **HB1281**

Books of historical interest now available in Grafton Books

David Daiches
Edinburgh (illustrated)   £1.95 ☐
Glasgow (illustrated)   £3.95 ☐

Paul Johnson
The National Trust Book of British Castles (illustrated)   £4.95 ☐

Nigel Nicolson
The National Trust Book of Great Houses (illustrated)   £4.95 ☐

Frank Delaney
James Joyce's Odyssey (illustrated)   £2.95 ☐

Stan Gébler Davies
James Joyce: A Portrait of the Artist (illustrated)   £2.50 ☐

To order direct from the publisher just tick the titles you want
and fill in the order form.   **GM681**

All these books are available at your local bookshop or newsagent, or can be ordered direct from the publisher.

To order direct from the publishers just tick the titles you want and fill in the form below.

Name _____

Address _____

_____

Send to:
Grafton Cash Sales
PO Box 11, Falmouth, Cornwall TR10 9EN.

Please enclose remittance to the value of the cover price plus:

UK 60p for the first book, 25p for the second book plus 15p per copy for each additional book ordered to a maximum charge of £1.90.

BFPO 60p for the first book, 25p for the second book plus 15p per copy for the next 7 books, thereafter 9p per book.

Overseas including Eire £1.25 for the first book, 75p for second book and 28p for each additional book.

Grafton Books reserve the right to show new retail prices on covers, which may differ from those previously advertised in the text or elsewhere.